PRAISE FOR M. I

A fabulous soaring thriller.

— *TAKE OVER AT MIDNIGHT,* MIDWEST BOOK REVIEW

Meticulously researched, hard-hitting, and suspenseful.

— *PURE HEAT,* PUBLISHERS WEEKLY, STARRED REVIEW

Expert technical details abound, as do realistic military missions with superb imagery that will have readers feeling as if they are right there in the midst and on the edges of their seats.

— *LIGHT UP THE NIGHT,* RT REVIEWS, 4 1/2 STARS

Buchman has catapulted his way to the top tier of my favorite authors.

— FRESH FICTION

Nonstop action that will keep readers on the edge of their seats.

— *TAKE OVER AT MIDNIGHT*, LIBRARY JOURNAL

M L. Buchman's ability to keep the reader right in the middle of the action is amazing.

— LONG AND SHORT REVIEWS

The only thing you'll ask yourself is, "When does the next one come out?"

— *WAIT UNTIL MIDNIGHT*, RT REVIEWS, 4 STARS

The first...of (a) stellar, long-running (military) romantic suspense series.

— *THE NIGHT IS MINE*, BOOKLIST, "THE 20 BEST ROMANTIC SUSPENSE NOVELS: MODERN MASTERPIECES"

I knew the books would be good, but I didn't realize how good.

— NIGHT STALKERS SERIES, KIRKUS REVIEWS

Buchman mixes adrenalin-spiking battles and brusque military jargon with a sensitive approach.

— PUBLISHERS WEEKLY

13 times "Top Pick of the Month"

— NIGHT OWL REVIEWS

Tom Clancy fans open to a strong female lead will clamor for more.

— *DRONE*, PUBLISHERS WEEKLY

Superb! Miranda is utterly compelling!

— *BOOKLIST*, STARRED REVIEW

Miranda Chase continues to astound and charm.

— BARB M.

Escape Rating: A. Five Stars! OMG just start with *Drone* and be prepared for a fantastic binge-read!

— READING REALITY

The best military thriller I've read in a very long time. Love the female characters.

— *DRONE,* SHELDON MCARTHUR, FOUNDER OF THE MYSTERY BOOKSTORE, LA

NIGHTWATCH

A MIRANDA CHASE ACTION-ADVENTURE TECHNOTHRILLER

M. L. BUCHMAN

Copyright 2023 Matthew L. Buchman

All rights reserved.

This book, or parts thereof, may not be reproduced in any form without permission from the author.

Receive a free book and discover more by this author at: www.mlbuchman.com

Cover images:

E-4B Nightwatch © US Air Force

Northern Lights in Iceland © surangastockx

SIGN UP FOR M. L. BUCHMAN'S NEWSLETTER TODAY

and receive:
Release News
Free Short Stories
a Free Book

Get your free book today. Do it now.
free-book.mlbuchman.com

Other works by M. L. Buchman: (* - also in audio)

Action-Adventure Thrillers

Dead Chef
One Chef!
Two Chef!

Miranda Chase
Drone*
Thunderbolt*
Condor*
Ghostrider*
Raider*
Chinook*
Havoc*
White Top*
Start the Chase*
Lightning*
Skibird*
Nightwatch*
Osprey*
Gryphon*

Science Fiction / Fantasy

Deities Anonymous
Cookbook from Hell: Reheated
Saviors 101

Contemporary Romance

Eagle Cove
Return to Eagle Cove
Recipe for Eagle Cove
Longing for Eagle Cove
Keepsake for Eagle Cove

Love Abroad
Heart of the Cotswolds: England
Path of Love: Cinque Terre, Italy

Where Dreams
Where Dreams are Born
Where Dreams Reside
Where Dreams Are of Christmas*
Where Dreams Unfold
Where Dreams Are Written
Where Dreams Continue

Non-Fiction

Strategies for Success
Managing Your Inner Artist/Writer
Estate Planning for Authors*
Character Voice
Narrate and Record Your Own Audiobook*

Short Story Series by M. L. Buchman:

Action-Adventure Thrillers

Dead Chef

Miranda Chase Stories

Romantic Suspense

Antarctic Ice Fliers

US Coast Guard

Contemporary Romance

Eagle Cove

Other

Deities Anonymous (fantasy)

Single Titles

The Emily Beale Universe
(military romantic suspense)

The Night Stalkers
MAIN FLIGHT
The Night Is Mine
I Own the Dawn
Wait Until Dark
Take Over at Midnight
Light Up the Night
Bring On the Dusk
By Break of Day
Target of the Heart
Target Lock on Love
Target of Mine
Target of One's Own
NIGHT STALKERS HOLIDAYS
*Daniel's Christmas**
*Frank's Independence Day**
*Peter's Christmas**
Christmas at Steel Beach
*Zachary's Christmas**
*Roy's Independence Day**
*Damien's Christmas**
Christmas at Peleliu Cove

Henderson's Ranch
*Nathan's Big Sky**
*Big Sky, Loyal Heart**
*Big Sky Dog Whisperer**
*Tales of Henderson's Ranch**

Shadow Force: Psi
*At the Slightest Sound**
*At the Quietest Word**
*At the Merest Glance**
*At the Clearest Sensation**

White House Protection Force
*Off the Leash**
*On Your Mark**
*In the Weeds**

Firehawks
Pure Heat
Full Blaze
*Hot Point**
*Flash of Fire**
Wild Fire
SMOKEJUMPERS
*Wildfire at Dawn**
*Wildfire at Larch Creek**
*Wildfire on the Skagit**

Delta Force
*Target Engaged**
*Heart Strike**
*Wild Justice**
*Midnight Trust**

Emily Beale Universe Short Story Series

The Night Stalkers
The Night Stalkers Stories
The Night Stalkers CSAR
The Night Stalkers Wedding Stories
The Future Night Stalkers

Delta Force
Th Delta Force Shooters
The Delta Force Warriors

Firehawks
The Firehawks Lookouts
The Firehawks Hotshots
The Firebirds

White House Protection Force
Stories

Future Night Stalkers
Stories (Science Fiction)

ABOUT THIS BOOK

As the Arctic melts, the fabled Northwest and Northeast Passages are opening. But are they opening to war?

A Chinese freighter attacked. A sabotaged passenger jet crashed in Quebec. And high overhead an E-4B Nightwatch, America's fortress-in-the-sky, sees all.

With nations shifting to high alert, Miranda Chase lands once more in the midst of the fray. But first she must fight battles of her own. Can she conquer the emotional chaos her autism unleashes amid the loss of her past? In time to save her team? —And avert the disaster playing out under the Northern Lights?

A tale of high adventure, airplanes, and espionage.

A list of characters and aircraft may be found at:
https://mlbuchman.com/people-places-planes

PROLOGUE

Sea Level
77°10'50" N / 67°42' 23" E
20 km north of Severny Island, Russia
Arctic Ocean

Captain Yú Ling never saw the missiles that struck his ship, though they hit in broad daylight at 0300 hours local time.

An hour before, Ling had woken at 0200 during the depths of the soft twilight that served as night this far above the Arctic Circle. He often shrugged on a parka to stand out here on the bridge wing of his ship to observe his first voyage through the Arctic Ocean. The complete lack of true night made sleep feel almost irrelevant.

Worries drove him from his bed as well. This maiden voyage of a new ship through the Arctic without an icebreaker escort would become a highlight upon his record as a sea captain. All of his previous journeys had taken the forty-eight-day southern route past Southeast Asia, India, and up through the Suez Canal. Never before had such a large container ship sailed unescorted through this nineteen-day Northeast Passage from Shanghai through the Bering Sea to pass over Russia to Europe. A full *month* faster. Knowing it for fact made it now less amazing.

Ling could only shake his head at the modern wonders. To travel Beijing to Rotterdam so quickly was unimaginable until only the last few years. And now the melting Arctic ice was making it a reality. The new Polar Silk Road would let China sell more to the hungry maw of Europe faster and with much lower transit costs than ever before.

He much preferred the peace here in the high Arctic. The waterways along southeast Asia and up through the Suez were clogged with constant traffic. Even the vast stretches of the Indian Ocean were hazardous as hundreds of massive cargo and oil ships jostled for the most fuel-efficient route. Here they traveled these waters alone, except for the occasional Russian oil tanker or fishing boat.

The September air was so fresh and crisp, matching a cold winter day in Beijing, a few degrees below freezing but none of the throat-catching pollution. It made him daydream of soft snowfalls. He could almost pretend he heard the crackle and smelled the smoke of long-ago wood fires.

Standing out on the bridge wing of the *Lucky Progress,* he could see the far white horizon of the pack ice to starboard as little more than a thin white stripe between the dark blue of the ocean and the deep blue of the sky. They were in a land and time of no true night, but the aurora danced in brilliant greens and smooth pinks. They faded with the slow rising twilight and disappeared, though it would be hours before the sun crested the ocean's surface.

His wife's photographs of their vacations by the sea always looked the same. They must have a thousand pictures of a stripe of sand, a stretch of ocean, and a sky of blue. She could never explain in a way he could understand how each wove a unique image, but the thought of her taking such photos made him smile in this barren place. She certainly still looked fine in her sleek black one-piece. She rarely went in the water now except with their grandchild, even then rarely past her own knees, though the girl at six was as fine a swimmer as her grandmother had been.

Someday they would have unrestricted bandwidth from anywhere in the world. For now Ling took a photo with his phone to send to her the next time he was in port. The curiously dark sea, the distant white line of ice pack, the crisp blue of the morning sky.

He leaned out to look down the twenty-story steel cliff of his container ship's side. Waves less than a meter high and no free ice at all—they'd left that behind twenty-one hours and eight hundred kilometers ago in the Vilkitsky Strait. His ship—with the strengthened hull to brush through the occasional patches of new ice at speed—had worked flawlessly. Here lay nothing but clear water to the distant horizon.

He crossed the seventy-five meters through the warmth of the main bridge and out to the far end of the port-side bridge wing. The sea ran much the same, but the view of the horizon held more interest. Twenty kilometers due south, Severny Island shone brilliantly white. It boasted the largest glacier in all of Europe. As the northernmost extension of the Ural Mountains, he could actually see their transition from Asia to Europe happening while churning past this island.

It was also where the Soviet Union had exploded nuclear bombs totaling a hundred times more than all of the ordnance of WWII, including the two American bombs. The largest bomb ever built had been exploded here. He didn't take a photo as he had of the polar ice to starboard. His wife wouldn't appreciate the irony of so much destruction now being replaced by Chinese commerce.

Then he looked ahead. Like his father had told him on his first sailboat when they would venture out on Chao Lake in Anhui Province, *Put your nose into the wind, Ling.* He split the wind with his nose, turning his head until the breeze landed evenly on both his cheeks. Now he was facing exactly into the apparent wind—ten degrees to port of straight ahead. Knowing that the ship was making twenty-three knots told him they faced only the lightest of winds from the southwest, a fact confirmed by the faint ripples upon the sea far below.

Despite the cold, a few degrees below freezing, he stayed out on the bridge wing to watch the world and his ship. Maybe those photos were how his wife found inner peace. He himself cherished these quiet moments with only the low thrum of the ship's engines and the cry of curious gulls to keep him company.

At 0230, an eager *zhong wei*—a new-minted lieutenant (junior grade)—brought him a thermal mug filled with his favorite jasmine tea, which was much appreciated despite the brief disturbance. Reading his mood with a delicacy that boded well for the girl's future in the merchant service, she retreated and left him to his thoughts. Voyages were long, and so few crew were required that living together required the greatest diplomacy.

Could she think in knots at all? She could convert their forty-two kilometers per hour in her head readily enough; he trained all of his crew to do that. But to *think* in knots? That was becoming a lost art over the three decades he'd spent largely at sea. That too was progress of a kind.

Again he studied the ship. Designed to the very limits of the Suez Canal's abilities, *Lucky Progress* measured precisely a tenth of a meter under the four-hundred-meter limit in length and the same under the maximum beam width. She carried twenty thousand TEU of containers. Yet another arcane measure—twenty-foot-equivalent units. The power of the Americans to keep the world locked into the outdated English units system rankled.

The *Lucky Progress* carried her twenty thousand TEU, as ten thousand forty-foot-long containers. And they had to be forty feet or they wouldn't fit the cranes, trains, or trucks of the Western world.

He sighed. It couldn't last. One decade, perhaps two, and then China could dictate the international standards of measurement.

Do not expend focus on that which is outside your control, Ling.

And he did. The entire horizon glowed pink and gold as the sun skimmed close below the horizon to the north-northeast, mere minutes from rising. His ship had cruised the Northeast Passage above Russia's frozen wastelands without slowing once. North from Shanghai, past the Koreas, Japan, and along the Arctic length of Russia. Only Murmansk and the Scandinavian countries remained before he turned south once more. They had cut twenty-four percent off the trip distance from Shanghai to Rotterdam, and because of the open sailing, sixty percent of the time as well.

With a route twenty-five hundred kilometers shorter, they'd saved time, payroll, and twelve hundred tons of fuel. They'd avoided pirates operating in the Malacca Strait of Malaysia, the entry to the Red Sea past Iraqi and Arabian squabbles, and past the Somalis. They'd also saved the six-hundred-thousand-dollar transit charge to pass through the Suez Canal.

He patted the railing he leaned upon to thank the *Lucky Progress* and to let his ship know they were through the worst of it. From here, the sea was reported clear all of the way to Rotterdam.

On track for a record speed run, all twenty thousand TEU would be coming off in the single port of Rotterdam, rather than five thousand here and five thousand there. Then they'd take on nineteen thousand of empties and one thousand more of luxury items before retracing the same route.

He checked his watch, 0255. Another hour closer to his destination. When they were done, it could be the fastest round-trip ever recorded.

There were rumors he might make senior captain if he succeeded in breaking the record. His wife would very much like the status and pay of that. He must find a new beach for her to photograph as a celebration.

THE UPGRADED CASC RAINBOW CH-5 UAV HAD BEEN BUILT in the Anhui Province of Eastern China. The HALE—high altitude / long endurance—unmanned aerial vehicle had been aloft for thirty-two hours to reach the Arctic Ocean and to loiter twelve kilometers high, watching for signs of a particular ship type passing below.

Due to its heavy load, it only had enough fuel for three more hours before it would have to dump a half-million US dollars of unused missiles into the ocean to save weight and make the trip home. But a lot of hard work, and more than a little luck, had placed it in the sky above the newest jewel of the Chinese cargo fleet.

Its distant operators spotted the *Lucky Progress* at thirty kilometers, when it was no bigger than a bright dot on the distant sea.

Satcom messages flashed back and forth with the command-and-control center but with little verification necessary. The ship fit the mission profile perfectly.

As the AR-1 missiles it carried were only rated to a maximum of eight kilometers, the Rainbow UAV circled down until it flew ten meters above the ocean's surface.

At seven kilometers off the stern of the ship, it fired.

LIEUTENANT (JUNIOR GRADE) SŪN JIĀ STOOD AS ASSISTANT officer of the watch on the bridge of the *Lucky Progress*. She wished she could have found the nerve to stand by the captain and enjoy the passage in silence, but she hadn't. Though the captain had never shown anything but kindness, she still had trouble speaking in his presence.

She should have asked the captain a question, she had a thousand of them, but...she hadn't.

So, after offering him tea, she retreated to the bridge and

watched Lieutenant Chen standing his watch. She was supposed to observe and learn, but Chen was lazy. A farmer's son from Henan province, he was content to set the autopilot and perform only the minimum of required checks—at least those received his proper diligence. She had already learned more than Chen would ever know. Not that she could ever admit that aloud.

He had made a pass at her, but even that had been more perfunctory than enthusiastic.

On the radar scope, there was a faint green blip astern.

Crews of non-military ships rarely paid attention to what lay aft of them. Lieutenant Chen most certainly did not.

Sūn Jia noted the new signal off the stern. It was neither big nor bright, definitely not a ship. Barely even a boat. But she remembered the stories her first captain had told her about Somali pirates taking huge ships with little more than a day-fishing boat.

"Excuse me, Lieutenant Chen. But what do you think this is?" she pointed at the screen.

He glanced down and shrugged. "Did we drop a container overboard?" Highly unlikely in this calm sea. The radar atop the bridge was high enough that their visible horizon range reached over twenty-five kilometers—the object lay only seven astern.

"It moves quickly."

"Maybe it's a whale," his tone warned her that this conversation was over. Daughters of her generation were still the unwanted children of the one-child policy. Her father's generation, and still most of hers, never thought a woman could have value.

Chen was not worth the effort.

The only other deck crew member awake was the captain out on the port bridge wing.

She moved to the end of the starboard bridge wing and looked aft.

At 0259:40, the CASC Rainbow CH-5 fired all six of its AR-1 missiles. Each measured a meter-and-a-half long and carried ten kilos of high explosive.

By 0259:41 they reached Mach 1.

Nineteen seconds remained until the missiles reached their target.

The UAV turned away to the south—briefly reflecting sunlight off its belly and toward the ship—then climbed rapidly. Within moments, it flew above the maximum height of the *Lucky Progress'* surface-scanning radar. The low-resolution weather radar would not show the UAV on Lieutenant Chen's screen, even if he cared to look down. The next weather check wasn't scheduled for twenty-seven more minutes. He didn't look.

Besides, he was too busy admonishing himself. Next time he talked to Sūn Jia, he must not turn into the babbling idiot he always became around her. *Maybe it's a whale?* She certainly hadn't laughed as he'd intended. What had he been thinking?

Second Lieutenant Sūn Jia saw a bright flash of the departing UAV far astern at precisely 0259:43. The sun catching an iceberg? She didn't think so as there were no other icebergs about. But she couldn't be sure.

For ten long seconds, she continued to lean out to watch astern, but saw nothing more.

She hurried once more into the bridge, wondering if she should disturb the captain from his contemplations. She could see that he once again faced forward and would have seen nothing.

As she crossed behind Lieutenant Chen, she thought she saw—for the briefest instant—a flash on the surface radar. A piece of ice bobbing up astern?

The motion was wrong, it approached the ship.

And very close astern.

But then it was gone below the radar's lower horizon.

THE SIX AR-1 MISSILES PERFORMED EXACTLY AS PROGRAMMED.

They'd flown at sea-skimming levels half the height of the UAV's passage, a mere five meters above the low Arctic Ocean waves.

At 0300:01—a hundred meters and a third of a second before reaching the ship—they angled down and plunged into the waves. Fired in a spread to assure a hit, the left-most missile and the three on the right missed the ship. Their detonations weren't observed by anyone.

At that moment, Lieutenant (junior grade) Sūn Jiā was looking for her binoculars. It would be several seconds before she discovered them, not in her drawer where they belonged, but close by First Lieutenant Chen. Too lazy to discover where he'd set down his own, he'd taken hers.

First Lieutenant Chen was watching Sūn Jia while trying to decide whether to speak and what to say if he did.

Captain Yú Ling faced Severny Island off the beam and didn't see the fountains of water blown upward astern. He didn't see the island either. Instead, he recalled the look of contentment on his wife's face. She often slept at the beach. But he never did, for the simple joy he took from watching her easy contentment that he found so difficult.

The vast circles of turbulence from the exploding missiles and the water they threw aloft were erased within seconds by the stern wake as the ship continued forward. The ocean muffled most of the low thump of the explosion, the rest sounded as no more than a murmur above the engine noise.

In the engine room, the watch officer didn't hear anything as he leaned close to inspect the Number Three hydraulic pump.

The two remaining missiles struck the Number Two blade on the three-story-tall propellor.

Damage to the blade was not initially apparent on the bridge—the hundred-and-twenty-ton propeller continued to turn at eighty-percent revolutions, moving the ship ahead at the twenty-three-knot designed cruise speed. There was no shock transmitted along the ship's hull and up to the command bridge to alert anyone.

The watch engineer paused, having heard something. So much ice had scraped down the length of the hull earlier in the crossing that he was past any greater reaction, or remembering the odd sound at all when it ceased with no further sign of trouble.

One missile struck in the middle of the vast copper-aluminum-iron alloy blade. It created a cluster of microfractures, but nothing that would be significant in the next half-million kilometers of normal usage—if that was the only damage.

The other missile almost missed the blade entirely. If it had, it would have struck the outer hull plate at the ship's stern a glancing blow and caused a leak in the outer hull, easily managed by the bilge pumps until it could be fixed. However, it caught the leading edge of the Number Two blade and knocked off a piece smaller than a person's head—an insignificant area on such a large blade.

Yet with each turn of the blade, the fractured surface cavitated more and more. Instead of smoothly slicing into the water, the blunt surface of the break impacted the water like a sledgehammer, creating a high-pressure zone. As the water escaped past the broken edges, the sudden drop in pressure caused the water to explosively vaporize. Each molecule that did, carved a molecule out of the alloy as well.

Fifty kilometers later, long after the UAV had flown high and turned for home in what the controllers assessed as a failure; the cavitation had scored a deep groove in both sides of the propellor blade. Still, it would have been easily identified and fixed at the next inspection—if it hadn't joined the impact point of the first strike.

There, the cavitation-carved grooves radiating along the blade's surface from the second missile's impact point intersected with the deeper microfractures caused by the first missile's strike. The combination resulted in an abrupt loss of material integrity. With deeply compromised support from the leading edge to the middle of its structure, all of the strain on the five-meter-tall blade was shifted onto the trailing half.

Then the trailing edge.

The blade failed catastrophically seventy-seven minutes and fifty-three-point-four kilometers after it was initially struck. Had it failed during the upstroke of its journey around the propellor's hub, it would have impacted the bottom of the hull, causing significant damage. But the *Lucky Progress* lived up to her name. The blade separated at the very peak of its journey around the driveshaft.

Flung sideways, its shape and angle of momentum caused it to briefly surf onto the tops of the waves.

Captain Yú Ling was counting how many more years he would be at sea before he could wake beside his wife each night.

Lieutenant Chen cringed and stared studiously ahead after Sūn Jia picked up her binoculars and replaced them with his own—without a single word or gesture of recrimination—yet radiating a deep-rooted annoyance his best efforts would never abate.

Lieutenant Sūn Jia raised her binoculars to look aft just as the broken blade sank beneath the surface and began its final journey to the sea floor. She would never forgive Lieutenant Chen for robbing her of what she would forever be convinced would have been her first whale sighting. Instead, all she saw were the great rings the blade had formed in the ship's wake after plunging into the depths.

Most of a propellor's weight lay in the hub and the thick base of the blades.

But when the Number Two blade failed, sixteen thousand kilograms broke off one side of the propellor. The uneven loading set off immediate alarms on the bridge and in the engine room.

As soon as Captain Yú Ling heard the reports from the bridge officer and the engine room officer, he knew what had happened. The pictures from the UUV—unmanned underwater vehicle—that they lowered into the water held no surprises.

They'd thrown a propellor blade.

Three hours of careful testing and they were able to proceed forward at six knots, eleven kilometers per hour, a quarter of their normal speed.

With the blade gone, they also lost any chance of a record-breaking run.

But *how* had they lost a blade?

Was it poor manufacture?

That would be vehemently denied by the shipyard, of course. And they had the security of servicing long-term large military contracts as proof of their skills. They were safe, wielding the political heft to brush aside his question with as little notice as his ship might encounter overrunning an errant snowball.

Had they struck something out in the middle of the Arctic Ocean?

Not even Lieutenant Sūn Jia's whale should have broken that blade.

He'd been watching the open sea ahead at the time it happened. There had been no ice, no Arctic hazard.

Not that he would be believed.

As captain, the blame would land squarely on his shoulders.

Instead of being four days from Rotterdam, they were now fifteen. When they finally limped into port, they would have to wait weeks, perhaps months for a repair.

He searched for any bright light in the disaster. He had to

stand at the rail for a long time, with the wind so light on his cheeks from the ship's passage it might as well have been anchored, before he found it.

Well, perhaps he would be able to wake up beside his wife every morning sooner than he'd expected.

1

"This is beyond amazing, Jeremy." Taz waved a hand at the late afternoon sun skimming over the trees that surrounded Lac Brome in southern Quebec. Or perhaps the brilliant blue sky above reflected in the lake's waters. Maybe the ducks and geese clustered along the shore honking out their curiosity.

"Um, yeah." It seemed unlikely she was talking about the Embraer 175 passenger jet lying half on the beach and half in the lake.

Simply because he didn't see what made Taz so excited didn't matter. He'd long since learned that it was always safer to agree with her—especially lately. Since she'd become pregnant, she was even less predictable than usual. Though neither of them had figured out that reason for her slightly manic reactions until two weeks ago.

The whole becoming-a-father-in-seven-months concept made his head hurt. They weren't even married yet. He'd proposed, even producing the ring he'd been trying to find the right time for, before they'd discussed the implications.

He'd never seen her cry before his proposal and wasn't buying her declaration that it was merely hormones.

And you thought I was hair trigger before. With a mini-me on board, look out, Jeremy!

Then she'd turned into a maternal lunatic. Dinner conversations were about picking out boy versus girl room colors: soothing if a boy, otherwise vibrant and inspiring. All room color meant to him was that it would reflect some wavelength between 380 and 750 nanometers—the bounds of the visible spectrum for the human eye.

"I mean, just look around you!"

He did...again. They'd been sent by the National Transportation Safety Board to inspect a crash, and, yep, here it was. The jet, configured for seventy-eight passengers seated two-and-two across a narrow aisle, had gone down. For reasons they were here to determine, the hundred-foot-long jet had catastrophically lost power an hour into an hour-and-twenty-minute direct flight from Boston to Montreal.

The pilots had managed to land the plane relatively intact on a lake. It hadn't caught a wing and tumbled—instead they'd managed as picture perfect a landing as that Airbus jet on the Hudson. Better even. The Airbus had been left floating in the middle of the river. The Embraer, by luck or planning, had parked on the only sand beach along the whole shore.

The passengers—except for the few idiots who'd declined to put on their seatbelts—had stepped off the plane onto dry sand. One idiot was removed on a stretcher and two more in body bags.

"The pilots did a good job."

"A good job? *A good job?* Jeremy, wake up, you're standing

on the shore of Lac Brome in Knowlton, Quebec. Birds are singing in the trees."

He could hear one...no, two. A chickadee in one of the park's trees and a duck along the lake edge. The kids playing in the park on the far side of the police caution tape were making far more noise.

"It smells like summer. I can taste every bloom on the air."

The air smelled like sunbaked metal. The crash had happened in the morning, but they hadn't arrived from DC until late afternoon of the brilliantly clear day. No leaking kerosene-based Jet A fuel, which was good. He shot for a safe response, hoping it proved sufficient. "Uh-huh."

By Taz's eye roll, it wasn't. "That does it. I'm taking away your aircraft structural manuals until you read a couple of real books."

"*Real* books?" Again he tried for an even tone. Again, it didn't help.

"My favorite murder mysteries ever are all set right here! This is the land of Inspector Gamache."

"I don't think anyone was murdered here other than a few sandcastles. Besides, I read real books."

"Science fiction aren't real books."

"And your murder mysteries are?" He knew it was a mistake as soon as he said it. She was likely to turn away from the TV, prop her feet on his thigh, and pull out her phone to read a book whenever he watched a science fiction movie.

She offered a disdainful sniff and turned her attention back to the plane.

It took up about half of the beach, but the local police had taped it all off. The first phase of people had come and gone before they'd arrived. The passengers and crew were all gone. A couple of Mounties stood around, mostly to keep the locals in the grassy park and away from the plane. Kids long since frustrated that the unmoving plane hadn't done something more exciting, like blowing up, were playing on the gym set.

An airline rep rolled up and checked in, but he wasn't an engineer.

Taz gave him the task of getting some fuel trucks to drive over from Montreal to empty the fuel tanks. "Then call the manufacturer and get some people and equipment here to figure out how to remove this. I don't think anyone other than the kids want this to remain here as a fixture."

He eyed the kids, then his beached thirty-million-dollar jet, and was on the phone in seconds.

2

"What do you think about children?"

Miranda stopped slipping cedar shingles under the still fist-sized squash before they rotted on the damp soil of the Pacific Northwest, and turned to face Andi.

She'd forbidden Andi to come past the dual Adirondack chair placed two steps inside the garden gate, which she now sat in. Her girlfriend had proven not only to have no measurable green thumb but to have an actual black thumb.

Miranda had become convinced, after careful statistical analysis, that any plant Andi tended had a thirty-seven percent chance of survival, plus or minus six percent. Against all reasonable expectations, careful training hadn't increased that, but rather decreased it to twenty-nine percent with a mere four-point statistical uncertainty to testify to her data's veracity.

That's when Miranda had set the boundary—the chair. Only zucchini appeared immune to her influence, but then she'd never heard of anything that could kill one of those.

Banning her partner outright from the garden had

apparently hurt Andi's feelings badly for reasons she'd been unable to explain to Miranda. Her own emotional inabilities often left them at an impasse in such discussions. They'd compromised on the chair two steps inside the gate.

"Children?" Miranda looked down at the squash she'd just shingled. "I usually think of these as *baby* squash. I've never thought of them as child squash."

Did the plants take Andi's delighted laugh personally, and that was part of the problem? She considered the challenges of creating a next-level non-plant-destructive simulation, but ultimately concluded that would indeed be a highly complex task. Personally, she enjoyed the sound.

Then she wondered if that was sufficient reason to abandon a potentially plant-saving test. Yes. Curtailing the occurrence rate of Andi's laughs was not something she'd pursue without better reason—or new evidence.

"No, I meant human children. Like Taz and Jeremy's."

"Oh." Subject changes always disoriented her. She could now navigate their twists and turns with some degree of reliability, but she had to be careful how she set aside her current thoughts before starting along new ones or she'd never find her way back. Noting them in her personal notebook had proved largely ineffective. She'd filled all of its pages with questions and tasks that largely remained unanswered and unfinished. She was experimenting with physical triggers for more reliable results. Picking up the next cedar shingle would hopefully prove sufficient. She held onto it tightly. "What was the question?"

"What do you think about human children?"

"I don't." At least Andi had learned to not ask her how she *felt* about something. She could never answer that with any degree of confidence about anything.

"You don't like them or you don't think about them?"

"You asked if I think about them. I don't."

"Well, you'd better. You're going to be an auntie is seven months."

"I don't understand. I'm not related to either Taz or Jeremy. They each worked on my air-crash investigation team, but that doesn't make me an aunt, as that requires a blood or married relationship."

"An auntie is a common slang term for an older female-type person who takes an interest in raising someone younger."

"Like a teacher?"

"Like a friend. You call your former governess Tante Daniels."

"Starting after my parents died in the crash of TWA 800."

"And Tante means…"

Miranda didn't understand why Andi was asking as they both knew that in German it meant…*aunt.* "Oh."

And again Andi's laugh sounded through the garden.

Miranda looked down quickly but couldn't see any change in the foliage. No leaf curl or browning edges. Good aphid-eating ladybugs didn't flop dead to the ground from their patrol on her tomato plants. The freshly weeded rows still smelled of compost and rich dark soil.

"I'm still confused. What do I think about children? I have no basis for answering that question. The last child I spent any significant time with was myself. The one with next highest frequency was an afternoon with a male child while investigating the crash of a Hercules C-130 Ghostrider before you joined the team."

"Did you enjoy that?"

There was one of the questions she had trouble with.

Misidentifying an emotion had almost cost her Andi as a teammate and lover. Emotions were like very boggy ground filled with unmarked pitfalls. Since then, she'd staged a tactical retreat from attempts to pinpoint her emotions.

"He was very knowledgeable about aircraft in general."

"So you liked him."

"I didn't dislike him. He was an intelligent and inquisitive nine-year-old. But I don't see how that follows." If she didn't dislike someone, did that mean that she *did* like them?

No, that discounted the neutral state of neither liking nor disliking. But she had no idea by what calibration she was supposed to measure those three disparate states.

"I didn't dislike him," she reiterated. That relegated her feelings to only one of two states. Interesting. In some situations, repeating herself *did* serve a purpose of emphasis rather than time-wasting reiteration. She set down the cedar shake and pulled out her personal autism notebook to record that observation.

After she'd tucked it away, she considered if Andi might be enquiring from a state of concern? Perhaps fearing Miranda would dislike Jeremy's child. How could she know that without meeting it first? Which would be difficult as it wouldn't be born for seven months, plus or minus a range of uncertainty spanning several weeks.

Or—

"Are you asking because you'd like to have a child?"

3

"No!" Andi slammed her head against the back of their chair hard enough to make her sting. She reached back to rub her head but it didn't make the insides feel any better.

"Okay." Miranda picked up the shingle and turned her attention once more to the rows of zucchini that filled the gap between them, turning over leaves and brushing at the soil. How could she ask such a crazy-ass question, then turn back to her gardening?

Andi was an ex-US Army Night Stalker helicopter pilot, for crying out loud. She was a member of the most elite air-crash investigation team in the entire National Transportation Safety Board—Miranda's.

And her girlfriend of the last eighteen months, again Miranda, was utterly insane.

"Holy Hell, you sound like my mother."

"I have a Chinese accent?" Miranda at least stopped with the gardening thing.

"Yes. No. You don't. But she's always asking when I'm going to give her a grandchild."

"Why would you give her your child?"

"I don't have a child."

"Then how could she want you to give it to her if you don't have one?"

Andi closed her eyes and counted to ten. Then backward to zero. Continuing to minus ten offered no greater aid. Maybe if she tried counting irrational numbers: square root of two, Euler's Number *e*, pi… She sighed, opened her eyes, and stared up at the high horsetail clouds that preceded an incoming storm. The first heavy layer—Pacific Northwest storms arrived in layers—was already shadowing the western sky. The afternoon sun was fading rapidly. Which meant that the storm would be hitting soon and hard.

"Mother badgers me constantly to *have* a child so that she can be an auntie to it."

"You mean a great-auntie."

"Yes." Conceding that point was a minor victory in understanding.

"And you don't want to do this for what reason?"

"Do you want to have a child, Miranda?" Andi figured the best defense was to duck and run away from the question as fast as she could.

"There would be a high statistical likelihood of a child of mine being autistic. I don't know if that's a good thing."

"But you're wonderful. I'm the one who's an utter basket case." And if Andi ever found out which god to talk to about that latter point, she'd give them a royal ass kicking.

"Statistically—"

"Screw stats."

Miranda's face blanked. Andi knew she hated being interrupted but couldn't stop herself. And Miranda did love her data.

"What if I gave birth to my mother? That would be a thousand times worse."

Miranda's frown implied she was probably considering parallel universes and time machines.

"I meant, to a kid *like* my mother."

"Oh," Miranda nodded to herself. "Your mother is a very successful woman. She's a top attorney and the senior manager of one of San Francisco's oldest and largest law firms."

"She's also a heartless, conniving bitch." And for reasons that Andi still couldn't fathom, two days ago she'd announced her imminent arrival in Seattle to visit her daughter. Which exacerbated the craziness in her head at least tenfold. There had to be some way that she could avoid Mother, perhaps by calling the President and requesting that he declare a global emergency. Either that or he could declare the Wu household a national disaster area. She tried to recall the last time they'd been in a room together without fighting? It certainly hadn't been at birth, Mother always said what a battle that had been.

Only two more hours before they had to leave to pick her up at the airport. Could she arrange to be temporarily dead within the next two hours? Maybe.

Ching Hui Wu never approved of anyone in her middle daughter's life, including her middle daughter. For several years after Andi had announced her preference for women, Mother had suggested various *cures*. Not the shortsighted *treatments* some parents talked about. Ching Hui would never send her daughter to a retraining center or pray over her. Instead, she'd suggested marrying sons of other wealthy Chinese business owners and she would adapt to it with time. The number of *surprise* dinner guests had been staggering as Mother had worked her way down the San Francisco social register every time Andi was home on leave.

When that had failed, she'd engineered a *chance* meeting with a particularly wealthy Chinese heiress who had recently been outed by her ex-girlfriend. Andi had considered calling the ex to ask what she'd seen there in the first place—the woman made the dark goddess of war, Jiutian Xuannü, appear benevolent.

And it didn't help that last week Mother had returned to the question she'd finally dropped a decade before. *You know, Andrea, I have set up estate plans for several lovely lesbian couples...for their children.* Mother never stated anything directly when it could be passive-aggressively suggested.

Nobody on the team had this pressure. Well, except Jeremy. But his parents had loved Taz at first sight and were ecstatic over the recent news.

Mike was an orphan. Holly's parents had died last year. And Miranda's and Taz's had been dead since they were each in the early teens.

Andi's own mother had been built from adamantine steel. Maybe she was a Terminator with a coating of human flesh sent back to make Andi's life a misery until Ching Hui Wu rusted away in some unknowable future.

Miranda remained kneeling on the soil, probably waiting for Andi's thoughts to settle. As she did, she kept inspecting the plants.

"You're not going to find a baby growing there."

"I was inspecting them for ill effects from your reaction and brooding."

"I'm not brooding."

And she wouldn't have bought into her own adverse

effects on the garden—if Miranda hadn't produced charts and statistics to prove her point.

"Okay." Miranda always took Andi's word about emotions. Which, in this case, felt like a lie. *Was* a lie.

"Fine. I'm brooding. But I'm not enjoying it and your plants don't care."

"That remains to be seen. The lack of instantaneous ill effects doesn't preclude longer-term impacts."

Andi buried her face in her hands. It was far too easy to imagine Miranda with a young daughter at her side. She'd be an amazing parent. But if Miranda didn't want to have the child, then having one would be up to Andi herself. That, at least, made the decision easy. *No way!* Not motherhood, not even for Miranda.

At eighteen months, her relationship with Miranda was already twice any previous record. Partly by choice, but mostly because being a Wu of Wu and Wu Law meant that the most avaricious in school had targeted her—those wanting to marry their way into the family firm. The rest were too terrified of her mother to come anywhere close. Later, as a US Army Special Operations pilot, she'd never stayed still enough for a longer relationship.

Eighteen months was one thing, but even talking about a kid had moved this to a whole new level. A commitment stretching...twenty or more years? Talk about an elephant trampling through the garden.

And if their child was hers to bear... "Who in the world would be the father?"

She hoped Miranda hadn't heard her.

"That's obvious." Miranda didn't elaborate.

No way was Andi asking—because she was *not* going to have a child.

Miranda was inspecting the cedar shingle in her hand as if she'd never seen one before.

"Baby squashes," Andi whispered, reminding her of what she'd been doing.

"Oh!" Miranda brightened and turned back to tending her garden.

Leaving Andi as the one stuck with the thousand and one questions as the chilly breeze presaged the storm clouds gathering overhead.

4

"Jeremy?" Taz sat down beside him on the Embraer's wing. Propped out of the water by the mostly submerged engine. Through the long afternoon and evening, the park had slowly emptied until only the Mountie remained, sleeping in his car.

Before heading off to buy them all dinner, the airline rep had mobilized everyone and told them help would be arriving soon to remove the jet. Which meant time was short and he had to make sure he had all the information he needed from the jet while it remained in place.

"Uh-huh." He studied the graphic on his screen. Something had happened to the passenger jet up at thirty-one thousand feet above southern Quebec. Both of the twinjet's engines had failed, with no clear evidence as to why. No bird strike. No recorded mechanical failure.

He'd waded out into the lake far enough to reach into the engines. The fans spun, reluctantly, probably because they were half submerged. He could feel no mechanical resistance or grinding as he'd forced the blades to rotate more like a paddlewheel than a jet turbine. No broken fan blades in evidence.

"Jeremy?"

"Uh-huh." According to the readout from the Quick Access Recorder, the throttles hadn't been untimely retarded. No alerts in the cockpit. One minute the plane had been on time en route to Montreal, the next it had begun falling out of the sky. In quick succession, the engines had both flamed out despite multiple redundant systems. Then an unheard-of pressure seal failure at the rear cargo door, followed by a loss of cabin pressure.

When he'd first seen the plane down in the lake, he wondered why the pilots hadn't rerouted to any of the nearby airports. There was a lot of glide time between thirty-one thousand feet and the ground. Now he knew why. They'd been too busy due to a whole series of successive failures that—

An abrupt push had him sliding down the back side of the wing. He twisted to toss his laptop to safety. Taz's hands were already there. She slipped it from his hands and smiled—the moment before he slid into the lake.

Only a few feet deep this close to shore, he quickly found his feet as the water sluiced out of his hair and over his face. An angry duck yelled at him before herding her ducklings away along the length of the wing.

"Why did you do that?"

"I got your attention, didn't I?" Taz waved the dry laptop at him.

He considered grabbing Taz's ankle and dragging her in after him. Anticipating his move, she folded her legs out of reach and sat like a perfectly content Latina elf.

His attempts to climb back onto the top of the sloped

wing were foiled by his own soaked clothes turning it into an ice-slick surface. He dove under the wing rather than slogging around the far end, where the mother duck still glowered at him.

Taz walked along the wing to the fuselage, through the open over-wing emergency evac door, and met him by the nose after coming out the main passenger door onto the dry beach.

He considered shaking himself like a wet dog and spraying water all over her. But he didn't want to be thrown back into the lake. He might be five-seven to her four-eleven, but he knew he was no match for her. Probably hadn't been before she'd spent twenty years in the Air Force and earned her Taser-based nickname. Also, she was still holding his laptop.

She handed him a towel.

"Thanks." He began drying himself off. "What was that for?"

"Next time I need to ask you something, don't try brushing me off with a grunt."

"I did? When?"

Taz sighed, then kissed him. That's when he noticed she was almost as wet as he was.

He began rubbing the towel in her long hair.

"I was swimming around in the cargo hold."

"Uh-huh."

"Jeremy!"

"I'm listening. I'm listening." He made sure that he had a buffer zone between himself and the water. Before he could turn to face her again, she swept his legs, dropping him to the sandy beach. He stood, but there would be no getting rid of it, the grit stuck to everything. He walked back into the water and rinsed himself off.

When he emerged, Taz handed him the already sopping-wet towel.

As he rubbed ineffectually at his own face once more, she reached into a small bag sitting on the sand and handed him a box that fit in the palm of his hand. "Look what I found installed in the cargo hold."

"It's a hose timer." His mother used them in her garden. They had an onboard timer with controls to turn a watering hose on for a preset amount of time. This one sported a little wi-fi symbol that meant it could be controlled by an app.

"Where did you find it?" Then he looked at the dead airplane spreadeagled on the beach in front of him. "On the main fuel line?"

"And the auxiliary. And on both engines. I bet we find another couple of timers associated with each step of that cascade failure you were looking at. What do you think? Four on the fuel lines. Two electronic cutouts on the hydraulics pressure pumps. More to shut down the nav and flight computers. I figure a hundred bucks at any hardware and electronics store."

"Pressure seal on the rear door as well. Must have made the pilots nuts as system after system shut down for no visible reasons. The Embraer 175 is fly-by-wire. That explains why they went for the lake rather than trying to reach an airport."

Taz nodded. "Terrified that the next thing to go away would be the electronics operating their flight controls and they'd make like a brick." She pantomimed dropping one onto the beach from a height.

"Sabotage. That finally fits the QAR data." Jeremy felt

better knowing that. "If the saboteurs were smart, they'd have set up a switch to shut down that recorder early."

"But they clearly didn't care if we found this evidence so there was no need to shut down the recorders. They simply wanted the plane down, or perhaps they wanted to make sure we found out it was sabotage. Either way, this shifts the pilots from incompetent to victims."

"But it raises the new question of who sabotaged this plane. It had to be recent."

Taz nodded. "And who paid them enough to do it."

Jeremy stared at the plane, so clean and white, perched on the beach and colored by the pink-and-orange sunset sky. To get it out of here, they'd have to pull the wings and fly in a big Chinook helo to lift out the smaller pieces, the fuselage would be ugly times ten—too heavy for a helo. It certainly wasn't going to travel out through the park and along the narrow country roads they'd followed to get here.

"This must be what Miranda feels like."

"How's that?" Taz wrapped an arm around his waist as she leaned against him and faced the sunset.

"I'd be much happier if this was a simple plane crash. Instead, we're now in the territory of calling the FBI and the Mounties."

"You really think they'll find the answer?"

"It's their job, not ours."

Taz made one of those thoughtful hums like the ones when he asked questions about their upcoming wedding.

Miranda always found the perpetrator when there was one. Taz's hum suggested that pursuing the perpetrators perhaps wasn't up to him.

But she was wrong.

5

READY FOR TAKEOFF, ANDI WANTED OUT.

Normally she was happy flying in Miranda's Cessna Citation M2 jet. It was almost impossible not to be. Eight seats including pilot and copilot, it was the epitome of a luxury light bizjet. That Cessna had given the multimillion-dollar plane to Miranda as part of a safety consulting package was crazy, but the team used it well. It let them arrive at crash sites all over the western US with minimal delay.

It also pushed the very limits of what was possible on Spieden Island. The short grass strip on Miranda's personal island had been intended for one of the jet's baby cousins, like a four-seat prop-driven Cessna 172. She'd expanded it to the M2's requirements, though with little extra to spare.

Andi had to admit this time was different. Why wasn't hard to figure out now that she'd thought it through. From the moment they were aloft, they'd be under fifteen minutes to arriving at SeaTac, where Mother's flight was landing just now. By the time she had her baggage, they'd be there.

"We need parachutes." Andi decided.

Miranda was taxiing up to the northwest end of the runway close by the tall Douglas fir trees that covered half the island. The deer and sheep that populated the island could be seen scampering into the trees to escape the noisy invader. They never grew used to it.

"If the plane was to fail in flight, we'd be safer attempting to glide to a landing than jumping out of it." Miranda spun them around at the head of the field and began the final departure checklist.

The first of the rain pattered against the windshield. The storm had arrived faster than anyone predicted, but not fast enough to trap them here.

It wasn't until they'd rushed down the runway and the trees to the west gave way to the island's lush grass meadows that the full lash of the storm hit them broadside. Not enough to disconcert a pilot of Miranda's skill, but enough to wake Andi from her dark thoughts. *Crap!* She could have jumped out during the runup; wouldn't need a parachute for that at all.

Miranda took the gusty crosswind in stride and they were aloft well before they passed the main house. However much her autism made her unpredictable, nothing could dangerously distract her while piloting. To a former Night Stalker helicopter pilot for the US Army Special Operations Forces, Miranda's level of skill was incredibly sexy.

Sterile cockpit rules during takeoff and landing meant no side chatter during those crucial operations. So Andi couldn't discuss Taz and Jeremy's kid to distract herself. She couldn't wonder aloud how Holly and Mike were handling their first vacation together. At least not until Miranda had climbed out and pivoted south over Shaw

Island, which thankfully happened very quickly in the zippy little jet.

"Right now a Hawaiian beach sounds very inviting. Let's go there instead. Check in with Mike and Holly."

"The Citation M2's range is insufficient to reach Hawaii. Even if we were to route through San Francisco, it lacks seven hundred miles of range. Of course why would we go to San Francisco if your mother is flying *from* there to see you?" Miranda climbed quickly to ten thousand feet, then bolted south. The storm kicked them hard, several times, forcing Miranda to make far more corrections than usual. Rain squalls drove against the plane in heavy fusillades, muffled to a benign patter by the heavy sound insulation.

"That strikes me as the perfect reason to head for San Francisco. Besides, she isn't coming to see me. She's coming to meet you."

Andi was unsure if the plane's next motion was storm driven or Miranda had momentarily bobbled the controls.

"Meet *me*? Why would she want to meet me? Is there a plane crash she needs investigated?"

Andi couldn't help working a laugh past the knots in her gut. "Because you're my girlfriend. My longest relationship by a factor of three or four."

"Other than my year of on-again, off-again with Jon, you're my only relationship longer than seven days."

"Really?" Andi had always assumed that she was the neophyte in this situation.

"You're the only one who has ever tolerated my peculiarities this long."

"One, I like your peculiarities; they make you be you. And two, there are the others on the team."

"Yes, but I'm not dating them. I'm dating you." Then she

began communicating with SeaTac approach, once again ending the conversation just as it got interesting. The storm, coming in from the northwest but unable to move at four hundred knots, had fallen behind like a curtain drawn. But it would catch up with them soon.

Unable to speak during final approach, Andi contemplated that this adventure mapped new territory for both of them. That *did* draw down the fear factor.

Miranda landed smoothly and followed ground guidance to the main terminal. And there, waiting beside an airport security guard, was the worst idea in a long time.

Ching Hui Wu, the elegant matron of the San Francisco Wu clan, wore an emerald-green vintage Versace pantsuit. Her shoes and handbag matched, of course. *You can never overdress if your target is the high-end client.* And Wu and Wu Law was *the* intellectual property law firm for Silicon Valley and so many others. Their clients were very high end.

"She looks just like you." Miranda hadn't looked up from securing the plane since the airport marshal had crossed his batons telling her to stop. But, as Andi now knew, just because she hadn't looked didn't mean Miranda hadn't seen.

"No way."

"Based upon observability at this distance, the similarity is quite striking." Miranda continued scrolling through checklists that Andi was fairly sure she didn't need. They weren't staying, so there was no need for engine shutdown and warm start, but that didn't stop her.

"All Chinese look alike to Westerners." And she felt like a total heel the moment she said it.

Miranda raised her gaze slowly to stare at her face. As far as Andi knew, hers was the only face that Miranda ever looked at directly. "No, you don't. But you do look like your mother."

Touched by the former—and *deeply* disturbed by the latter—Andi unbuckled and stepped aft to lower the side door and greet her mother.

"Andrea, dear." Mother's scan of her jeans, t-shirt, and unzipped REI rain slick spoke volumes. "How nice of you to dress up for my visit."

Andi cursed, silently to herself. She'd known better, but the whole baby discussion with Miranda had blown that out of her mind as effectively as a Hellfire missile.

She offered a half bow as if taking a curtain call. This was who she was and Mother would finally have to take or leave that.

6

"No, don't!" Taz called out.

"What? Why?" All Jeremy had done was call Clarissa Reece, the Director of the CIA. "We're in southern Quebec. The sabotaged Embraer is therefore outside of direct FBI jurisdiction. The CIA covers international problems."

"But calling her direct?"

Jeremy shrugged as the ringing tone continued. "How many hours fighting our way through their bureaucracy do you want to do?"

"Christ! They *are* worse than the Pentagon. But—"

"Clarissa here. What do you want, Jeremy?" Sounded in his right ear as Taz spoke in the left.

"—I so hate that bitch."

"Tell her the feeling is mutual," Clarissa spoke without missing a beat.

"She says the feeling is mutual."

Taz's eye roll said that he probably shouldn't have repeated that part.

Clarissa's laugh agreed with Taz.

Jeremy explained the situation.

"Give me one reason why I should care. Let the Mounties and the Boston cops deal with it."

"Ernie Maxwell."

Stone silence over the phone and Taz squinted at him.

"What about him?"

"Isn't he the CIA Director of the Middle East Desk that you—"

"I know who the hell he is, Jeremy. What about him?"

"He was on the flight and is now in critical condition in a Montreal hospital."

"Which seat?" Taz whispered.

"2A."

And Taz sprinted into the plane.

"No, he said he was headed to Atlanta." Clarissa shouted at someone in the background demanding clarification from someone on Maxwell's whereabouts. He tipped his head to try and get some water out of his ear. It didn't work, but he became acutely aware of gritty sand under his collar—now sliding down his back. He tried to pull the sodden shirttail out before the sand was routed into his underwear, but his clothes were all so wet that all he did was give himself a wedgie.

"Shit!" Clarissa's curse confirmed that it was the right Ernie Maxwell at the same moment Taz returned. She was holding one half of a seatbelt, actually a quarter of one as she'd undone the buckle. Actually, three seatbelts.

"Strap cut most of the way through. Ernie," she held up one of the severed ends. The break was clean except for the few outer threads which had torn. Then she held up the other two. "And the two body bags."

"Director Ernie Maxwell *did* have his seatbelt buckled."

Jeremy fingered the edge of all three. Cut, then brushed lightly with a flame source, perhaps a lighter. It showed none of the inevitable fraying of cut polyester that might have been noticed. Yet the slice's unevenness said it was done fast. Still, it had proven sufficient to the task. "But someone cut it. Planned ahead of time, sealed with a lighter. Knew which seat he'd be in," he told Clarissa.

Taz spoke up. "Someone wanted to make sure he didn't survive the crash, just in case sabotaging the plane wasn't enough."

"Who were the other two?" Clarissa asked.

Jeremy pulled up the seat manifest and read off the names.

"Nope! Not mine. Maybe someone cut their belts to distract attention from Ernie."

"Or perhaps they were unsure of his seat, so they cut the three most likely." Taz always saw variations that he missed. She grabbed the phone and set it to speaker. "Good man or bad man?"

"Ernie? Good," Clarissa didn't even pause before answering.

Taz grunted. "Now I just have to decide if your definition of good matches mine."

Clarissa snorted but didn't argue. Maybe she'd already lost too many arguments with Taz in the past.

7

CLARISSA HUNG UP THE PHONE AND TURNED HER CHAIR TO HER office window on the top floor of the Original Headquarters Building.

Facing east along the Potomac, she wasn't gazing longingly toward downtown DC. Not anymore. Her political ambitions there had been crushed. One too many scandals—a few with hard evidence—wouldn't let her survive the press deep-diving her past as part of a political campaign. It was a point that President Roy Cole and the standing members of the House Intelligence Committee had made painfully clear.

She had enough dirt on the latter that they wouldn't move against her, but the *quid pro quo* they'd made crystalline clear: *If we go down, you go down.* The only thing that had saved their careers.

It was more than a little galling that Rose, her one friend—who had planned to run as her future VP—would make it to the White House without her. Not as an elected official, but as President Roy Cole's fiancé.

Rose and Roy had been completely transparent about their courtship, other than how soon after her husband's murder it had begun. The ex-Mrs. Senator Hunter Ramson's engagement last night was dominating this morning's news cycle—and America was eating it up. The widowed President finding true love halfway into his second term, and the reigning First Lady of DC's social scene becoming First Lady in title as well. Nobody seemed to be missing Senator Hunter Ramson at all, least of all Rose.

The news cycle timing worked well; it would bury the crash of the Embraer in Montreal to a mere a footnote. That would buy her time to figure out what the hell happened and why Ernie had lied to her about his itinerary.

No, she wasn't looking out her window toward DC. The three branches of government—legislative, judicial, and executive—were closed to her. Her fortieth birthday next month and she'd already reached as high as she would ever climb. However, expanding the power of the CIA, as it should be to protect all of those crappy little voter's way of life, would serve as ambition enough.

So, the distant glimpse of DC from CIA headquarters no longer drew her as it had when she'd married D/CIA Clark Winston and groomed him for the President's chair. Damn the bastard for getting himself killed.

Let it go, Clarissa. No matter how many times Rose gave her that advice, it had remained a fiery ball in her gut.

Enough of that shit. She was so done with the self-pity party.

As if her vision had cleared, Clarissa now gazed beyond the horizon—toward the Middle East, a third of the way around the globe. Out there, where the world feared the reach and power of the CIA, lay the future.

With Ernie in place, her attention had drifted. She'd focused west on China's final descent into demographic hell, doubly reinforced by a brutally authoritarian dictatorship. She'd be surprised if they lasted the decade. And east on that micro-penile ruler of Russia who could only jack himself off with war crimes and missile barrages.

And yet... Why was the Middle East always such a pain in the ass?

Ernie Maxwell in intensive care? Couldn't she catch a break?

His Assistant Director of the Middle East Desk lacked nothing in brains to run the desk effectively in her boss' absence, but she had no field experience. She'd risen through the bureaucratic side of the Agency, and Clarissa would have to vet her every choice.

Cutthroat enough to erase her boss to get the job? No, it didn't fit. He'd only recently elevated Marwa Samir to the position; it was too soon for such a move on her part. She also didn't seem the type—though Clarissa knew that they were the ones who needed the closest watching.

Someone had targeted Ernie specifically. Probably from outside the agency.

Who? And why?

Clarissa's history with him traced all of the way back to the torture black sites of the Afghanistan War. They'd processed plenty of Taliban and al-Qaeda through there together. Neither of them lacked for enemies.

If that was the connection, was she the next target?

But he'd also worked undercover in Syria, the American Embassy in Russia, and the Diego Garcia Black Site before she'd offered him the Middle East Desk. That island in the middle of the Indian Ocean was only the second time their careers had overlapped, but he'd done what was needed without hesitation.

There was that one escapee from Diego Garcia who remained at large: Paolo Ortiz, the self-proclaimed *Latin Wonder*. The other two escapees had been tracked and erased by the CIA's Special Operations Group—too dangerous to recapture and lock up again. It had also precluded any embarrassing explanations to Interpol.

Had Paolo resurfaced after two years to target Ernie Maxwell? She couldn't imagine how the man would know of Ernie's existence, much less care. Paolo's specialty was South and Central American coups—for a price. She'd tried to see if he was a part of the latest debacle in Peru but, if so, he'd kept an atypically low profile.

Yet someone had tracked Ernie on a flight from Boston to Montreal.

Boston to Montreal?

Why the hell would the Director of the Middle East Desk go to either one? And why had he lied about it?

She spun back to her computer and pulled up Ernie's bio. No travel to either recorded in his past. Montreal was *not* a hotbed of international intelligence cooperation. The CSIS, Canadian Security Intelligence Service, was based in Ottawa, which could be reached from DC direct. No reason for Boston or Montreal.

No personal connections to either.

No relatives.

No known Canadian mistresses, though there was a new girlfriend in Alexandria, Virginia, who'd been dutifully reported.

His wife had dumped him years ago—claimed she loved him but hated the hardship overseas postings that Ernie's career offered. They'd remained friends, which was more than she'd ever managed with an ex-lover.

So who the hell was he meeting there?

She placed a call to the CSIS and called in a favor. They promised her an agent would be at the hospital and call her the second Ernie woke up. She didn't even have to promise anything in return because Canadians were so goddamn polite.

8

ANDI LONGED TO SIT COPILOT BESIDE MIRANDA IN THE M2, even though she wouldn't be of any help. She flew rotorcraft, not fixed wing. But dutybound to sit with her mother in the cabin—and a knot in her stomach at having to—made her kowtow to the inevitable.

You're thirty-four, Andi Wu. You can be civil to your own mother for a few days. Keep your shit together. Now, soldier. Maybe if she was still a Spec Ops pilot the order would have worked—*Not!*

She entered the plane last after stowing Mother's luggage in the rear baggage hold, then hauled up and locked the flight stairs. That placed her in the tiny aisle between Miranda and her mother, making it almost impossible to introduce them. The ceiling was four-foot-nine, which meant even she had to duck five inches.

Feeling like a troll, she waved rearward. "Let's sit."

Miranda, of course, didn't think to step out of the open cockpit to introduce herself. Or even turn. It was the sort of social cue she never understood.

As soon as they hit the rear pair of the four facing seats, Miranda was on the radio requesting permission to taxi.

"She appears...preoccupied." Mother's tone, which could convince every member of a jury that an expert witness had lied, revealed the direness of Miranda's offense.

"No," Andi surprised herself with a sudden failure of her inbred familial meekitude. "First, SeaTac doesn't generally allow general aviation aircraft at its terminal, and they want us gone as quickly as possible. They do it as a special favor for her. Also," Andi took a deep breath and decided she should correct the real reason head on. "She's on the spectrum—Autism Spectrum Disorder. She would not intend or perceive rudeness. Instead, she moves to the next task."

"An emotionless automaton?" Mother arched one of her perfectly plucked eyebrows saying, *Why am I not surprised at such a choice.* Except the expression didn't quite fit. Was Mother simply surprised and no more?

"Not at all. She has plenty of emotions, maybe more than you or I. But they're an overwhelming confusing whorl."

"And this makes me confident in her abilities as a pilot how?" Andi was stuck as a hostile witness to be attacked on the stand.

"Because," she no longer rose to the bait, as she couldn't stop before she'd become a Night Stalker, "if a crisis hits, her emotions won't overwhelm her any more than they already do. She's the best civilian pilot I've ever flown with, and better than many military ones with far more training. And trust me, I'd know."

Curiously, that appeared to assuage Mother.

Miranda had taxied into place. She turned the M2 onto the active runway and ran the engines up for takeoff.

Mother's answer was to face forward and clutch the chair arms hard enough to permanently pucker the soft leather. Andi had forgotten she hated to fly. Perhaps nerves were why she'd opened with a frontal-assault gambit.

In a helo Andi had a terrible time relinquishing control, but in an airplane she always sat back and enjoyed the ride. Her pulse ticked up in anticipation of heading toward a new adventure, even when they were simply headed to the island. The power of a takeoff always made her smile.

They departed SeaTac to the south, climbing hard. The leading edge of the storm had caught up with them and the rain again pattered a light staccato on the hull. During the banked turn to the north, Andi glanced out the window, and square into the face of the storm.

She checked her watch. There should still be two more hours of daylight. But not to the north.

The storm had slammed in, dark and heavy past anything she'd seen since moving to the Pacific Northwest and joining Miranda's team two years ago. A brilliant flash in the heart of the storm illuminated the land below for the length of an eyeblink. Then another lightning strike and a third. Two years and she'd only seen three other thunderstorms in the Northwest—very rare here—and nothing like this.

Andi leaned out into the aisle and looked forward. The weather radar was painted in wide patches of intense-storm purple and heavy-rain red. She considered shouting to Miranda, but she had on a dual-muff headset—and it would scare the crap out of Mother.

Under normal conditions the jet was so small that communication inside the cabin wasn't a problem, but the drumbeat of the rain as they reached the true stormfront overwhelmed the plane's sound insulation. It must sound like a Dillon Aero M134 Minigun firing wide open on the outside. Inside wasn't much quieter.

She grabbed to release her seatbelt at the same time a gust slammed them aside. Mother screamed. Andi cursed as she tore a nail to the quick on the metal buckle, but was glad she hadn't released it as the jet plunged and twisted.

Seconds later, Miranda carved a turn back to the south.

The flight smoothed out in moments. They cleared the main body of rain and Andi could overhear Miranda calmly warning the local air traffic controller of dangerous wind shear conditions approaching SeaTac.

Andi reached over to rest a reassuring hand on Mother's—and received five-, then ten-pincer points for her trouble as she dug her fingernails into Andi's hand and forearm.

"I'm sorry, Mother. We're safe now." She glanced out the windshield and saw that Miranda was already approaching Tacoma Narrows Airport where the weather radar painted only scattered weak-rain green. A good choice as it lay a dozen miles south of SeaTac.

They'd be in the team hangar before the serious rain arrived there. Andi tried to remember if the team had left it clean after their last time there. It was never messy, as Miranda couldn't tolerate that, but at times their was a degree of frantic disarray during a crash investigation that they were occasionally slow to clear up.

Her mother's grip didn't ease until they were on the ground and had taxied into the hangar.

"See? Miranda's the best."

Her mother released her grip, and Andi felt the sharp tingle of blood rushing back into her arm. Mother's face had turned to stone.

Andi sighed. *Hello, Mother. Let me introduce you to my girlfriend who just scared you half to death.*

Someone up there hated her deeply.

9

When the Transports Canada rep arrived shortly after sunset, he had been very efficient. Or he wanted the negative news of the plane crash gone from Lac Brome's one beach as fast as possible.

A fresh audience from Knowlton, which Taz still had not seen though it lay less than a kilometer away, and the surrounding area gathered to watch the action. The children of the afternoon were replaced by families and people with phones busy posting videos to social media.

The fuel truck from Montreal arrived at the same time as an environmental team. Floodlights were set up, and in under an hour, the plane had been ringed by absorbent floats and pumped dry.

A team from Embraer arrived. It took them little longer to remove the wings. It was awkward as one end was propped up on the beach close by the fuselage, and they had to place jackstands underwater farther along. The horizontal and vertical stabilizers were next removed from the tail until nothing but a hundred-foot-long sleek bullet of the fuselage remained.

While a Royal Canadian Air Force CH-147 Chinook helicopter carried off each wing, a team of divers arrived. Luggage was retrieved from the partly submerged cargo area and loaded onto a waiting truck. They then repaired the door seal with a simple run of duct tape all around the seam. After that the local fire department pumped the airplane dry once more.

Before they towed it away, Taz swept through the onboard systems and recovered several more retail-grade controllers, all wi-fi compatible.

By the time she was done, the fuselage bobbed and rolled on the surface. Once she stepped onto the beach, a small fleet of Zodiac boats tied onto the fuselage.

Even with the water and cargo removed, the plane's fuselage was beyond the lifting capacity of any helicopter. So they were towing it three kilometers across the lake to where only a single row of power lines separated the main road from the water. A line crew, a pair of cranes, and an oversize flatbed truck would be meeting it there and everything would be gone by morning.

The environmental team checked the entire shore once more, and then the local fire department folded up the emergency lights and took down the No Trespassing yellow tape.

Taz checked her watch. Midnight. The crowd had diminished slowly, but the last few die-hards were gone.

Soon, the only sign of the day's activities were the numerous paths tramped on the beach and the deep groove where the fuselage had nosed ashore and knocked over the metal lifeguard stand. She was half surprised that the groundskeeper hadn't been rousted from bed to rake the sand back into conformity.

She sat on the sand at the apex of where the plane had reached, her butt on the loose sand and her feet on the hardpacked area where the nose had flattened and curved it into a parabolic trough.

Through it all, Jeremy had remained at a picnic table spread with his array of equipment for reading the QAR and the flight recorders. Had he even noticed it was dark or that the plane had been disassembled mere meters away? Having long since learned that asking him when he'd be done bordered on the absurd side of foolish, she lay back on the sand and stared up at the summer sky.

Orion, Cygnus, Lyra. Stars hadn't been of note in Mexico City, the barrios of San Diego, or living in DC and working at the Pentagon. But Jeremy knew and loved them. He knew how to perform celestial navigation with a sextant and tracked the planets and meteor showers. He'd even been one of the very first to apply for the one-way trip to Mars as a pioneer-settler when that had been a thing—which she'd never heard of.

So, she had learned the constellations. And enough of the planets to recognize the red of Mars transiting Gemini.

She'd always been a quick study, because her life had depended on learning English or Air Force politics or analyzing a plane crash. Horizons past surviving tomorrow were as far away as the sands of the tiny point of red glistening so far above.

Yet her hand rested on her belly.

For the nineteen years she'd maneuvered her way through Pentagon madness, she'd always had a go bag near and a preplanned bolt hole. The six months of her supposed death had proceeded day-to-day until Miranda's team had recognized her at a crash site. There was a time when survival choices had seriously downshifted, more like minute-to-minute, and twice down to mere seconds.

Long-term thinking belonged in the realm of aliens from those shining stars above.

Yet lately, when she hadn't been paying attention, she'd slipped out of survival mode.

She now had a role, a man who loved her enough to put a ring on her finger, and a life growing in her belly. What was this, the 1950s? Sooo disorienting.

Did she know how to think year-to-year? Lifelong? Taz had no more frame of reference to do that than she did about living on Mars. Actually, the latter possessed far greater clarity as Jeremy made her watch every show about living on Mars, no matter if it was a documentary or a ludicrous piece of science fiction.

Yet here she lay, much as she might in a spacesuit on Mars, staring up at the unreachable stars with Earth no more than a blue-white spark in the skies.

Her military life had been tip of the spear. As the assistant to three-star General JJ Martinez, she'd been his enforcer within the Pentagon bureaucracy.

As Jeremy's assistant, she'd become second fiddle. The Air Force hadn't fooled anyone when they'd re-upped her after her Presidential pardon. Instead of being the pariah she'd deserved, she'd retained her rank as full colonel and they'd assigned her to the Air Force's Accident Investigation Board. Now, as far as she could tell, she served only one purpose on the AIB; that of liaison to the two air-crash-investigation geniuses of the NTSB, Miranda Chase and Jeremy Trahn.

Second place was her role in life and she'd thought she was at peace with it. She'd thrived in a behind-the-scenes lifestyle, but with General Martinez, she'd been his hammer. With Jeremy, his connection to reality?

One thing was certain, nothing about a child was behind the scenes.

She tipped her head back, getting even more sand in her hair, if that was possible.

Jeremy still sat at the picnic table surrounded by his equipment; his face eerily lit by his laptop. He'd work through the night if his batteries lasted. Like Miranda, he was the master of detail. But the big picture eluded him almost as thoroughly as it did her. Miranda had a whole team around her to provide it, Jeremy only had herself.

Maybe it was time to reforge her role on the Jeremy-Taz team. With Mr. Detail Jeremy, she always had served another purpose. Not Martinez's hammer, but Jeremy's wider view.

So, Colonel Vicki Taz Cortez, she looked back up at Mars, *what is the big picture?*

A sabotaged plane.

A targeted CIA Director of the Middle East Desk. One who'd survived with a shattered shoulder, bruised ribs, and a concussion that he hadn't yet woken from—surgery on hold until he did.

Senator Hunter Ramson and possibly even Vice President Clark Winston had gone down due to a Saudi plot. A few princes had abruptly disappeared after those two events. Two of them had shown up in Macau, at least their bodies had. Three more had never been heard from again. Provable links traceable to the Crown Prince—who must have ordered it all? Didn't exist, of course.

Was Ernie Maxwell the next victim to fall beneath the long but clumsy arm of the House of Saud?

Or was it some other state actor?

Who would hate a CIA desk director enough to kill a planeload of tourists to remove him? Now there was a list as long as her arm.

She held it up into the night, a shadow against the stars. Okay, longer than her arm. Women who stood four-eleven didn't possess model-length elegant limbs.

If she wanted to anonymously remove someone from the CIA—like the D/CIA herself, Clarissa Reese, perhaps—there would be far easier ways than the eleven timers and switches they'd found rigged throughout the plane's systems. A bomb in the cockpit would have been far more effective.

In fact, several of the devices hadn't been triggered at all.

Done in stages? The failures hadn't been simultaneous, but rather a cascade of failures.

Which meant what?

Trip device Number One—engine flameout from fuel starvation. Didn't cause enough trouble. Trip Number Two—nav-comm out. More dangerous but not there yet. Trip Number Three—hydraulics...

Someone had to be aboard to judge that. And have some kind of controller.

"Jeremy!" Taz shoved to her feet and almost stumbled face-first into the water. Saving herself by inches, she raced up to the table he was working at and began shaking him.

"What? I heard you the first time."

"I never know how to tell. The timers!" She grabbed one of the plastic bags laid out on the bench beside him. Inside was the first hose timer she'd found. "They aren't manual control only. They had wireless capability. Someone aboard was controlling the failures one by one. We need an inventory of every item that was found loose in the cabin."

"Half of the bins popped open and dumped out into the aisle. *Everything* was loose."

"Pictures. I need pictures. No! The plane!" She twisted around to look out over the lake. The distant work lights were still aglow where they were extracting the fuselage from the water. "Now I know what I'm looking for. Hurry up!" She slapped his laptop closed and began pulling cables.

"Hey! You—" Jeremy stopped, then muttered, "Why would I try to argue?"

"Smart boy."

Between them they had everything gathered up in seconds and were racing toward the rental car.

10

"Shoot me now, please!" Andi collapsed on the bed of their Gig Harbor team house.

"I don't have a gun with me." Miranda wore a long flannel nightgown as she brushed her teeth. It was a very conservative nightgown that typically made Andi think about how much fun it would be getting her out of it. Not tonight.

"Pretty please." She'd survived the evening being all-polite with Mother, but it had been touch and go. Not some nice practice touch-and-go landing with wheels kissing the runway, then powering up to return aloft for another practice loop. It had been second-to-second desperation to teleport off the planet as far as possible. Alpha Centauri should be nice this time of year. It had been a good thing she didn't carry a sidearm herself.

Once they were inside the team hangar, Miranda had introduced Mother to both her helicopter and her vintage F-86 Sabrejet as if they were her best friends. That had led to a guided tour of the secure office space Miranda had installed in the back of the hangar.

Everything was neat and in place, because Miranda couldn't function any other way. But it was world weary. One wall had become a museum of part failures: a cracked engine block from a Zivko Edge aerobatics plane, a bent seventy-seven-inch propellor blade from when a C-130 had struck a FedEx truck, the half-ton core of a Pratt & Whitney turbine that had shattered a blade and destroyed a Falcon 7X bizjet, and more.

The workbench along the far wall showed a thousand scratches and scars from equipment analyzed there, especially flight recorders. The couches were threadbare along the edges after two years of exhausted team members collapsing on them for a few hours' sleep before dragging off to continue some investigation. Only Miranda's Victorian rolltop desk and Mike's espresso machine looked little the worse for wear.

Andi's Mini Cooper had been the only vehicle at the hangar for the ride into town. Of course, Mother had always hated her car with a passion.

What does it say to Wu and Wu's clientele that you drive such a car? If you had to go British, you could at least drive a Jaguar. She didn't say the words this time, but she'd said it every single time Andi had driven it to the office back when she'd been interning as a law student.

Pointing out that an Indian company owned Jaguar, and that her Mini was manufactured by the same German company that made her mother's chauffeured 7-series BMW luxury sedan hadn't been the road to familial peace. Pointing out that she wasn't a Wu and Wu lawyer or associate had also gained no traction. *You are my daughter and your choices reflect on our company.*

Dunagan Irish Pub & Brewery was a team favorite, but clearly not up to Mother's standard either. Andi's preferred Irish stew was bucking for release as she flopped across the foot of the bed. Miranda's shepherd's pie didn't appear to be bothering her in the slightest.

Miranda approached from the far side of the bed and looked at her upside down. "If I were to shoot you, you would be dead."

"That's the point."

"Am I right that would upset your mother in the morning?"

"Not half as much as it would upset me having to face her tomorrow morning."

Miranda sank to sit on the bed by Andi's head. "I don't understand. I try so hard, but I don't. I'm so sorry, Andi. I wish I was better for you."

"No, Miranda. Don't listen to me. I'm just feeling sorry for myself. Mother has always hated me—I literally can't remember a civil conversation. But I think she likes you despite herself." Andi reached up to tuck Miranda's hair behind one ear so that she could see Miranda's face.

"I don't think she hates you. I think—" Miranda pushed to her feet just as Andi was reaching for her, leaving her with empty arms when she simply wanted to hide her face against Miranda's belly.

Miranda strode over to her belongings lined up in a neat row upon the dresser. She picked up one of her ever-present notebooks and studied one of its pages for a moment.

The emoji page, Andi was willing to bet.

"This is the expression I think I detected on her face,"

she returned to the bed with the notebook and held it for Andi to see.

"Confusion?"

"Yes, I think it would be reasonable to conclude that you confuse your mother."

"Confusion?" Andi asked the ceiling. "Why would I confuse her?"

"I don't know. You're the one who is her daughter." Miranda placed her notebook once more in its proper place and climbed into bed, scooting her feet down close by Andi's head. She didn't say anything, but knew that Andi knew she was in the way of Miranda's preferred sleeping position.

She always slept along the exact centerline of her half of the bed, flat on her back, with her hands folded over her breastbone. The position was so uncanny that, early on, Andi would jolt awake in the night and watch carefully by the nightlight until she was sure Miranda was still breathing.

With a sigh, Andi headed to brush her own teeth, no closer to any answers.

11

The Embraer 175's fuselage dangled fifteen feet in the air as the truck drove underneath it. It was a strange rig. The hundred-foot fuselage couldn't be rested on a multipart trailer; it wouldn't bend in the middle. Instead, a big cross-country tractor truck pulled a sixty-foot low-boy trailer under the fuselage.

Taz and Jeremy had pulled over to the side of the road to watch as they were lowering it with the nose inching closer behind the truck's cab. The underside of the last thirty feet of the tail sloped upward, sticking well out beyond the back of the trailer. The plane itself was under ten feet wide, not counting the short stub remains of the wings that stuck out to either side. Maneuvering this contraption along the twisting two-lane was going to take a magician of a driver along with several spotter cars and an RCMP escort.

Jeremy was soon in the middle of the fray, offering advice on precisely where to place the support wedges in line with the frame members to avoid denting the hull's skin. It shouldn't surprise her that he knew as much as the Embraer reps, but it did, every time he or Miranda did something like that.

She followed along to make sure he didn't irritate anyone. No need to be worried. Once past their surprise, the techs welcomed his advice.

As they eased the fuselage closer and closer to the truck bed, apparently by the nanometer, Taz could do nothing but pace back and forth—waiting. Waiting was the worst thing ever. Watching Jeremy work lasted her six minutes. Going for a long walk down the road ended a hundred and three meters after she started, including the return. Impatiently tapping her foot served as a fine distraction for thirty-seven seconds. Other than that, all she could do was stay out of the way and growl at anyone who came near her.

Time was slipping by and that itch between her shoulders said that those minutes were becoming more important by the second.

The moment the fuselage touched the truck bed, before the first restraining strap had been heaved over, she clambered up on a wing stub and entered through the still missing over-wing emergency door.

Men shouted to stop her.

She didn't slow down enough to give them the finger.

The inside reeked of spilled coffee.

The moment she turned on her headlamp, she knew she was screwed. No water had entered the upper cabin, but it was still a mess. Detritus filled the aisle and spread under the seats in mounds of safety brochures, paper coffee cups, and snack bags. All the overhead bins were open and empty. No personal belongings lay in the aisle. The crew had cleared them out to return to the passengers.

Still, Taz moved to the rear of the plane. The smell was

stronger back here. In the rear galley she could see the coffee carafes that had dumped their contents into the carpet.

Could see it because there was minimal floor garbage here.

Why?

Oh! The plane had slammed hard enough into the beach to eject Mr. Middle East Desk out of his seat and smash him against the next seat forward once his seatbelt failed. Hard enough to kill the other two with sabotaged seatbelts. Anything on the floor would have shot forward as the plane slammed into the beach.

Taz turned around. Sure enough, as she moved along the aisle toward the nose of the plane, the junk layer deepened—a scattering, a covering, then small piles gathered around seat supports. Maybe what she was looking for had hit the floor and slid forward.

A burly man blocked her way when she reached the middle of the aisle over the wing.

"Miss, you can't be in here."

"I'm busy. I'm from the Air Force Accident Investigation Board. That's A-I-B." she pointed at the big yellow letters on her vest. Except she'd taken it off hours ago and realized she was pointing at her breast. *Real smooth, Taz.*

She debated simply pulling out her Taser Pulse and threatening to shoot him. Reaching for newfound patience she hadn't realized was in her, she fished out her Air Force ID.

"Accident Investigation Board."

He studied it carefully. She should have tazed him and been done with it.

When he finally returned it, she pushed past him and didn't bother to watch him leave.

Taz found a gift two rows later. Economy seats had given way to three rows of Premium Class offering the extra three inches that someone her size would never waste money to pay for. The aisle jogged left for the transition to First Class: two seats to the right and one to the left instead of two-and-two. At the transition, a solid bulkhead separated the classes.

That was the gift because all of the economy and premium junk had gathered against the back side of the bulkhead. A quick paw through unearthed nothing. Whoever had the money to pay to sabotage a plane—a little equipment but a lot of bribes there—and the balls to be aboard while they were doing it, wouldn't think twice about flying First Class. Especially not if their target was also up there in Seat 2A.

With a fresh start, she moved much slower to inspect the four rows of First Class.

Nothing.

Nothing.

Nothing.

Not even on the entryway floor or what little had slid through the flight attendant position into the cockpit.

Maybe it wasn't on the floor.

Tucked safe in someone's pocket? No. They wouldn't risk being caught holding whatever device had controlled the sabotage devices.

Jammed into a seat cushion? Nothing in the cracks of those twelve seats except for old salted almonds and a pink coffee stirrer.

Tucked in a seat pocket?

Nothing in Row Four or Three. Row One was up against the forward bulkhead and had no stowage.

Row Two? Unlikely. As that's where the target victim sat, where she'd found the partially severed seat belt.

But in the pocket on the back of Seat 1B—a phone. A phone with a custom app for controlling the various devices hidden in the plane's systems? Perhaps it belonged to the person in Seat 2B. Seemed kind of obvious.

Had whoever sabotaged the plane and Director Ernie Maxwell's seatbelt been sitting directly across the aisle from him?

She tapped it awake.

Locked, with plenty of battery life.

And a greeting screen background that she absolutely recognized.

12

Taz wore a path all the way through the linoleum flooring outside of the post-op recovery ward of Montréal General Hospital.

At least it felt that way.

If Jeremy suggested she sit down on the hard plastic seats next to him one more time, she'd throttle him just to have something to do. Besides, being four-eleven, her feet never touched the floor when seated. She hated that.

The changing shifts of a lone RCMP guard did nothing to relieve the tedium. They consistently took their post by the surgery recovery ward door, opened a book, and began reading.

The nurse from hell remained firmly planted at her station across the wide hall. She only roused herself to block Taz at every turn since her arrival.

Middle East Desk Director Ernie Maxwell had woken from his concussion enough for the doctors to put him back under for shoulder surgery. The nurse had tried to stonewall her on even that tidbit of information until

Nightwatch

she'd invoked CIA Director Clarissa Reese upon her head.

For eight hours she'd been waiting to get to him. Seven if she didn't count the drive from Lac Brome, but she did because that's where she actually *wanted* to be.

He'd now been out of surgery for twenty minutes, but they estimated several hours before he'd be even marginally coherent.

"What's going on?" Clarissa came clacking down the hall. Five-ten (six-one with the mid-heels of her black ankle boots), white-blonde ponytail to the middle of her back, and a blood-red power suit that Taz wholly approved of—if she stabbed the bitch, the blood would barely show. Too bad she had a bodyguard in tow.

"Since when do you care enough about anyone to fly to Montreal?"

"Since you suddenly showed such an interest in him that you're perched outside his operating suite like a carrion crow. Or perhaps a carrion sparrow."

"I might be a foot shorter and weigh less than your tits, but don't fuck with me, Clarissa. I've lost a night's sleep to this and I'm no longer easily amused. Worse, I had to bug out of Knowlton without even a chance to look around." Which was ridiculous in the face of a crash investigation but she threw that gripe at Clarissa anyway.

The woman squinted down at her.

"Shit! Doesn't anyone here read? Southern Quebec? Knowlton? Inspector Gamache?"

The bodyguard who'd arrive with Clarissa spoke softly, "Louise Penny."

"Thank you! My God, how did someone with a brain end up working at the CIA?"

The man offered her a flash of a grin before returning to being a somber non-entity scanning the halls for crazed scalpel-wielding nurses with even more of a hate-on for Clarissa Reese than she had herself.

Taz wondered if she could do Clarissa in and get off by claiming that she was all hormonal with her pregnancy. Probably not. A real pity as feeling like this…*mayhem* in her body should be good for *something*. The woman was as dirty as they came, yet she kept surviving. Taz had fought corruption and dirty dealers for nineteen years inside the Pentagon; she wasn't about to stop now.

The RCMP room guard held up the book he was reading to show her the cover. Despite his overly serious appearance, he was clearly paying more attention than she was. Another fan.

Taz held up the phone she'd found, close enough to make Clarissa's eyes cross. "I found this in a nearby seat—nearby Ernie Maxwell. I need his face."

"Why, if it wasn't his phone?"

She tapped it awake to show the lock screen image. "Recognize that?"

Clarissa cursed. The bodyguard leaned over to look around Clarissa's shoulder. His nod was all the confirmation Taz needed.

The phone's screen saver image was *Kryptos*. It was a beautiful and enigmatic sculpture that stood in the CIA headquarters' inner courtyard—past several layers of security Taz had never penetrated. But she'd certainly seen the miniature of it in Miranda's home garden enough times to recognize it.

"That phone is secured for a reason." Clarissa reached

Nightwatch

for it but Taz slapped her hand away hard enough to elicit a satisfying yelp.

"I have a theory and I need to test it. For now this is evidence."

"So, let's go. Because I'm not letting that phone out of my sight."

"Tell that to her," Taz waved at the nurse who'd been studiously ignoring them at her station across the hall.

Clarissa spoke a single word, "Kurt."

The bodyguard moved up to the desk ever so casually. Taz shifted close enough to hear him.

"Ma'am. The Director of the CIA wishes to visit one of her key directors. This is a matter of US National Security."

"He is my patient. And you will not disturb him without a doctor's direct order."

"And the doctor?"

"Is performing back-to-back surgeries and will not be available until at least—"

"Ma'am," Kurt said in that same implacable tone. "If you wish the next three minutes to go quietly, you will place your hands palm down on the desk in clear view and make no attempt to reach for any alarm. You will not raise your voice or move abruptly without my express permission. Are we clear?" He said it so calmly. It was familiar…

The pieces came together. Kurt, no bets on his real name, moved and spoke the way Holly Harper did when she wanted something badly. A former SASR operator—Australian Special Air Service Regiment—she was the single most lethal person Taz had ever tangled with.

Kurt of the CIA, threatening a nurse without hesitation, revealed his training similar to Holly's. He stank of SOG—Special Operations Group—the arm of the CIA specializing in assassinations, coups, and other illegal black ops. A group they'd tangled with during a crash on Johnston Atoll in the South Pacific.

The nurse glared, preparing to ignore him. But then she glanced her way and Taz shook her head very slightly. Taz was good, but she'd long since learned she couldn't begin to take on Holly. If Kurt was what she guessed, Taz wouldn't be messing with him either.

Making the same assessment, the nurse rested her hands on her desk, but didn't stop boring vicious-nurse-eye lasers at Kurt.

"If you value your hide, Kurt, you'd better keep the nurse away from scalpels."

Again that hint of a smile, there and gone.

The Mountie guard had his hand on his sidearm.

Clarissa handed her ID to the Mountie. "I'm CIA Director Clarissa Reese. I'm the one who put you here."

To his credit, he was careful enough to verify that against the orders in his pocket before he nodded. But he didn't return to his book.

"Masks, and wash your hands at the station on your right," The nurse called out despite Kurt's instruction to keep quiet.

When Taz waved for Jeremy to join them, he remained in his seat and looked a little green around the gills. The man could walk through a wrecked airplane and discuss the aerodynamics of spatter patterns of the victims' dried blood. But he couldn't walk into a hospital room without fainting. It didn't bode well for when she gave birth in seven months. That thought had even *her* feeling a bit queasy.

"Fine. Stay and keep the nurse from killing Kurt."

"Uh—"

She left him looking over at the SOG operator and led Clarissa through the swinging door. They masked up and washed their hands.

Once through the outer bastion, the attending nurses assumed they were supposed to be there and led them to Bed Six.

Taz had never been a fan of hospitals herself, not that she'd let Jeremy or Clarissa ever know that. Maybe she'd go for an at-home delivery. Though she liked the idea of having all of that nice technology surrounding her just in case.

The man lying on the bed was a big guy—not heavy, just big. No wonder he'd made a mess of himself when his seatbelt gave way. Forties? His dark hair was belied by the gray in his day's growth of beard. Hair dye. Fifties she decided.

He had an oxygen tube clipped in his nose, three bags of intravenous drips: a big bag of saline, and two smaller of an antibiotic and a painkiller. Each ran into a machine that metered them out. There were ranks of other equipment sitting idle, ready to pounce if something went wrong. She finally picked out a heart monitor, but the pulse was so slow that she figured he must still be asleep.

Clarissa looked paler than even her usual fair skin. "Christ, Ernie," she whispered to him.

He had several facial bandages. One arm in a cast that started at his first knuckle and went all the way past his shoulder. It had one of those weird rigs with a steel pole to support the arm in an immobile position attached to a harness around his midriff so that the arm stuck up into the air like a sick greeting wave from some zombie corpse.

Taz held the phone in front of his face and tapped the screen awake.

Nothing.

She propped open one of his eyes with her fingers and that was enough, the phone unlocked.

"Well?" Clarissa asked.

"Definitely his phone." The first thing she did was open the security settings and give herself a password. She didn't let Clarissa see that.

Then she swiped up to review recent apps and opened the one that had been active immediately preceding her access to the security settings.

13

"What the *hell?*" Clarissa couldn't make sense of what she was seeing.

A nurse shushed her. Patients, groggy with post-surgical drugs looked wild-eyed in their general vicinity with few managing to quite focus. Ernie Maxwell didn't move at all.

Clarissa told the nurse to go screw herself.

Taz spun Clarissa about by the elbow and shoved her, stumbling, out of Recovery and toward the outer nurse's station. She hated being manhandled, especially by a pipsqueak like Colonel Taz Cortez. But past experience had taught her not to fight back against the little Latina. She could still feel where the knife had rested against her throat when Taz had once threatened to cut her head off. Clarissa knew her record well enough to believe that sufficiently provoked, Taz might—then and now.

Once they were in the hall, Taz shook her. "Is that how you operate, arguing with a post-op nurse just doing her job? You're pitiful, Clarissa."

If she had claws, she'd slash open Taz's face. At least that feeling was mutual.

Kurt still waited beside the receptionist nurse, whose hands remained flat on her desk. Jeremy fooled with his computer as if they'd never left. The Mountie stood by the door where he'd been watching them through the window.

"Is there an empty room where we can talk?" Kurt asked.

"D804," the nurse pointed down the hall with one finger raised off the desk.

He nodded politely and led the way.

To fit into D804 they had to stand in a circle around the empty bed, like they were standing around a deathbed with the patient gone.

Kurt closed the door and leaned his back against it, that anchored one corner. She and Taz ended up along either side and Jeremy at the foot.

He dropped his laptop on the rolling table thing and Taz set Ernie's phone beside it.

Clarissa could only watch as he pulled a plastic evidence bag from his pack. Inside she saw a watering hose timer.

Taz tapped several controls on the phone until the timer gave out a grinding whirr that made Clarissa jump. It seemed to echo in the small room. A light on the display turned green. She tapped it again. It whirred in response and offered a red light.

"I repeat, what the hell?"

"This one was inserted into the Engine One fuel line. Amateur move, and dangerous to use a water hose timer on a line carrying Jet A, but effective." Taz didn't look up. Instead she and Jeremy repeated the act with two more controllers of types she didn't recognize but that had status lights which changed color on command once the appropriate control was tapped.

"You're telling me that my Director of the Middle East Desk sabotaged the plane *he* was flying on? And that he did it so poorly that he needed eight hours of surgery?"

Taz simply waved at the controllers on the table in their individual evidence bags.

Jeremy, like the little boy he sometimes was, continued pulling them from his pack one by one. Each time, he tapped the screen until he made it buzz, whirr, or blink in turn, then placed them in order.

Taz took the phone, opened the Contacts list, and punched something.

Clarissa's phone rang in her purse.

"How many people have that number?"

Clarissa glared at her as Taz let it keep ringing until she finally ground out, "Not many."

With Clark dead, there was nobody personal. Murdered only a year ago, and with him labeled a national hero, she couldn't even risk dragging some man into her bed without making headline news.

"Outside of my department heads, the FBI, and the top tier at the White House, no one has this number. And you lot, of course." Miranda's team continued to be annoying at every turn, even the ones who were no longer *on* that team.

"Final proof that it was his phone. He must have stuffed it in the seat pocket across the aisle when he realized things had gone wrong."

"Who sat there?"

Jeremy tapped his keyboard for a few moments. "Seats 2B and 2C were a retired couple from an old Montreal family."

Clarissa turned to Kurt. "Your work?"

Moving as silently as ever, the ex-Delta Force operator leaned over to inspect the app when Taz showed no sign of handing it over. Then he picked up each plastic bag in turn, setting each back on the dead man's dinner table precisely where he'd picked it up.

Jeremy also offered him three cut seatbelts to inspect.

Finally Kurt offered a shrug. "We could certainly do it, but it doesn't have the right feel." As long a sentence as he ever uttered.

Clarissa pulled out her phone, set it on speaker, and dialed the cyber twins—the married couple who headed up the CIA's cyber-security and cyber-attack assets. Heidi answered.

"Hi Clarissa. You haven't called in weeks, what's wrong now?"

"There's an app on Ernie Maxwell's phone. I need to know its origin."

"Is he bringing it down to us?"

"He's in a Montreal hospital. I've got the phone here. The number is—"

A rattle of a computer keyword. "I've got it. Is the phone unlocked? Oh it is, good, that makes it easier. Which app? The open one? Some kind of timer controller? Let me grab a copy."

The phone didn't flicker or offer any other indication that Heidi had just hacked it. Clarissa needed to make sure they couldn't ever do that to her phone. Of course, the people she'd need to make sure of that *were* the cyber twins. Fat chance.

"Did you know that between Google and Apple," Heidi continued rambling, "they control ninety-five percent of the app market. That's over eight million apps including games. That doesn't count sideloaded custom work like this one."

Clarissa sighed. She'd never found a way to stop Heidi's joy of computer trivia.

"Hi, Heidi and Harry," Jeremy spoke up. He didn't pause for a response—he and the cyber twins were like the nerd triumvirate. "Did you also know that even though ninety-four percent of the official ones are the free versions, the remaining six percent have a total worth over six trillion dollars, which is more than Japan's GDP, the world's third largest economy? That's if it happened all in one year instead of the last thirteen."

"Slick! Hi, Jeremy. So, we've got a plane crash involved here, do we? Oh, the Embraer 175 into a lake. Is it nice up there? Taz with you on this holiday?"

The rattle of keys over the phone didn't cease as Taz called out a "Hey there."

"This is a nice bit of code."

Jeremy had continued testing and shuffling the controllers around to match the order on the phone. "Huh, that's weird."

He was never a man who needed prompting to explain something.

"Each controller responds individually to its matching control. But when I select the fifth cutoff on the phone—one assumes that he worked from the top down—it triggers a cascade." He tapped the fifth button and the fifth controller in his line of plastic bags blinked from green to red. Two seconds later the sixth one flipped, then the seventh, eighth, and ninth. "He'd have thought he was causing incremental failures, but after triggering the fifth, the following systems would have failed rapidly making the plane only marginally controllable. Maybe it's a coding error."

More key rattles from Heidi. "Nope. Right here in the code clean as can be. There's a trigger on Step Five to launch a subloop tripping the next four at two-second intervals. Nasty. You know...this code reminds me of something. Harry," she called out, "look at this and tell me what it reminds you of."

"Huh. Remember that Turkish hacker?"

"Oh sure. The guy who cracked the GPS satellites and almost killed the VP—" Heidi finally paused. "Uh, sorry, Clarissa. I wasn't thinking. But he did...almost...back in—"

"Forget it. That was so two years ago. Is this the Turkish hacker come back?" Clarissa didn't need to be reminded of anything about Clark or how his first brush with death had made him a shoo-in for the Presidency. She slammed down a mental shield on her emotions on how his death had permanently fucked her path to the Oval Office.

"No, I know where he is and what he's up to. But there are similarities to his way of thinking," Heidi responded. "Something in the structure of the code that isn't, well, Western. Wild guess, and that's all this is, I wouldn't even bet a pizza on it—it's equatorial."

"Equatorial?"

"Western code is code in a hurry, and often a little sloppy. Bloatware at its worst." It sounded as if Heidi dumped a pile of jellybeans on the table close by the phone, sounding like gunfire. Her crunching noises confirmed that. "Eastern code tends toward the concise. Middle East, Africa, the lower Americas, even India tend to make code that gets there but isn't in a real hurry. Kinda a random rule of thumb but it's an indicator."

"That narrows it down for me nicely—only half of the damn world." Clarissa sometimes wondered why she bothered with them, even if they were the best hackers in the business. She stared at the empty bed. Who had last died here? And did she need to make sure Ernie never made it out of this hospital?

Harry started laughing, "Hey, this guy is still using WhatsApp. How old school is that? Wait...Ooo! Handshaking with the Telegram app. That's harsh."

"In *English*."

"Well, looking at the rest of this guy's phone, he ain't the savviest tech user around. The thing's a mess of installed apps, half not used since a day or two post-install, and not organized in any way that makes sense. Tells me that he couldn't have been the one to set up the secure messaging structure, as that's custom work. And he definitely didn't write the timer app. Someone is giving him a big hand up. Of course, that added cascade trigger offers him a big hand back down too."

"And..."

"There's no *and*, Clarissa," Heidi spoke up. "Telegram is world-class encryption. Even the CIA uses it. Might as well be a dead-drop. No tracing it."

"Fine. Call me when you figure it out."

Clarissa had the small satisfaction of hanging up in the middle of Heidi's squawk of protest. She looked at the other three.

"Okay, so what's next?"

"Nothing." Jeremy spoke up and, for once, didn't elaborate endlessly.

"What do you mean *nothing?*"

"We're done. Taz and I discovered not only what

happened to the plane but who caused it to happen. We are not police. The NTSB has no enforcement capacity. We can only observe, conclude, and advise."

Taz opened her mouth but Jeremy shook his head.

"No. I won't fall into the same trap Miranda does. Miranda does it unintentionally, but has been kidnapped, drugged, nearly shot down, and had to make an emergency landing on the National Mall in DC when her private plane was sabotaged. Don't forget spending a week trapped in a shot-down plane in Antarctica. You're pregnant. You're going to be the mother of our child. *We* will not be putting ourselves in harm's way knowingly or otherwise."

Clarissa could only stare in amazement as Colonel Taz Cortez turned from steel to potato-mush, sniffled, and buried her face against Jeremy's shoulder as he kissed her atop her head.

"Christ! Get a room, you two."

A flicker of a smile crossed Kurt's features.

"What?"

He nodded toward the bed. "They've got one." Then he opened the hospital room door and waved for her to precede him out.

14

Once they were aloft, Andi blessed the gods of the four winds that the Tacoma Narrows Airport lay only a nine minutes' flight from Miranda's island. She could manage that, then there would be many other distractions.

To fill the dead air in the cabin, she tried to make a joke about her odd ability to murder Miranda's vegetable garden at a distance.

"The flowers don't appear to suffer. I can walk within two feet of a rose or dahlia and it barely whimpers. Let me within ten of a green pepper and it will turn brown in three heartbeats. Peas shrivel in the pod if someone so much as says my name inside the fence line."

Calling Mother's expression *tolerant* would be a gross exaggeration but it was still a hint of a smile—Andi was taking that as a win.

"So we have The Bench. I may not have become a lawyer like you wanted, but I'm now relegated to a bench that—"

The plane jinked hard left then right. Mother's grip went white on the armrest.

Andi spoke fast to reassure her. "Must be a left-over bit of turbulence from last night's storm. The FAA notifications didn't report any, but it happens."

But looking out the windows, it shouldn't have. The storm had moved on leaving a high overcast sky. The water below appeared calm. She could see several sailboats on Puget Sound that looked as if they were barely moving. They certainly weren't heeled over in a strong wind or leaving white wakes. A pilot learned to assess wind conditions under any circumstances in case of an emergency landing situation, and there simply weren't any alarming indicators.

The plane began a slow roll and dive to port.

That definitely didn't feel right.

"Miranda?"

No response.

"*Miranda!*"

Nothing. The plane continued rolling, ten degrees became fifteen.

At twenty degrees, Andi unsnapped her seat belt, struggled out of her seat, and staggered forward. The plane was small enough that she could brace off the ceiling and chair seat backs but it still took forever to reach the copilot's seat—all of seven steps from where she'd been sitting.

Thirty degrees over and nosing down into a steep dive.

Aircraft first, she told herself as she leveraged her way upslope into the copilot's seat and buckled in. She placed a hand on the wheel and the plane responded. It returned to roughly level and began climbing back to altitude as well as she could—she wasn't an airplane pilot.

Why had Miranda lost control?

Andi tried to block the memories before looking over.

It didn't help.

Her last flight with Ken—her last with the US Army's 160th SOAR. Three meters above the ground, moving at a hundred and fifty knots in her MH-6M Little Bird. An undetected Russian patrol deep into US territory in Syria had shot them with a rifle-fired grenade. It lodged inside Ken's vest. Knowing he was dead, he'd turned from her, presenting his back and the back of his Kevlar vest, so that the detonation wouldn't kill her as well.

She'd loved flying with Ken, he'd been like her little brother, though he stood ten inches taller. He'd laughed every single time she called him, *Didi,* Mandarin for Little Brother. She'd loved *flying* with Ken—but she *loved* Miranda.

Please don't be dead.

It was the best prayer she had before turning to look.

Miranda sat unmoving.

Hands in her lap as if someone had simply dropped them there.

Staring straight ahead, and rocking.

Alive! Brain aneurysm or…

An autism reaction? Rocking faster and faster, mumbling something.

Andi turned to look out the front windshield.

Spieden Island lay dead ahead but most of it was obscured by smoke. A massive blaze had engulfed the north end of the island. Even as she watched it, the northwest end of the runway caught.

The brown summer grass accelerated it. And the windsock indicated westerly winds. The flames climbed and pulsed malevolently.

15

Andi had seen enough forest fires on television to know when she saw one. The island was burning. A lightning strike must have started a fire up near the north end. Slow to kindle through the night, it was on a roll now and headed southeast down the length of the narrow island.

The vast number of animals that populated the island raced out of the trees and headed for the south end of the island in an actual stampede. Deer, sheep, and a crazy variety of birds.

"The animals!" Miranda suddenly shouted and grabbed the wheel. "I have to help them!" And she drove the nose down. Not some out of control dive, this time she had them aiming at the heart of the island.

Andi pulled back but panic had made Miranda fearsomely strong. "There's not enough runway!" The Citation M2 used every bit of runway available on the island, including the part already on fire.

Miranda ignored the shout and fought her for control.

"Are you buckled in, Mother?" she shouted toward the cabin.

A shrieked, "*Yes.*"

"Stay that way!"

The radio crackled to life. "Aircraft in vicinity of Spieden Island please redirect immediately. You're entering a TFR."

Andi risked a moment's attention to see a helicopter with an underslung water bucket approaching the fire. Temporary Flight Restriction areas were set up for any number of events: air shows, Presidential visits, nuclear or chemical spills, volcanoes—and if her mind would shut up —aerial firefighting was the obvious one at the moment.

She grabbed for a headset to respond.

It was a mistake.

Miranda's dive for the runway continued at full flight speed. Moving at four hundred knots, not even a perfect landing would save them. They'd shoot out the north end of the runway and die in the trees long before the fire burned them to death.

Andi shoved against Miranda's shoulder but she was braced hard between the seat back and the wheel.

"C'mon, Miranda. Give me a break." The island filled more and more of the windscreen with each passing second.

Then she knew what she had to do. The angle was wrong for a slap. Besides, that would probably drive Miranda deeper into whatever mental hole she was in.

Instead, Andi raised her left arm, then brought it crashing down on Miranda's forearms.

A bone snapped.

Miranda yelped in pain, letting go of the wheel.

Now in control, Andi began easing out of the dive. Crap!

Why did she know nothing about fixed-wing flight? How fast a correction was too fast?

The sharp buzz of the stall warning told her soon enough. Then a stick shaker kicked in, vibrating the wheel to get her attention.

"You already got it, you stupid plane."

The view out the window said it wasn't enough. They were too close the ground for her to be sure of clearing the trees.

Add power to control a dive? Ease power to abate it? How was she supposed to know?

"Are you crazy?" someone shouted. The radio. She could ask him, even though he was a helo pilot like herself, he might know. But not without the headset.

"Miranda! Power up or down?"

"Huh? What?" She had her broken arm cradled against her chest. Yet she continued to stare out the window as if the pain out the window was greater than her arm.

"Power? What do I do? Now." She kept her voice dead calm and professional like the trained pilot she was.

"Uh, ease." At least that's what Andi hoped she mumbled.

She eased the throttle, using the wheel to ride the very edge of the stall buzzer. The two-hundred-foot Douglas fir trees were big enough that in a moment she'd be able to count needles.

Without warning, Miranda stomped on one of the rudder pedals.

Andi didn't even have time to swear. Mother's scream was plenty clear, though.

Her stomach gave that sickening lurch of an unbalanced turn. She turned the wheel to compensate. And they shot clear of the trees and headed toward the water. Except the two-hundred-foot trees and the two-hundred-and-eighty-foot height of the island itself gave her five hundred more feet of maneuvering room.

Mother's panic sounded again, but Andi could do nothing to ease her terror.

It was sloppy. Andi barely missed ramming Cactus Island a half-mile to the north, but she kept them aloft and alive. Then she began climbing.

How had she been with Miranda so long and never taken fixed-wing flying lessons? Because Mike was always her copilot. But the unhelpful bastard was presently lying on a Hawaiian beach—the very one she'd suggested to Miranda but been turned down on. She struggled back up to two thousand feet, then three, circling above the island.

Miranda's forehead rested against the side window as she looked down. The vibrant, brilliant woman she so loved looked like no more than a shattered street person huddled in a doorway rather than the cockpit of a five-million-dollar jet.

Andi looked past her as the fire reached the hangar. Flame wrapped around the building and she saw the helo approaching it with a load of water.

"My father's plane," Miranda whispered.

Andi remembered the Mooney presently parked in the back of the hangar. They usually flew the Citation jet and the helo presently at Gig Harbor far more often. For space reasons, Miranda kept her historic F-86 in the Tacoma hangar. But her most precious plane—her father's—was kept here on the island.

"Oh crap!" Andi scrabbled about until she found the headset snarled under her feet. The instant she had it on, she swung down the boom and found the microphone trigger in the same place as her helo, on the backside of the wheel.

"This is Citation M2 to firefighting helo. Back off! Back off! Back off! Stay clear of the hangar." She could see the fire melting through the steel siding.

The helo peeled hard to the south. "About time you responded. Do you have any idea how much trouble you're in with that goddamn stunt? You missed me by two rotors."

She had? Military helo pilots measure distances in rotor diameters and his Black Hawk's was only sixty feet across. She'd passed him within two rotors at five hundred miles an hour and never seen him? Andi was never touching a fixed-wing plane again.

"Roger that." She'd earned the heat; she'd take whatever came. "Just stay clear of that hangar. There's a couple hundred gallons of avgas and Jet A in there."

"Christ! You trying to start a war?"

"In a plane and some storage drums. It's all—"

She didn't have time to say *legal* as the fire breached the sheet metal walls and poured into the building, accelerated by the high vents. Something gave. The fireball blew the rolling hangar doors out onto the field, roiling out and up, straight through where the helicopter would have been.

The only sound in the plane were the low hum of the engines and Mother's quieting sobs.

16

"Mother of God," First Lieutenant Henry James whispered over the intercom.

"No shit," Donny Draper his copilot whispered back.

They came to stable hover five rotors away from the fireball that ate the airplane hangar. The heat pouring through the windscreen heated his face worse than any Afghan summer sun.

The reenergized fire raced down island.

It was hopeless.

He'd been part of the Army National Guard team working a fire just twenty minutes away on the Olympic Peninsula when the call came in. Some rich bastard's private island was burning, spotted by a passing boat. By the time he'd arrived, the trees had been heavily engaged.

His Black Hawk could only move a thousand gallons of water at a time, so he'd tried to save the structures. No ponds or streams on the rocky island, he slid offshore and dipped salt water. It was hard on his gear and would corrode anything it touched, but it was the only chance of saving anything.

Two close calls inside of sixty seconds was three too many.

He'd settled enough to dip the bucket into the ocean, then shifted sideways to tip the flexible bucket at the lower end of a hundred-foot line and watch it fill. When he'd looked up, he'd almost eaten the wing of a sleek little bizjet. The wake turbulence had tossed them hard.

The tail number had been and gone too fast to recognize, but he'd find the gawker. Christ, he was sick of sightseers who wanted to buzz a fire.

But he'd recovered and headed for the hangar, only to be warned off before it blew all to hell.

Okay. Okay.

To prove to himself that he was okay, he moved over the house and dumped his load there.

The jet had climbed to circle high above. Looked like they were going to stay out of the way instead of trying to kill him again.

"Pilot of jet, identify yourself." Because he was sure as hell going to report their ass. If not for the abrupt end of his first Army National Guard tour overseas—the mayhem of the closing days of the Afghan War—he might not have been able to dodge the jet's dive at all.

"Captain Andi Wu, Retired. Please accept my apologies. I'm not trained in fixed-wing flight."

After he completed the dump on the house—forward slope of the roof so that the water spilled down the front of the structure and onto the ground immediately before it— he glanced upward.

The plane now flew three thousand feet above him. But

watching long enough, he could see it wasn't tracking smoothly.

"Captain of what? Crunch cereal? Jack Sparrow's pirate ship?"

"US Army 160th SOAR."

He glanced over at Donny as they headed for more water.

Night Stalkers? Donny mouthed at him. Henry would wager that his eyes were wide behind his Ray Bans.

Holy hell. He'd never met one of those in the flesh. He'd heard of them, of course. The best helo pilots in the Army, in *any* army. Not even in his deepest fantasies could he imagine ever qualifying for them.

"What are you doing at the helm?"

"The pilot, uh, had a problem."

"No shit!"

"That's her family home."

Henry was easing in with a fresh load of water, he'd done enough firefighting in the Army National Guard that he could talk at the same time.

He was a hundred and fifty feet from a side building that had already caught fire—which shot out a massive tongue of flame. Though he had plenty of height this time, he hauled back on the cyclic to a hover so he could watch from a place of safety.

"And what was in that side building?"

"More fuel. A tractor, lawnmower, snowcat, and a golf cart among others."

"A golf cart?"

"Island transportation," the woman circling above informed him.

"What crazy person lives here and has all this stuff?" He

doused the outbuilding to little effect. Even the punch of a thousand gallons wasn't going to snuff this fire. It had already raced toward the main house. There was nothing more he could do to help so he pulled back farther.

"It belongs to Miranda Chase."

Henry twisted to find the plane circling above. There! To the south.

"What's the big deal about that?" Donny asked.

Henry shook his head to clear it. He'd been closer than he realized when he'd joked she was the captain of Jack Sparrow's pirate ship. Captain Jack *The Pirate* Spahr had been his best friend at the ANG. Until he'd gone down over a forest fire two years ago in his Chinook. The NTSB investigator who'd figured out what happened—he'd studied the reports desperately seeking some clue as to how a pilot as good as Jack had died—had been one Miranda Chase.

"Uh, give her my thanks for the work she did on the Chinook out on the Olympic Peninsula."

"I'll...pass that on." Then after a long pause. "Do you know anything about how to land a Citation M2 jet?"

He glanced aloft once more. The plane wobbled badly, but then stabilized again...mostly.

"No, ma'am. I'm sorry." Donny shook his head. "Neither of us do. You'll have to call the tower. And ma'am, thank you for your service." Because what the hell else could you say to a Night Stalker. They flew way beyond any rational limits and were good enough to come back.

"Uh, thank you for yours."

He double-clicked his mic to acknowledge that. Sounded as if she had enough trouble on her hands. They were all alive, in part thanks to the Night Stalker warning him off overflying the hangar he'd taken for a machinery garage. This might be a great story, but he didn't think it was one he'd be telling in the bar any night soon.

She double-clicked the mic back in thanks.

He turned his attention back to the fire, but there was nothing more he could do. Driven by the fire from the outbuilding, it launched across the yard toward the house.

Henry hoped the owner wasn't attached to her garden the way his wife was.

While he'd been talking to Captain Andi Wu, the fire engulfed it—not a single plant would survive.

17

WHEN HE WAS IN DC, DRAKE COULDN'T WAIT TO GET OUT. Every time he left, he wondered what was wrong with him. He was out now and his emotions were exactly on track—half exhaustion and half deep frustration.

He closed the door to his office aboard the E-4B Nightwatch and dropped into the chair. The madness of DC didn't cease simply because he was out trotting the globe. Worse, every time he left the country, he dragged a hundred other people with him on the fifty-year-old 747.

He closed his eyes and tipped his chair back, trying not to think of the last couple days. Which, of course, meant he couldn't think of anything else.

A full day at Kadena Air Base on Okinawa—as close as the Chairman of the Joint Chiefs of Staff could get to Taiwan without escalating international tensions. The old 75th Ranger in him wanted to land in Taipei and give the People's Republic of China the finger up close and personal. The older and hopefully wiser four-star general in him...still wanted to do it.

Nightwatch

Of course, the Chinese had been sufficiently ticked off when the military leaders of Japan, Taiwan, the Philippines, and Vietnam had come to Kadena to meet with him. With that list of attendees, it was plenty obvious that they were strategizing what to do if the PRC was stupid enough to attempt the annexation of Taiwan. Good. He hoped they'd been listening, good and hard.

He'd also hoped for some sleep en route to JBER. Joint Base Elmendorf-Richardson in Anchorage lay practically under the flight path to his next stop and it would have been a wasted opportunity to not stop in. The problem was that each of the leaders he'd just spent a day with were then flying home with their own staff. This led to a dozen follow-up calls and questions and new virtual meetings from the onboard conference room.

His day at JBER had been equally hectic. As the sun finally set on the Pacific Rim, it rose over more developments in Russia's love of death spreading over Eastern Europe.

The Nightwatch had been designed for one purpose, its ability to run a war from the air. Aptly named for the Rembrandt painting of *The Night Watch* protecting a town, this plane had been designed to protect the country.

The four identical so-called Doomsday Planes had none of the comfort and niceties of Air Force One. What it lacked in luxurious fittings, catering staff, and press area, it made up for in communications and surveillance gear. It could talk to satellites or submarines running silent and deep, all the while monitoring everything from cyber attacks to the status of the national power grid—in almost any country.

The entire US military could be commanded from one of these planes. Which is why there was always one parked within a hundred miles of Air Force One every time the

President left the country. It was also the international plane for travel by the Secretary of Defense and himself.

The meetings at JBER had been mostly about the Russians. They weren't doing anything untoward in the Pacific, unlike in the old Eastern Bloc countries, but if they did, the forces at JBER were the keystone. They were also the secondary perimeter forces if a Chinese or North Korean attack targeted Japan.

JBER to Tonopah in Nevada gave him less than four hours' break.

He opened one eye and glanced at the array of clocks above his desk. Ten a.m. in DC. Thank God.

He picked up the phone that connected to the comm center and called the Director of the National Reconnaissance Office.

"General Gray," she answered on the first ring. Gods but he loved the sound of her voice.

"General Lizzy Gray. Have your people developed that transporter beam yet so I can come home to you right now?"

"They have, General Drake Nason," her voice softened, "but there's a small bug. It turns former 75th Rangers into hamsters."

"Hmmm... How would you feel about being married to a hamster?"

"Well, you'd be all soft and cuddly, I suppose I could learn to live with that."

"I—" The console beeped and a message from the comm center displayed on his screen. *Urgent call. CoS(AF).* "Crap! Ralph's calling. Gotta go, bye." He punched for the blinking line. Someday he'd manage a leisurely phone call with his wife, but this wasn't the day. So far, this hadn't even been the trip. Each of his prior attempts had been cut off by some aide, call, meeting..."

"Hey, Ralph." When the four-star Air Force Chief of Staff labeled something urgent, he wasn't some two-star panicking, he meant it.

"I have some bad news, Drake. A flight went down en route from Boston to Montreal seventeen hours ago. I only just heard."

Drake felt a sudden chill.

"Two fatalities. Lewis and Gerald."

"Accident or..."

"Unknown. I called you the moment I'd confirmed. The AIB dispatched a Jeremy Trahn and a Colonel Vicki Cortez. Wait? Is that Taser Cortez?"

"Soon to be Cortez-Trahn according to the wedding invitation."

"Well..." Drake could hear the unvoiced curse, probably averted only by Drake obviously being a friend. Which perhaps was too strong a word, but he and Lizzy had been touched by the invitation nonetheless. Even if Taz didn't easily engender friendship, he'd certainly learned to respect the team the two of them made.

Senior Air Force staff, on the other hand, had spent two decades learning to face her visits with deep trepidation as the woman was a true force of nature ready to destroy anyone who didn't measure up to her impeccable standards.

"Have you seen a report yet?"

"No. I can call the Accident Investigation Board and try to reach them but—"

"Don't bother, Ralph. I have their numbers. You get on with Lewis and Gerald's families."

"You'll need a replacement for the Greenland meeting at Thule Air Base."

"I'll think about that in a minute. Draw me up a list of..." Drake hesitated.

"...possible replacements?" Ralph filled the pause while Drake's mind churned. "Not many of their caliber in flight design. I'll—"

Drake tapped his console for the Nightwatch's flight map and allowed himself a thin smile. "Don't bother, Ralph. I'll call you back if I don't have it covered."

He hung up by punching for the cockpit.

"Captain, change of plan. We're stopping at JBLM."

"Ah," the captain hesitated. "No problem. Yes sir." And hung up. Mere seconds to verify that their position and fuel actually placed them in easy range of Joint Base Lewis-McChord in Washington State.

He punched out his next call.

18

THE BLAST OF THE PHONE RINGING IN THE DEAD SILENCE OF the cockpit made Andi bobble the controls. She hadn't dared do anything more than circle above the burning island. She was slowly getting the feel of the jet, now able to maintain the banked turn and only a little wobbly on the altitude. At first even hitting the microphone switch to talk with the helo pilot had caused problems. Not big ones, as she was high enough not to interfere with the lone helo working the fire, but problems.

Miranda had finally turned away from the devastation to cradle her broken arm, hang her head, and weep silent tears.

Each time Andi tried to reach out to comfort her, the plane had other thoughts. Two-fisted white-knuckling the wheel felt like it was the only thing keeping them aloft.

The phone rang again. All Miranda did was flinch.

Andi saw a microphone symbol blink on the radio screen. Thank God Miranda kept her phone synced to the plane's comm system.

She freed one hand long enough to tap it, which cost her an abrupt hundred-foot climb. "Hello?"

"Who is this?"

"I could ask the same. You called us."

"Miranda?"

Andi wondered at what degree of panic she was in to not recognize Drake Nason's voice. A glance to the side. "Uh. She's incapacitated at the moment. This is Andi Wu, General."

"Is she there with you?"

"Technically." As if shaken from her own state of mind, Andi started wondering if she could land the plane without killing them. All of them. Her mother still sat alone in the cabin. God, she'd forgotten all about her.

"Captain Wu. What is going on there?"

"Fire. Spieden." How was she supposed to explain what she'd witnessed? What they'd witnessed? Miranda's home had become her home, the one place she finally felt like herself outside a helo's cockpit.

Now it was gone.

The fire had turned from the garden—somehow it had to be her fault that the fire had destroyed every plant Miranda so loved—before it took the house. The lone Black Hawk had doused it hard, but the roof and windows were gone. The stout log walls might be recoverable, though they still smoldered even as he hit them again. Done with the house, the fire had stalled, turned as the morning winds shifted, and died against the steep cliffs and Puget Sound on the southwest shore.

For all Miranda's panic, most of the animals had remained safe on the unburned southern half of the island.

The helo shifted from dousing the structures to killing various hot spots.

"I need to talk to Miranda." The general insisted.

"Not going to happen." Miranda showed no sign that she heard anything. "Mother!" Andi called back into the cabin.

"Yes?" Her voice cracked.

"Miranda needs help. Could you get the medical kit? It's on the wall directly behind her seat."

"Is it safe?"

"For now, yes."

Mother edged into view and opened the med kit.

"An arm sling and painkillers," Andi told her.

At her last word, Miranda shrieked loud enough to hurt Andi's ears over the intercom. "No shots! No shots! No shots! I don't want any drugs. Never! Never! Never!"

Andi reached out and flicked the boom mic up over Miranda's head, which switched off the microphone, which dropped her flight level three hundred feet far too abruptly.

Once Andi had corrected that, she spoke again. "We're a little busy here, General."

"Andi, could you please explain what is going on and how I can help?" There was no denying that suddenly dead-calm battle-commander voice.

"I can't imagine how, General Nason, unless you have a pilot able to coach me on how to land a Citation M2 jet without killing us."

Her mother, who had given up on the arm sling and was now gently tucking in a flight blanket for extra support, twisted around to stare at her.

Andi mouthed a, "Sorry."

"Take a breath, Captain Wu, and explain your situation."

Right.

Captain.

Of the 160th.

Her heart rate *was* far too high for a trained Special Operations pilot. She'd flown through worse. The fact that she couldn't remember when at the moment didn't make it any less true. At least her copilot wasn't dead. Instead her lover was whimpering with pain from the arm Andi herself had broken.

She forced her heart rate down and slowed her breathing.

"We're in the air. Over Spieden Island. Miranda's island. In her Citation M2." *Complete sentences. C'mon, soldier.* "There is," she risked tipping the wings enough to look down at the island, "*was* a forest fire. It's wiped out most of the island, including her home and airplane hangar. Miranda is injured and I don't know how to fly a fixed-wing aircraft. We're safe at the moment but as to how to land a jet without killing everyone aboard…"

"Let me check with my pilot. Hold please."

"Button," a voice said faintly. A woman's voice but not over the headset so she could barely hear it through the earmuffs.

"She said *button*," Mother repeated more audibly.

Andi felt a wave of relief that Miranda had somehow dug herself out of her hole to offer up even that lone clue.

Andi looked at the console of the jet. Three large computer screens, each ringed by buttons. But just like a helicopter, they would only change the view of the displays.

Two smaller screens below, one for the pilot and a matching one for the copilot, with whole menus of choices within choices. Not one she saw said, *Get me the hell out of here.*

Below those were throttle and flap levers.

Letting her gaze travel back upward, she spotted switches to the left and right of the menu screens, again duplicated for the pilot and copilot.

But Miranda had said button.

At the very top of the console, above the central screen, were dials and switches for controlling lights, buttons labeled *Eng Fire R* and *L*...

And a lone button on her side of the cockpit, not mirrored on Miranda's side.

Only for the person riding copilot.

Emergency Autoland.

It was behind a plastic cover. Taking a deep breath, she lifted the cover and pressed the button.

It turned red.

19

EMERGENCY AUTOLAND ACTIVATED.

A computerized female voice filled Andi's headset and the cockpit with a soothing tone as the same words flashed up on the console's central screen.

The Emergency Autoland System is controlling the aircraft and will land automatically at the safest nearby airport. Please remain calm. Avoid touching the flight controls which may interfere with...

It kept talking.

Andi, finger by finger, released her death grip on the wheel. When she finally managed to release both hands, she hovered them near the wheel, which began to twist and turn on its own, the rudder pedals shifted to create a smooth coordinated turn. Then the throttle levers eased back by a third without her touching them.

The plane turned east and settled to straight-and-level flight all on its own.

The display changed as the voice continued, *A safe airport has been identified. The plane will be landing in seven minutes.*

Emergency Autoland has already contacted air traffic control. You may press the blue microphone button on the display if you wish to communicate with the tower.

Andi pushed it and it turned green.

"Citation M2." Then she lifted her finger to release the mike switch. It didn't appear to change anything. The plane was taking care of even the push-to-talk switch.

"Bellingham Tower. Please state the nature of your emergency."

"Sorry for the trouble. The pilot is…" and what was Andi supposed to say that wouldn't immediately cost Miranda her license as well. "Is, ah, incapacitated. I'd like to request an ambulance meet us at the terminal."

"Roger. Please state nature of medical emergency."

She glanced at Miranda. The trick now was minimal information. "The pilot has a broken arm." Andi could see the bend in it. "Displaced fracture, don't think it's compound as I don't see any blood."

"Roger," the tower clicked off.

Andi tapped the green microphone button. It went back to being blue.

"How did Miranda break her arm?" a different voice asked.

Andi looked wildly around the cockpit for a moment then remembered she was still on an open call with General Nason. She double-checked that the mike to the tower was off. "I, uh, broke it for her, sir, to regain flight control."

Five minutes to landing. The voice kept saying soothing things, which she tuned out. She kept her hands close by the wheel though she had no real idea what good she might do if there were any problems.

"Okay. I'll call you in twenty minutes. I'm sorry, it's all the time I can afford. This is a matter of national security."

In case Miranda had a flight recorder running, she didn't want to say more than necessary, like *if* Miranda's brain was okay within twenty minutes.

"Understood, General." What else was she supposed to say.

"You take good care of her, Andi," Nason's voice went soft.

"I will, sir." If she'll let me.

There was a sudden silence in the cockpit after Drake cut the call.

"Does this mean we're going to be okay?" Mother rested a hand on her arm from where she squatted between the pilot seats.

Andi rested what she hoped was a reassuring hand over her mother's. "Yes. The plane will take care of everything. You'd better go buckle in for landing. I'm sorry, but I think I should stay up here. It will be okay."

Her mother nodded carefully, then edged once more into the cabin.

Out the windshield and on the flight instruments, Andi could see that they were lined up on a distant runway. Her hand was moving toward the center console when the landing gear extended with a soothing triple clunk and the flaps extended halfway.

The voice calmly announced *Two minutes to landing.*

And once they landed?

No way was any of this going to be okay.

20

Clarissa hurried out of the hospital into the September morning sunshine with Kurt on her heels.

The parking lot wasn't far enough—not *near* far enough. She was only aware of striding across the two-lane road beyond when a car screeched to a halt. She ignored it. Over the road, her way blocked by a wall of trees climbing the face of a steep hill, she turned right along the sidewalk. A trail led up into the trees and she took it.

"God! I *hate* hospitals!"

Kurt nodded. "While it's nice to not be the one in the bed, always seems harder when it's one of yours lying there." His quiet words reminded her of his years as a Delta Force operator before the CIA had scooped him up. And the time since hadn't been all roses.

"No. I was fifteen the last time I was in one. I—" She clamped her teeth shut until the muscle at the back of her jaw throbbed. Fifteen. In that hospital bed was the day she began plotting how to kill her father.

She left the silence and Kurt didn't question her.

Dead, buried, and unmourned for twenty-five years, still she felt a desperate need for a shower to scrub her father's slime-mold off her skin for even thinking of the bastard.

The paths wandered in long, lazy switchbacks beneath thick shade trees poked by shafts of sunlight. Here and there, broad sets of weathered-wood stairs jumped upward, but she kept to the wide gravel. Volleying between tourists, late morning joggers swirled by, mostly mothers with big-wheeled baby strollers. The pre-work crowd were now ensconced in the offices and shops of Montreal, visible below through gaps in the trees. Benches along the trail were mostly occupied by old men talking in the slow way they did, a state she hoped never to decay to.

A trail map placard said they'd wandered up into the Parc du Mont-Royal.

"Famous cemetery here," Kurt pointed at one of the labels, *Cimetière du Mont-Royal.*

"Are you suggesting we bury Ernie Maxwell there?"

In her peripheral vision, Clarissa could see him studying her profile for several paces, then shrugging.

"Not until we know more." She wanted to be clear on that.

"Okay."

"Thoughts?" she asked.

Kurt might lead the Special Operations Group but he'd never aspired to being more than a warrior. He was one of the few senior people at the CIA who wasn't in a political position, offering potential avenues to unseat her from the directorship.

They negotiated a switchback turn, busy with cyclists, baby joggers, and walkers cluttered together. He didn't speak again until they were well on the way along the next straightaway.

"Not a complex job to rig the plane. But it takes some financial heft and planning. Timing is the main issue. The right aircraft, setting the timers probably required an hour, less if it was a pro, less than that if it was a team. But a team is harder to hide and these smaller planes stay busy. Finding time alone in the cargo space is hard." Not *would be* but rather *is*. The voice of experience.

"You'll find out the last time the plane stopped long enough or was in for service?"

He nodded. "Ernie was a field agent far longer than you were. He'd know exactly what he was doing—maybe not the technical execution, but the planning. Except for the cascading trigger in the software."

"And the tampered seatbelt?"

Kurt shook his head. "Different method. I'd have thought it was all his setup if it weren't for the software trick and the belt. He was on one mission and someone else set him up for another. Someone who knew about the first one."

Clarissa nodded, their thinking synced up.

A big gray squirrel raced across their path, making her catch a heel in the gravel. She wasn't used to being outdoors. Clark had liked the country, or so he'd claimed, but she'd never lived outside the Beltway except for her field years on CIA Black Sites in the hell that was Afghanistan.

The rodent carried a peanut in the husk, probably tossed by the old-guy cluster at the bench ahead. She kept her thoughts to herself until they were clear of the bench.

"So, let's focus on the first one. Why would he sabotage the plane he himself flew on?"

Kurt kept his silence through the entire next switchback.

She didn't interrupt as she could see him shifting through every element of the puzzle.

Her legs were aching. The exercise was so different from her usual 5K on the treadmill. The heels weren't helping. How had she ended up climbing a mountain, even a citified one, in Louboutin ankle boots? There had better be a road and a taxi to get them back down.

At the top stood a grand stone structure. Closer inspection showed it was no more than a lofty meeting room, probably for mountaintop wedding parties. She turned to survey the other direction and had to admit it had its points.

A vast tiered patio of concrete paver blocks that could seat five hundred easily was backed by a sweeping view of Montreal.

She and Kurt strolled among the grandparents with grandkids in tow, all of whom must have come up in a car—a good sign. The young included overly intent hipsters or whatever they were called in the digital age, hunkering over laptops and tablets, pretending they were working remote.

The heavy stone balustrade at the far edge of the sprawling patio hung over a drop-off that told exactly why her calves were sore. Trees spilled in great cascades of lush green down to the city. The tops of the towers of downtown were ranged below them. The busy waters of the St. Lawrence Seaway curving across the background of yet more wooded hills.

She and Kurt stopped by a large bronze book mounted atop the concrete railing. The metal was cast as if open to a middle page.

Kurt pointed at the date.

"*October 2nd, 1535,*" Clarissa read. "*Jacques Cartier*

discovered Canada. Stood here and called it Mount Royal, which became Montreal. When was Jamestown? 1609?"

"Before they mostly died and left. It's only called the *first settlement* because they met the long-delayed supply ship just offshore and turned back."

"Christ but America is so young. I forget that sometimes."

"Especially when people like Ernie Maxwell make you feel old."

She sent a scathing look at Kurt but he ignored it. Instead, he leaned on the rail beside the metal book and stared out over the city.

"What did he have to gain by such a stunt?" Kurt had finally sifted enough pieces to speak.

"Assuming he survived?" Clarissa puzzled at it.

She'd known Ernie for over twenty years, since the early days of the Afghanistan War.

Ernie's predecessor, the unfortunate scheming bastard Gavin Chalmers, had been trying to frame her for a massive multifold intelligence failure. Frame her so that he could take over the Directorship.

"Was Ernie preparing to frame me for attacking his flight and him personally?"

Kurt, who'd been moving in his normal calm-and-steady mode since she'd called him to meet her at the airport this morning, twisted to stare at her.

Not wanting to see, she kept turned to face him anyway.

His slow nod, visible peripherally, confirmed it—the pieces fit.

At least Ernie's part in it.

But whoever set up Ernie to fail, with rigged software and the sliced seatbelt, remained hidden.

21

Taz jolted and cracked the top of her head against Jeremy's chin when the phone in his breast pocket rang moments after Clarissa and Kurt left them alone. She'd been having more hormonal tears with her face pressed there—when it had gone off like a siren against her face. Jeremy always kept it turned up so *loud*.

He began cursing, in his typically mild Jeremy way full of *gosh darns* and other such extreme expletives, as he cradled his jaw. His instinctive clutch had also gathered up a goodly hank of her hair, pinning her in place against his chest where she'd turned unaccountably mushy just moments before.

The phone blasted her face again. It echoed in the small hospital room.

A quick poke in his ticklish spot had him clasping his hands to protect his rib cage.

Freed, she extracted his phone and punched Speaker to silence the thing.

"Jeremy Trahn's receptionist. How may he help you

today?" No way was anyone else going to hear how mushy she'd become about the sweet man she'd found.

"I have nineteen minutes, Taz. I need to know everything about the fatalities on the plane crash you're investigating."

She and Jeremy looked at each other. General Drake Nason had never directly called either of them before.

"The fatalities? There were two on an Embraer 175 flight from Boston to Montreal."

"Great, you've now covered what I know, except that their names were Gerald and Lewis. Tell me what I don't know."

"We, uh," Jeremy rubbed at his chin one more time and, being a cautious man, kept the other hand protectively over the ticklish spot on his lower ribs. "We haven't investigated the fatalities."

"Then what the *hell* are you doing there?" It wasn't like the general to get pissed.

Taz reached for her normal response, meet anger with anger, but didn't find it. Like she'd lost some key part of herself. Was this what pregnancy did to a woman? If so, she didn't approve at all.

Jeremy began to explain. "The flight went down because the Director of the CIA's Middle East Desk sabotaged the plane. He was seriously injured as his seatbelt was intentionally damaged, presumed to be done by an unknown third party. He finished surgery less than thirty minutes ago."

"A senior CIA director sabotaged his own flight?"

"Yes sir. Though perhaps not his seatbelt. We found evidence that his sabotage of the flight itself was, in turn, sabotaged by that unknown party I mentioned. We've turned that part of the investigation over to the CIA."

Though she understood Jeremy's choice, Taz still wasn't

comfortable doing that. Her entire career had been about getting to the bottom of matters herself. Though there'd been little choice, to hand it off—to Clarissa Reese of all people—was galling.

"The seatbelts of the two fatalities were also cut. We thought they were a byproduct of the secondary sabotage of Director Maxwell."

"Well, think again, Jeremy. Those were two critical US Air Force assets, traveling under deep cover, or at least what we thought was deep cover. You're two of the top cause-and-effect investigators we've got. I lost two good men on that flight and I damn well want to know the how, why, and especially the who. And if you find out that they're somehow tied to Maxwell…" He left the threat hanging.

"We're on it, sir." Taz had always felt a certain connection to the general for their shared distrust of Clarissa. Being all tall, blonde, built, and beautiful didn't cut shit in her book.

Maybe she could tie the tampering of Ernie's app and seatbelt back to Clarissa. Perhaps she'd flown up to Montreal to stop Taz from doing precisely that.

22

Miranda's phone rang far louder than any of the equipment in the ambulance. No siren for a mere broken arm.

Andi had never ridden in one and was surprised at how little room there was in the boxy truck, even for such small women as herself and her mother. Thick cabinets of supplies that Miranda didn't require remained closed, for which Andi would gladly bow to the gods in thanks if she knew which ones were listening.

Miranda lay on the stretcher, her eyes tightly closed and her arm in a temporary splint—one with a distinct bend in the middle of the forearm, which made Andi want to gag each time she saw it.

The EMT sitting by her head had hooked up only the basics: heart monitor and blood pressure. So unworried that he was shooting the shit with the driver who annoyingly kept to the speed limit. For herself, Andi leaned more toward the whirling-lights blaring-sirens full-blown-panic side of the equation. Who knew that panic smelled of antiseptic and bleach?

The big stretcher left her and Mother at Miranda's feet on a bench seat meant for one American, which forced them hip-to-hip like Siamese twins. More contact than she'd had with Mother any time since…breastfeeding?

She wanted to rest a comforting hand on Miranda's calf, but didn't know how Miranda would react. Some autistics, including Miranda, couldn't tolerate a gentle touch at all but a firm one was usually okay. Upset like this, Andi had no idea how she'd react.

Miranda had certainly been plummeting toward an… episode as fast as the jet had been diving toward the island. Yet she'd dragged herself out enough to save all of their lives with the kick to the rudder pedal. Andi had no idea what to think.

The phone rang again.

"Are you going to answer that?" Mother asked.

Andi looked at her hand in surprise. She'd been clutching onto Miranda's phone like a lifeline. She tapped Accept and held it up to her ear.

"Miranda's phone."

"Andi?" She recognized the cheery voice.

"Hi, Jill. Yes, it's me."

"Is Miranda there?"

"Yes, but she can't come to the phone at the moment." Miranda still lay unmoving, unnaturally so as her body was held in place by the straps. She and Mother kept bumping against each other at each turn as the ambulance came off the highway and headed onto the surface streets.

"That's okay. Are either of you available for a launch? I've got a weird one."

"How weird?"

"A small bizjet did one of those emergency autoland things which triggered the FAA calling me. Those are exceedingly rare outside of testing and the FAA wants full interviews and details. The manufacturer was on me seconds later. It's in your neighborhood or I wouldn't bother Miranda as there wasn't really a crash."

Andi closed her eyes and felt she understood Miranda's desire to shut out the world a little better. "Let me guess, Bellingham International Airport."

"Right! So, you're already on it?"

She didn't know whether to laugh or cry. "I can't investigate myself."

"It was *you*? What's going on? Is everyone okay?" Jill's instant concern somehow made everything ten times worse. She'd busted Miranda's arm.

And one or the other of them would never fly as pilot again.

If the truth of Miranda's panic attack—that's what Andi would call it, *not* autistic episode—came out, the FAA would yank her license anyway. It was an amazing testament to her skill that Miranda had been certified to fly at all given her mental challenges. In a single swipe, this would negate decades of hard work.

The only other option was to claim the incredibly dangerous dive as her own action. *I broke the pilot's arm to take control, then dove the plane so dangerously that I almost killed both of us and the firefighting helo pilots before I came to my senses.* How fast would her own license be yanked? Would it earn her jail time for air piracy?

"We're all…okay. Miranda has a broken arm and we're on the way to the hospital." They were all a complete mess.

The phone announced another incoming call. She pulled it away to see who.

Drake.

She so wasn't ready for this. "I have to go, Jill. I'll call you later."

"'Kay. Bye. Tell Miranda to be more careful and heal fast."

Yeah, more careful in who she chooses as a girlfriend. But Andi kept that thought to herself.

"Will do." She switched lines. "Hello, General Nason. It's still Andi Wu here."

"You're all down safe?"

"Yes sir."

"I'll want the full story on this, at some other time. Right now, I need Miranda."

"I'm not sure she can help you at this point, sir."

Mother tapped her arm and pointed.

Miranda's eyes were open and looking at her.

And now she understood some of an autistic's problem of looking at someone's face. Was Miranda's mouth in a grim line, or merely at rest? Did condemnation burn in her eyes, or perhaps sadness at the loss of her home? It was all very confusing. Each emotion, perceived or real but not understood, whiplashed her own emotions about far harder than the out-of-control jet.

"Can you talk to Drake?"

Miranda nodded.

Andi wished she could use the speakerphone but the EMT was right there, not paying them any attention—but there. Earlier General Nason had said it was a matter of national security. Instead, Andi tried to hand over the phone. But Miranda's right arm was in the splint. With her left one she cradled the right one with no indication of being willing to let it go.

Andi had to scoot forward, lean on the gurney with her elbow against Miranda's hip, and hold the phone against her ear. Her hair softly brushed the back of Andi's knuckles. She tried to hold the phone steady without touching Miranda but the swaying of the ambulance defeated her and she finally rested her fingertips, firmly, against the soft skin of Miranda's cheek and jaw.

And all she could do was cry and listen to Miranda's occasional, "Uh-huh," "Yes, Drake," and her final articulate, "I'll want to see all of the flight data on that."

23

With two fatalities from the Lac Brome plane crash in a morgue a hundred kilometers away, Taz figured they should start locally first. She reached for a deep officiousness before exiting hospital room D804 and returning to the post-op nurse's station.

It turned out to be completely unnecessary.

The battle-ax nurse's sigh of resignation heaved her large chest, despite wearing heavy starch-whites, as she waved them by. The RCMP guard didn't look up from his book until the last second when his hand snaked out to open the door for them. Masked once again, and with fresh-washed hands, they returned to Bed Six.

Ernie Maxwell was coming out of it, squinting at his arm suspended in a cast above him. "Whad da shell?"

A nurse was instructing him to lie still, as if he had a choice with the raised side rails and the massive arm-and-shoulder cast pinning him to the mattress.

"I need to ask him some questions," Taz informed her.

"But—"

"Yes. I understand he's still groggy and drugged and all that. But he holds the clues to two deaths that I've been ordered to investigate."

"He—"

"Jeremy," Taz said and turned her back on the woman before she felt all sympathetic and backed away.

"What?" Jeremy was staring fixedly at Maxwell's cast, either calculating the structural inconsistencies of forces on Maxwell's body, or trying not to be ill.

Taz sighed. Either way, one hundred percent her Jeremy. "Please escort her somewhere else. Anywhere else."

"Oh! Okay. Why?"

"Jer-e-my!"

"Right. Don't argue. Just do it." He mumbled to himself before turning to the nurse. "Arguing with her never works. Trust me, she's my fiancée and I know."

His fiancée. Crazy words. Marriage was another item that had never been on her radar.

As soon as they were both gone, Taz started the voice recorder on her phone and held it close. "Why did you sabotage the plane, Ernie?"

"Didnut..." But even drugged, his dodging eyes gave him away.

She plopped her phone on his chest and pulled out his own. Both Clarissa and Kurt had missed her keeping it. She tapped in her own security code, then turned it to face him.

He grunted when he saw the sabotage app, "Pd."

"Paid?"

He grunted once, which she'd assume was an affirmative.

"How much?" What was the price to buy a CIA director these days?

"One half befoe. Two aft."

"Million?"

Another monosyllabic grunt.

Cheaper than she'd thought. Far cheaper actually, as the second round of sabotage said they never expected to have to pay the two million after he finished the job. No need to pay the dead.

"Plus, Clrsa chob." And Clarissa's job? Not as cheap as she'd thought.

While Taz would have thought she'd prefer anyone else in the D/CIA's chair, she'd actually take Clarissa over this waste of space.

"Who?"

He shrugged. Or tried to. The lance of pain across his face said that the drugs were wearing off. Which meant she was running out of time.

"Guess!"

"Egyp'. Is reel. Saud-a-bia. Lega… Leb… Liba…"

"Lebanon or Libya?"

"Bode." He nodded. "All fuh-in' nutso."

"What about the two guys in the first row, other side of the aisle?"

This time when he squinted at her, she could see him start to wonder who she was. She wished she'd studied medicine more, or at least the machines. The IVs were dangling from a pole above a blue contraption. But it wasn't clear how to turn up the dose even if she understood which bag was the goofy juice.

"Wha shoe guysh?"

"Two men. Traveling Boston to Montreal. Ahead to your right. You probably spent most of the flight looking at them when you weren't fucking around with your little phone app."

He rocked his head back and forth in denial.

Sadly, she believed him.

"Why I know?"

"Because whoever sabotaged you—your app and the seatbelt were both tampered with—did the same to them."

"Is tha wha happnd?" He squinted at her again. "Who are sho?"

"No one. I was never here."

She turned off both phones and pocketed them. Then thought of one last question. After that, she was done.

The nurse hovered not far away.

"I think you need to turn up his pain meds a bit." Maybe he wouldn't remember she was here at all.

The nurse hurried over.

"Anything useful?" Jeremy whispered as they left and headed for the elevator. He took her hand, which was utterly ridiculous and she rather liked it.

"Yeah. Not only is the guy cheap, but he's an idiot. He doesn't know who he's working for. Yet when they promised him Clarissa's job, he believed them."

"What next?"

"I think we need to go visit a couple of dead guys."

And in addition to the kiss Jeremy placed atop her head, she had another reason to be happy.

The two corpses' morgue was back near Lac Brome. Maybe she'd finally get a chance to visit the area.

24

ANDI COULDN'T BE SURE IF THEY HIT A GAP IN THE Bellingham ER's typical influx or her threat to call the President *back,* if they didn't hurry, earned them the results —but it worked. The fact that it hadn't actually been Roy Cole on the phone was something they had no need to know.

Miranda was admitted, x-rayed, given a local anesthetic (once Mother talked her into it), and had her bone reset and re-x-rayed in record time. The doctor didn't disappear between each step, but hovered instead. After the hospital was done, the three of them ended up standing outside in the midmorning sunshine watching the ambulatory patients entering the ER and the occasional ambulance rolling another in.

Andi dropped onto a bench and wondered what the hell came next. Miranda had remained atypically passive and Mother atypically nonjudgmental. She had no idea what she herself was being—atypically hesitant?

Andi couldn't decide which was the most confusing of the three.

Well, hesitancy was not the word of the day.

"We need to get you—" she bit off the word *home* before it could slip out. "To, ah, the office."

Miranda nodded but didn't speak. She hadn't shied away from Andi's presence or touch when she was holding the phone, which she'd take as a good sign of Miranda's mental state. But did going nonverbal mean she was emotionally exhausted? Or did it mean she was retreating into some preverbal autistic state? Andi simply didn't know enough about ASD to guess.

Reading a few books had mostly taught her that each person on the spectrum followed their own unique pattern, kinda like everyone. At that point Andi had tossed all the books aside and decided to treat Miranda as Miranda.

"How long a drive is it?" Mother rescued her.

"Over two hours, probably three with Seattle traffic. Except we'd hit downtown at lunchtime so maybe four."

"How long to fly?"

Andi could only blink at her in shock. "Uh, fifteen minutes in Miranda's jet, but I don't know how to fly it."

Miranda still didn't speak, even if Andi would let her fly it one-handed after what she'd just been through.

Mother gave her one of *those* looks. "Then hire someone to fly it for you."

Andi smacked her forehead and yanked out her phone. "First, a taxi."

Before she'd finished voicing the thought, Mother stepped to the curb. A taxi pulled up and someone stepped out to enter ER. She climbed in without asking the driver first, "The airport."

Action! The universe rewards action. Everyone from her mother to her Night Stalkers instructor had echoed that one. She coaxed Miranda into the back seat and climbed into the front.

Then she buried herself in finding a pilot during the ten-mile trip back to where they'd started.

No one handy to fly the jet.

All the sightseeing helos were fully booked.

They were rolling into the airport by the time she'd dug her way down to flight schools. She started to book the annoyingly slow one-hour flight in the only plane available, a Cessna 172 four-seater, plus its empty return. Regrettably, the instructor was not certified in jets. Thinking better of it, she booked it as a one-way lesson in fixed-wing flight.

They were bound to pull her license. The slash of pain at losing the chance to fly? No time for that now, though she could barely breathe past the agony in her chest. But she would never be caught out again.

Feeling helpless in the face of Miranda's panic had created a fist crushing tighter on her heart than never piloting again.

It might be her last-ever fixed-wing lesson, but she'd damn well get her first one.

25

Miranda looked out.

Not out the window of the Cessna 172, her eyes had been doing that for a while.

Not at Andi struggling to adapt one set of reflexes to another under the guidance of a flummoxed flight instructor. The poor man didn't know what to do with Andi's familiarity with flight and flight controls that he could never hope to match—paired with her complete lack of instinct for fixed-wing flight. Miranda could see her improving by the minute as they practiced level flight, banked turns, and stalls on their way south.

Miranda now understood that old saying: *We see through a glass, darkly.* She looked out from the depths of a long remove from the vista of Puget Sound and Andi's flight.

Her parents' home, *her* home had burned. She'd witnessed it, not as some nightmare vision but as a horrid, unimagined reality. That house had been the one true anchor in her life.

Her parents dead. Tante Daniels her governess-guardian-therapist-friend departed after Miranda entered the NTSB. Her team, built over the last three years, still brand-new by almost every measure—Taz and Jeremy's recent departure only emphasizing its ephemeral nature.

Yet Miranda could also see how close she'd come to killing them all. They would write it off as an autistic regression, a loss of previously developed skills, sometimes called autistic burnout. But that would be an inaccurate assessment of the occurrence.

Her actions had been a pure panic attack.

It wasn't until today's fire that she understood how much her view of her father had changed. Tante Daniels had told her of the drug regimens her parents had used to control her early on—an abuse that Tante Daniels had replaced with a kind voice and behavioral therapy.

How much of her past was real and how much imagined? She had no idea. Mom was a mostly passive memory. But had she been passive in Miranda's life, or maybe simply overwhelmed by her daughter's autism? She remembered so many good moments together in the gardens. Yes, she'd choose that memory to focus on.

Andi had twice tried to console her over the loss of her father's plane, but it wasn't even his plane. Twenty years ago she'd crashed that in the remote Idaho wilderness due to engine failure—and replaced it twice since. She didn't think she'd be replacing it again. A past she'd been holding on to so hard.

When she'd dived the plane, maybe she'd been trying to hold onto that memory. Or her home. Or protect the animals she could see running from the fire in an all too familiar panic. The panic of a child overwhelmed by her environment had briefly overwhelmed the adult.

The shot of pain as Andi broke her arm had cleared away so much, as if shattering that dark glass.

That was past.

And yet she had been unable to stop her actions, unable to face the shame after Andi had to break her arm to regain control. Miranda couldn't stop cradling the cast, not in pain but in memory of Andi saving her. Saving them all.

She turned to Andi's mother and whispered to her below the noise level that might carry her voice to the front seat over the sound of the small Cessna's Lycoming IO-360 engine. "You have an amazing daughter, Mrs. Wu."

Ching Hui looked at her in some surprise—at least that was the look on her face that would match the emoji in Miranda's reference notebook. "This from a woman who receives calls from the Chairman of the Joint Chiefs?"

"Drake called?" She'd forgotten about that. "Did Roy call too?"

Ching Hui's expression shifted from surprise to...shock? "You call the President by his first..." she trailed off. "Yes, the Chairman of the Joint Chiefs called. No, the President did not."

"Lately I seem to find it challenging to differentiate memory from current events."

"That the President might have called you?"

Miranda tipped her head one way and another but couldn't see any more clearly through the past. She knew her actions, but it was as if her hearing had become as superfluous during the fire as the past, future, or any sense of present self-preservation. She'd been...

Was that what the temporarily insane experienced? A

full and complete logical disconnect? She never wanted to be insane if that was part of the required experience. It was even more fractured than being autistic on a bad day.

"I recall…speaking with Drake, now that you mention it. Flight data! Oh!" The rest of the memory came back. That was comforting.

And she focused on where they were for the first time. Andi was practicing turning-around-a-point, a point that was three thousand feet below, over central Vashon Island. She held the wing rock-steady in the bank.

"Andi," she called forward. "I need to get to JBLM."

"You're talking to me?" Andi bobbled the controls as she twisted to look back over her shoulder; it was the first time the flight instructor had to grab for the wheel in the entire flight.

"Yes. Though perhaps I shouldn't have if that's how you react while piloting."

Andi made a weird face.

Miranda winced as she recalled that the same could definitely be said of her a few hours previously. Oh, Andi's expression had probably matched hers: horrified at her momentary lapse in pilot-in-command protocols. They would damn Miranda for that, pull her pilot's license and perhaps end her career as an air-crash investigator.

That was too overwhelming to think about at the moment.

And with her arm broken, she had no way to note it down in her personal notebook. Well, it was of sufficient importance, she was sure it would come up again on its own.

"Joint Base Lewis-McChord is military restricted air space, ma'am." The flight instructor spoke up.

"Gray Field or the main runway at McChord?" Andi overran him.

"McChord." It lay just fifteen miles ahead, only ten miles past her office at Tacoma Narrows Airport where Andi had been taking them.

Andi dialed in the tower frequency from memory and began talking to the controller, who began echoing the flight instructor's protest.

"Tell him we need to meet Drake. He's on an E-4B Nightwatch."

Much to the tower's consternation, the controller easily verified that they were expected. Within those few moments, his behavior completely changed.

Miranda remembered the first time she'd landed here. The controller had been far more obstreperous on that occasion though. In retrospect, that most likely had been due to the crash she'd come to investigate—a C-5 Galaxy that had destroyed the airport control tower before bursting into flame.

She let Andi and the flight instructor worry about the tower and the security of landing at a military airfield.

One thing had become absolutely clear. Despite Miranda's…lapse, Andi wouldn't desert her. Miranda *knew* that she trusted Andi more than anyone in her life. More than herself, as she'd always found herself to be an unreliable referent for normalcy even at the best of times.

Andi leveled the wings with a neat snap. It lagged, as a Cessna 172 was designed to treat the most rank beginner pilot gently, but it responded. Then her rotorcraft instincts had her nosing down to the south to descend rather than easing her throttle. From her perspective, Miranda could see Andi moving her left hand as if to lower a helicopter's collective, except in a Cessna there wasn't one to hold. It was the correct action, in the wrong aircraft.

Miranda turned to share a smile with Ching Hui. Her mother must not understand the joke. Come to think of it, Miranda was surprised as well. She herself *never* understood jokes.

26

Security at the loading stairs had balked about their new passengers. Despite his urgent need to be airborne, Drake descended from his office to clear up the matter. A short set of stairs led him from the mid-deck to the lower deck of the Nightwatch. The 747 had her own staircase that had folded out from the lower deck to the ground. Beside the bottom step, an armed SF, the Air Force's police security force, blocked three women from boarding. None of which reached his shoulder.

"Hello, Miranda. Thank you so much for coming. Captain Wu," they exchanged salutes. He didn't need to ask about the third, her looks said it all. "You are obviously Andi's mother." Andi looked pained, but the woman smiled.

"Ching Hui Wu at your service, General Nason." They shook hands. She had the same delicate build as her daughter, with a studied elegance that Andi made no attempt to achieve.

"How's the arm, Miranda?"

"Broken, Drake." Her tone said, *obviously,* except he

knew she wouldn't have meant it that way. He hadn't seen her in six months and it was easy to forget her ways.

"We're running terribly late as we were almost overhead before I called you. Had I realized you were at a different airfield, we could have picked you up there."

"That's in the past. I'm ready now."

"I need you sharp, Miranda. What painkillers are you—"

"She won't take any stronger than aspirin, General," Andi cut him off quickly with a worried glance toward Miranda.

At his questioning look, Andi answered with a glare. Apparently neither an issue *nor* a topic for discussion. "Captain Wu, if you're available to join us, I'm sure that Miranda would appreciate your assistance where we're headed." Because he'd seen how Andi could interpret Miranda's needs before anyone else. "Your expertise in rotorcraft probably would not go amiss either."

"Yours to command, sir." The soldier's answer, not the woman's, but it was all he needed.

"I, uh," he turned to the older woman. "Ms. Wu. I'm afraid that you lack the clearance to—"

"General," her accentless English was soft yet brooked no dissent.

What was it with small Chinese women cutting him off today?

"You may be unaware that I handle intellectual property rights for several organizations that are perhaps familiar to you, including Lockheed Martin's ADP, more colloquially known as Skunk Works. I assure you that my security clearance is in excellent standing."

"Well, now I know where Andi came by her unstoppable force of character, straight down the matrilineal line."

Ms. Wu nodded. Andi kept her eyeroll to herself, mostly—he spotted it.

He didn't waste time arguing. "Could you all please show your security clearances to the SF officer?"

Andi's mother opened a purse that he'd wager cost a significant portion of his monthly salary and handed the card to the security guard as Miranda and Andi handed over theirs. The guard took a step back so that no one could surprise him, lifted a scanner from his belt to the cards, and studied the display. He returned the cards and nodded to Drake. "All cleared Top Secret with discretionary code-word clearance, except Ms. Chase who is cleared Yankee White."

Ms. Wu aimed a surprised glance at Miranda that the latter utterly failed to notice. Drake kept his smile to himself; clearance to be armed around the President was very rare outside the Secret Service.

He considered for a moment.

Aboard that crash in Quebec he'd lost the foremost thinker about military aircraft capabilities in the business and a negotiator known for forging agreements. Miranda and Andi could stand in for the former, perhaps as well as the man himself. He had figured that he himself would lead the meeting. But it was with a group of allies who didn't always see eye-to-eye. A disinterested third-party viewpoint could be very useful.

"Ms. Wu—"

"Ching Hui."

"Ching Hui. We are headed into a very important international negotiation of a highly classified nature. Ms. Chase and Captain Wu between them constitute an asset of some brilliance—"

"But my daughter lacks delicacy. A shortcoming I was never able to break her of."

"Mother!"

"Precisely," he couldn't help teasing Andi.

She glared at him as her mother continued.

"And Ms. Chase, as I've observed…"

Andi went up on her toes ready to do battle. Her mother noticed and apparently reconsidered her approach with only the slightest sign of hesitation.

"…has little use for tact, preferring to remain utterly forthright."

Caught with nothing but the simple truth to face down, Andi was slow to ease her guard.

He nodded. "Could you spare three days for your government? You would be compensated at professional rates, of course."

"As I am on vacation to see my daughter, my schedule is open. As she is traveling with you, that would serve my personal agenda as well."

He nodded his thanks as Andi opened her mouth to protest, found nothing, and closed it again.

"If you would fetch your luggage…" But the Cessna 172 had already departed.

"I fear that such as we had, solely my own, remains aboard Miranda's jet parked in Bellingham. You will have to take us," she brushed at her jacket as if it came from Goodwill instead of some elite designer, "as we are."

"My crash site investigation bag," Miranda turned to look north and took a step as if ready to walk there to fetch it.

"Right here," Andi slung off the knapsack she'd had draped over her shoulder. "I knew you'd miss it."

"Where's yours?"

Andi grimaced. "I didn't think *that* far ahead. It's still on your plane along with both of our go bags of clothes and such." She held out Miranda's site pack.

Rather than taking it, Miranda leaned in and kissed her.

Drake noted that it was not the least bit hurried or perfunctory. Ching Hui Wu watched that most intently.

"You carry it for me," Miranda whispered in such away that Drake could feel himself blushing for overhearing it.

27

As she climbed up the steel stairs into the E-4B Nightwatch, Andi didn't know whether to be charmed that Miranda was so happy at Andi thinking of her feelings and trusting her with the pack far more important to her than any plane. Or to be annoyed with Chairman of the Joint Chiefs of Staff General Drake Nason for exactly the same two reasons: *You make such a perfect servant, Andrea Wu, anticipated my main asset's every need. Carry Miranda's luggage while you're at it.*

Isn't that what she'd been doing with the flight instructor? Learning fixed-wing flight to become yet another safety factor around Miranda?

At least she knew Miranda didn't think that way, couldn't think in head games. Her kiss had spoken volumes that Miranda might not be aware of but Andi hadn't missed.

Neither had Mother. Yet she hadn't hit her with a dose of the Wu and Wu stink-eye.

She'd braced herself for battle this week, but each time she dug in, it wasn't there.

Ching Hui Wu was leaking into her life. *Oh, you look just like your mother. Nastiness straight down the fucking matrilineal line.* Her mother: the genetic toxin she could never purge from her psyche.

Except Mother hadn't been nasty once since commenting on Andi's attire. And that had been more knee-jerk than nasty. Not even after one of the scariest moments in flight Andi had ever experienced other than being shot at in warzones.

Andi would certainly rest more easily if Mother had been dumped at JBLM and taken by taxi to SeaTac for a flight home. She wouldn't quite wish a plane crash on her mother's head, but she wouldn't argue against some serious en route turbulence.

Drake led them to the right and into his cabin at the nose of the aircraft.

Andi had been aboard a Nightwatch almost two years ago, as she and Miranda had rushed to investigate the Vice President's death. That time they'd been restricted to a small conference room that lay to the left.

She'd stopped at the threshold without intending to.

"Something wrong, Captain Wu?" Drake asked.

"Not what I expected, sir."

"Yes, my luxury home in the sky." A small wooden desk, little more than a slab bolted to the inside of the hull, dominated by a large comm gear panel that belonged in a museum and could probably do less than a modern cell phone. There was a sofa of three flight seats opposite Drake's chair.

Drake picked up a phone, punched a button, and passed instructions to the pilot as Andi concentrated on getting Miranda and Mother settled and belted in.

He must have noted her gaze as he waved them to a couch with three sets of seatbelts directly across from his chair.

"The comm gear isn't merely old, it's also not based on wi-fi, touchscreens, or any of that. We have all that, but everything aboard is hardwired as well. It's less susceptible to an EMP, an electro-magnetic pulse from a close-proximity nuclear blast. This console is wired with fiber-optic, ethernet, and good old copper phone line. We even have teletype in the communications bay."

Andi nodded. She knew about the Doomsday Planes, but her first trip aboard had been restricted to a conference room.

Miranda pointed toward the forward end of the deck above with her good hand. "The cockpit is all old-fashioned circular dials for the same reason. You're sitting inside a plane-sized Faraday cage and every piece of sensitive electronics is in a shielding case of its own. No payload spent on luxury here. This is a command-and-control center of last resort."

"The functionality matches the name," Mother observed. "The ones who keep watch, even in the darkness of night."

Drake's nod affirmed that as, done taxiing, they headed aloft with a gut-shaking roar of the engines.

"We've changed our route. I was scheduled to stopover at Tonopah, but due to the unanticipated delay, we'll make a brief stop, then proceed directly to our destination at Thule Air Base, Greenland. There we'll be meeting with all seven nations claiming direct interest in the Arctic, with the exception of the eighth, Russia, of course. The EU will also be sending an observer."

"And what is the purpose of this meeting, General?" Mother was naturally in full lawyer-mode.

"We have a broad set of topics, but our main focus is building a specification consensus for the rapid design and development of a blended security force-and-rescue aircraft best suited to the unique needs of the Arctic. In the past, this has been relegated to the LC-130 Skibirds of the 109th Airlift Wing of the New York National Guard. Also various small civilian aircraft contracted from cold-weather specialists such as Kenn Borek Air. Climate change and the resultant opening of the Arctic are drastically altering those criteria."

"Long range due to few bases," Miranda spoke up. "Ability to make rough field landings on newly exposed but ungroomed tundra. Exceptional cold weather performance."

"And," Andi sighed, "enough hardening and firepower to take the fight to anyone who gets out of line." No need to say who, as it was a secret meeting with Russia not invited.

Drake nodded. "Precisely. That's why I need your military expertise along with Miranda's technical know-how. How do we land on rough seas, unreliable ice pack, or whatever you think we'll encounter? How do we maintain functionality in such a harsh environment? Nothing's off the table at this point. But time is of the essence."

And there was a phrase with a heavily loaded meaning to both the lawyer and the military pilot. It had implications beyond *hurry up*. To both her and her mother, it would mean fast deadlines that *must* be met. The impossible triangle: speed, precision, cost. You could pick any two but never all three.

Miranda had taken her hand as if it was a normal, unthinking gesture, except Miranda had never done that before and she did *nothing* by instinct. She was the most conscious-living person Andi knew.

Then Drake frowned at some thought. "And as much as I'd like to give you all a rest, I need answers on who killed the people you're replacing."

"Why ask us?" Andi faced him but couldn't figure out how she'd suddenly become a detective.

"Because Mr. Trahn and Colonel Cortez are presently investigating the plane crash the two died on. They've said it was sabotage. I need to know who's responsible."

The plane, barely ten minutes aloft, began to descend.

Andi didn't need to be a fixed-wing pilot to recognize the change in the engines. *In the engines.* She wanted to smack her forehead. She should have known to pull the throttle to descend the small Cessna rather than nosing down.

"I thought we were headed to Greenland?"

"There are very few clothing stores in Thule. We're stopping in Bellingham to fetch your luggage. Specialized cold weather gear will be provided, of course."

28

"What do you mean *they're dead?* I know that. That's why we're here." Taz was feeling the depredations of not sleeping last night. In the hour drive from Montreal, she'd had to fight to stay awake to help Jeremy stay conscious.

"I mean just how I say," the head coroner of the morgue at the hospital in Cowansville, Quebec, sported a nearly incomprehensible French accent that he mumbled through a thick, unruly beard and mustache. Prominently displayed above his desk, with its own little spotlight, was a placard for Third Prize at last year's Festival du Voyageur's Beard Growing Contest.

The air was redolent with chemicals that almost convinced Taz morning sickness should not be restricted to mornings alone. Midafternoons were her newest candidate for prime time.

"I know they're dead. I want to know why." If his attitude didn't change in short order, Taz was going to pin him to the floor and shear his face like a sheep. She was way too tired for this.

"Because their necks, *chkkkk!*" He made a sound unnervingly like a neck snapping and flopped his head toward his shoulder.

Regrettably it was a sound she knew from her youth in the barrios and would never forget.

"The face," he slapped a palm into the other held up vertically, like a face impacting a wall, then cocked his wrist as if letting his hand flop bonelessly to the side. "Dead. I need not the autopsy to see this." He settled back into his chair and did his best to look deeply bored.

She tried several different tacks, but none appeared to be moving her any closer to useful information beyond broken necks.

The coroner had obviously noted that she thought his beard was utterly ridiculous and had begun stroking it like a pet dog to annoy her. They were rapidly becoming each other's least favorite people.

When Jeremy's phone rang, she half listened in while she considered her next move.

"Hi, Miranda. How are you? ... Your arm hurts? I'm sorry to hear that, I hope it gets better soon. ... You broke it?"

Taz paid closer attention to the call than the annoying coroner seated in front of her.

"*Andi* broke it? Why?"

The coroner stopped making love to his beard and leaned forward to listen as well. Maybe he had a fetish for broken bodies. Duh! He was a coroner.

"Too much to explain now," he whispered to Taz as she turned to face him. "She's... uh, with Drake. Sure," he said back into the phone. "I've uploaded everything I've found onto the server. So if you've been through that... Oh good, you have, then I don't have anything else at the moment. I haven't had time to review the flight recorder but as the Quick Access Recorder was recovered intact, I felt that was a low priority. Good. You saw that too."

Jeremy began digging for something in his bag as he pinned the phone between his shoulder and ear. When it predictably slipped away from him, Taz caught it and held it up to her own ear.

"I also have some recordings for you, Miranda. An interview with CIA Department Director Ernie Maxwell. He was injured in the crash and is the flight's primary saboteur. And you can tell Drake that I'm sitting less than ten meters from his two corpses here in Quebec but the local," she bit down on what she wanted to say, *weasel*, "coroner can't be bothered to look at them."

Miranda said something off to the side and then asked for the coroner's phone number.

Taz grabbed the phone from his desk and read the number off over his protests.

"Hold please." Miranda didn't mute the phone.

She heard Drake talking in the background. And the heavy throb of plane engines.

"Where are you, Miranda?"

"King William Island, I believe."

"That's a new one on me."

"Northern Nunavut. It's in the Arctic Ocean above central Canada."

"Oh!" was all that Taz could think to say. Miranda in the Arctic. A short while back she'd been in the Antarctic and that had been harrowing enough to hear about. "Be more careful this time."

"Okay."

The morgue director's desk phone rang.

In the background, Taz could hear that Drake had stopped talking.

"You'll want to answer that," she told the man when he didn't move.

He offered her a scoff before answering, "*Oui?*"

Then he jolted to his feet. His answers were brief and in French. Not one of her languages but she did enjoy watching the blood drain from his face.

"Who's he talking to?" she asked Miranda.

"Drake called the Surgeon General of Canada who called their Minister of Health. Something about a person interfering with an investigation that could affect Canadian national security."

The coroner hung up the phone very slowly. Then he looked at her with a puzzled expression, one asking who the hell this little Latina bitch was, and was there a way he could hate her even more than he already did.

"I don't care what you think," she told him. "As long as you get it in gear—now!"

She might have shot him with her Taser for how fast he moved. He rushed off, calling to his assistant about, "*Deux autopsies. Les Américains. Vite! Vite!*" He yanked a mask from the dispenser and hurried through the heavy steel door, battered and scarred where corpse-bearing stretchers had been slammed against it.

"He's with the program now." Taz reported. "National security, though? It isn't like Drake to be telling fibs."

"He isn't. Please send the recordings. And call me the moment he has anything to report." And Miranda was gone before Taz could ask for details.

National security? Sure, someone getting to the CIA Middle East Desk's director. But the two dead guys from the

Embraer flight? What were she and Jeremy snarled up in now?

And now? Here Taz was, her ass parked in the basement morgue of the Hospital Brome-Missisquoi-Perkins, stuck not fifteen kilometers from Knowlton, Quebec, where she wanted to be. Gamache would have to wait.

Crap!

29

At its famous Kiel shipyards, Germany built the Type 209 submarine strictly for export. Sixty-one have been built and sold to thirteen world militaries. The fifty-second one sold at a bargain price of two-hundred-and-eighty-three million US dollars. That was only one tiny piece of what made Germany the world's largest arms exporter that wasn't also one of the five permanent members of the UN Security Council.

Two-thirds of a football field long with a diameter no greater than a full-bed Ford F-150 SuperCab from front bumper to trailer hitch, the diesel-electric engines could drive the sub halfway around the globe and travel fifty straight days without replenishment.

At three hundred meters below the surface, it skimmed close enough to the bottom of the Arctic waters to disappear in the noise clutter that any down-facing ship's sonar might see. They would be concerned with the icebergs floating on the surface far above. Down here, rocks, underwater mudslides, and other irregularities would return as bright a signal as the submarine as long as it continued to move slowly.

It hadn't come all of the way to the Arctic Ocean to be seen.

It was up to him as the sonar technician to make sure they were neither found nor collided with anything. He was the eyes and ears of the submarine whenever it was submerged.

And for two weeks they'd been lurking where Lancaster Sound emptied into Baffin Bay close by Canada and the middle of Greenland. Hundreds had died here, perhaps thousands, vainly seeking the Northwest Passage over Canada to the Orient. The former captain had made it clear that he felt they were all idiots. *They only needed to wait for the ice to melt. Now tourist ships make the transition.*

That was before the former captain put that bullet through his brain.

The sonar tech felt the pressure outside the hull, squeezing in on them the same way everyone else did, but to—

Through his headphones, he heard a soft rumble. It faded in and out, but not like any whale call.

"Captain, sonar contact." Without asking, he put it up on the speakers as the new captain stalked over from his station. He'd been in command less than two weeks but was *not* an idiot like their former captain.

He knew that the captain wanted details, but he didn't have any yet. And this one knew he didn't have any yet, so he didn't ask, though he hovered like a hawk. He was built that way too, tall, lean, and slightly stooped from banging his head on hatchways too many times.

The man seemed permanently worried. He himself

would take the sonar station chair any time. Listen, analyze, report.

Besides, the Arctic was like no environment he'd ever encountered and he still learned new facets about its acoustics every day.

Lancaster Sound funneled the noisy, melting, crashing-mad Arctic Ice as it flowed west-to-east through the fourteen-hundred-kilometer-long Parry Channel and dumped into Baffin Bay. The surface flow of frigid freshwater from the annual polar cap ice melt, pumping through the eighty-kilometer maw of Lancaster Sound, ran especially thick and heavy in the late summer.

Less dense than saltwater, the freshwater floated on top despite being significantly colder. That temperature inversion created an acoustic barrier like a horizontal sound mirror deep in the water. Signals bounced and refracted in unusual ways and arrived from angles he couldn't yet predict.

Fifteen long days they'd been lurking at the mouth of Lancaster Sound, awaiting the right opportunity. He and the captain were probably the only two of the thirty crew not bored out of their minds.

He knew very little, except that the new captain was waiting for a particular type of ship—and was becoming increasingly dangerous due to not finding it. This captain was a smart man but *not* a patient one. Three men were on bread-and-water rations for minor offenses and two were handcuffed to their bunks for banging a watertight hatch one too many times instead of closing it silently. This was a big problem for the other sailors who were supposed to hot bunk there in eight-hour shifts.

He'd found two ships in thirty-six hours...ten days ago. Neither had been what the captain sought.

For both they'd surfaced, but the captain didn't care about the fishing boat or the Canadian ice breaker.

They'd also made the long climb from depth when he'd misidentified an American C-130 Hercules aircraft with skis passing low enough over the sea to sound like a ship.

"What do we have this time, Sonar?" The captain would call him *Sonar* even if they met on their deathbed. He often wondered if their commander knew any of their names, the foreigner who had been serving as First Officer until the captain's suicide certainly couldn't pronounce any of them properly. Everyone followed his example, of course. After a month at sea, he felt as if his birth name was Sonar.

The captain started the sub on a slow climb up to the base of the thermocline. At fifty meters they cleared the thermocline and the sonar gear was able to get a clearer fix.

"Exiting Lancaster Sound now, Captain," he announced. After all this time listening, he'd learned the variations of sound as it reflected off the sides of the channel opening out into the width of Baffin Bay. He heard the tone change. "A large surface ship, single screw. Moving away from us."

The captain brought them to periscope depth only after he reconfirmed the tone change thirty seconds later. Neither of them had forgotten the third day of the voyage. They'd been in the Mediterranean, surfacing at night to run the diesel engines to charge their batteries, when they'd almost been struck by a US Navy Arleigh-Burke destroyer. A warship like that could have sliced them in two, if they'd been ten meters shallower, and sent their boat to the bottom in seconds, sustaining minimal damage itself.

Most ships, except those who were particularly paranoid

like submariners, only looked forward for obstacles. Non-military skimmers, as submariners called surface boats, were especially susceptible to this. They almost never thought to look behind. Surfacing behind this ship, even in the near-constant daylight that was September north of the Arctic Circle, should be safe.

Neither he nor any of his thirty other crewmates had breathed fresh air in weeks or seen anything beyond the walls of this steel can—except the captain. Whatever he saw out of the periscope made him smile.

"Launch a surveillance drone." Command wanted imaging of their torpedo attack.

The drone tech, who was also the assistant cook, climbed to the top of the conning tower as the captain broached the surface. Lucky dog. He would have a moment in the air, with a horizon that stood more than five meters away.

But the drone tech knew the captain's temper, so returned inside before he possibly could have done more than launch his toy.

They all knew the drill now.

Once more they settled beneath the surface, all except for the radio mast. This would have left a visible wake if they'd been moving with any speed. They weren't. At two kilometers per hour they were moving just fast enough to keep steerage control, but little more. They'd released the drone when they were a kilometer aft of the ship. Seven minutes later the ship had pulled out to five kilometers ahead with the drone only a kilometer behind.

Tubes One and Three had been loaded with SeaHake Mod 4 torpedoes purchased from Germany along with the submarine. As they had during their two practice runs, they set the torpedo's programming to dive deep, keep out of sight, then rise to destroy a blade of the massive cargo ship's propellor.

For reasons that no one told a lowly ping jockey, Command wanted any Chinese freighter transiting the Northwest Passage to be struck. A damaged propellor could leave a cargo ship limping for weeks along a voyage that should have finished in days. In extreme cases, calls would have to be placed for terribly expensive deep-sea tugs.

The captain didn't fire the torpedoes in Tube One or Three, he fired Tube Two.

The one-point-five-million-dollar UGM-84 Harpoon missile built by Boeing spit out the front of the tube. Once it was clear, it fired its solid-propellent booster. The protective case that had kept it safe from seawater intrusion peeled away as it punched through the surface.

At eight hundred kilometers per hour, it tore after the Chinese cargo ship. He had to clear his throat several times before he managed to speak.

"*Missile* away, Captain." He was unsure why they were being so stealthy if they were simply going to fire a missile.

"Aye, Sonar." The captain paced forward to look over the drone operator's shoulder, then jerked to a halt and asked without turning, "Did you say *missile?*"

The captain turned slowly until they could see each other's shocked expression.

"Aye, Captain," he spoke the words very carefully. "Tube Two was loaded with an American Harpoon missile."

The blood drained from the captain's face until he was whiter than sea foam, then he spun forward once more.

"Splash the drone!"

"What?"

"Into the ocean. Get rid of it."

When the man hesitated, the captain ripped the controller out of his hands. For an instant there was a very detailed view of a wave on the monitor, and then nothing as the small surveillance drone destroyed itself.

"Sonar! Abort the missile!"

He hit the abort key, but knew it was too late. A SeaHake torpedo traveling at a hundred kilometers per hour would have had a transit time of three minutes to reach the ship. The sea-skimming Harpoon had covered the distance in twenty-one seconds.

They were seven seconds too late. Too late even before they splashed the drone.

The explosion might be in visual range, but the captain didn't raise the periscope. Instead he spoke very softly, "Dive the boat. Get us home."

30

THE THREE-HUNDRED-METER CARGO SHIP *FORTUNATE PROGRESS*—sister ship to the *Lucky Progress* currently transiting the Northeast Passage over Russia and northern Europe—had successfully navigated the much trickier Northwest Passage over Alaska and Canada also without an escort ice breaker.

This summer, the Arctic ice had melted so much that they hadn't need one. The strengthened bow for pushing aside float ice while traveling at twenty-two knots had proved sufficient to the task. Only twice had they slowed significantly to ease through heavier ice.

Thirty percent less distance than transiting the Panama Canal from Beijing to New York. That meant thirty percent less fuel, time, and salaries. And also no canal fees. As she was a Neopanamax, designed for the maximum of the new Panama Canal locks opened in 2016, that alone saved a three-hundred-thousand-US-dollar transit fee.

The captain marveled at the change. For now the passage lay open only a few months a year, but five years ago such a transit had remained unthinkable without a heavy icebreaker escort. In five more years he might make this passage year-round at speed. His country's economic power—

He felt a shudder of impact where his hand had been resting on the breakfast table in his cabin. No mere piece of float ice could cause such a vibration in a hundred-thousand-ton class ship. There was nothing to strike as they were in deep water, hundreds of meters clearance lay below the hull.

He stuffed a *baozi* pork steamed bun into his mouth and rushed onto the bridge. Out on the port-side flying bridge—the only place he could look down to the sea, eighteen stories below past the vast bulk of the stacked containers—lay nothing but ocean.

No sign of ice of any size.

No air bubbles indicating they'd been holed.

He turned to look across the bridge and out to the starboard flying bridge where his second-in-command also stared down. Though they stood fifty meters apart, he could tell that his second saw nothing either.

In unison they turned to look aft.

31

The UGM-84 Harpoon missile had behaved precisely as designed. As it flew, a radar altimeter assessed the varying wave height and period. The waters where Lancaster Sound opened out into Baffin Bay were currently running at very modest sea state 3 with the tallest measured wave one and a quarter meters high. With no float ice in the area, this allowed the missile's autonomous programming to fly a mere five meters above the sea.

The duck-and-splash setting, to strike the ship below the waterline, had not been turned on, so it flew straight and true.

It struck the *Fortunate Progress* precisely on the stern's centerline, three meters above the upper edge of the double-reinforced section of the hull.

The two-hundred-and-twenty-one-kilogram warhead did not ignite on impact. By design, it punched through the thin steel plate at the stern as well as four sets of containers before it exploded eight-hundredths of a second later.

The impact itself was as nothing to such a huge ship.

The initial shock felt on the bridge marked the explosion of the warhead. That effect was buffered by the small air gaps between rows and layers of containers.

Had it hit a single container row higher, it would have punched a hole in the stern and destroyed four of the thirty-nine containers filled with a board game destined to be the next big hit in America.

However, by pure chance, the missile ignited inside a container filled with thirty-three tons of the newest generation of lithium-sulfur rechargeable batteries. They were destined to launch the first car manufacturer in an American state called Massachusetts since 1989.

The lithium, exposed to oxygen through the shattered casings, formed an exothermic reaction. Being exothermic—releasing more heat than required to sustain it—the lithium would keep burning until completely consumed.

The Harpoon missile warhead's explosion had breached the casing of thousands of batteries simultaneously and exposed them to a heat source sufficient to ignite them.

The resulting conflagration—hot-pink and carmine-red with burning lithium—expanded upward explosively, destroying containers of games, stuffed animals, and polyester pants.

The residential tower, topped by the command bridge, was built where a fifth row of containers would have been stacked, placing it next to the exploding container. Flashover shrapnel killed thirteen of the twenty-one crew in their bunks.

Burning at two thousand degrees Celsius, thirty-six hundred Fahrenheit, the conflagration also bored down into the propellor shaft area like a gigantic glowing gopher. Had it landed on one of the propellor casings, it would have melted the top layer and merely destroyed the shafts.

But it landed on an open section of deck. There it rapidly melted through the double-plate hull.

The sea pounded upward like a fountain shot from a three-meter diameter fire hose driven by the ship's hundred-and-twenty-thousand dead weight tonnage. Three of the remaining eight crew didn't survive in the engine room long enough to make any difference.

On the bridge there was yet little evidence of the disaster unfolding below except for the sudden sounding of multiple water alarms.

The engines still spun and the propellor still drove the ship ahead.

That's when the ship began to die.

The fountain of seawater pounded upward through the newly bored shaft and entered the container of burning lithium-sulfur batteries.

The water didn't extinguish the fire. Instead, the chemical reaction shifted. The lithium atoms broke the water molecules into a strongly negatively charged -OH hydroxyl group—forming a caustically basic alkali chemical solution—and a plume of hydrogen gas as a byproduct.

Unable to dissipate rapidly in the confines of the container stack, the hydrogen flashed over explosively.

This tertiary explosion, after the warhead and the battery fire itself, destroyed the anti-flooding bulkhead between the stern and the second to rearmost compartment directly below the bridge.

The *Fortunate Progress* had been stoutly built to withstand the ice. It presented a properly engineered double-bottom hull for safety and boasted both standard and high-capacity emergency bilge pumps. But when the engines drowned, the bilge pumps stopped.

No emergency radio call was made.

No one escaped the blast that had ripped into the residential tower at the moment of flashover.

The three survivors of the second-stage ignition blast on the bridge couldn't breathe after inhaling the thick sulfurous smoke that enveloped them—another byproduct of the burning lithium-sulfur batteries.

The captain and his second in command, standing exposed on the two bridge wings, were blown so far through the air that they impacted the ocean's surface ahead of the ship. The Second's neck was broken when the blast caught him but the captain survived, making him the longest-lived member of the entire crew. The whole catastrophe had escalated so quickly that he'd have choked to death on the half-chewed *baozi* bun stuck in his throat except he impacted the freezing ocean first.

Within four minutes of the missile's launch, the Arctic waters once again flowed placidly out of Lancaster Sound into Baffin Bay, except for seven floating containers that were blown clear. Most were well and properly lashed into place and were dragged to the bottom of the Arctic.

The sonar operator on the Type 209 submarine knew he could never bear to go to sea again. Stunned as he listened to the distinct sounds of shipboard containers passing below crush depth and the successive blasts of air bubbles boiling upward like crackling fireworks in his headphones.

32

The E-4B Nightwatch flew high above the land of the midnight sun north of the Artic Circle. The highly modified Boeing 747-200 didn't boast any stealth capability, yet it was one of the hardiest planes in the entire US Air Force fleet.

Tamisha Ward had fallen in love the first time she'd seen one plowing aloft out of Offutt Air Base outside Omaha, Nebraska. She hadn't even been supposed to be there, merely an airman hopping a cross-country military flight that had a stop there.

She'd been given twenty minutes to stretch her legs when she'd seen it. The beast was dressed in the same blue-and-white and the bold *United States of America* as Air Force One. All it lacked was a bit of blue around the nose and a Presidential Seal on the door. It had plenty else going on to make up for that, her kind of plenty else.

A site security honcho at the outer edge of her permitted stretch-it-out zone had given her the skinny on the big fat bird.

The thing was old, ancient—a few years shy of fifty. Even

Iran had retired the Dash-200s in 2016, and that was saying something. But the Nightwatch was too unique to kill. A high second hump behind the first-class cabin contained the heavy-duty SATCOM gear. There were enough additional antennas sticking up along the spine to put anything less than a killer whale to shame. Flare housings for defensive measures and, the security honcho insisted, enough heavy comm and surveillance gear inside to run a world war.

She was so down with that next-level shit.

It had taken her another three years since then, but Staff Sergeant Tamisha Ward now parked her butt at Desk Eight in that beautiful bird along with twenty-nine other operators in the battle-staff cabin that filled the middle third of the plane.

The brass had a cabin forward. A small conference room and a large briefing room filled the rest of the front third of the plane. Up the circular stairs—which still had the little chandelier of the original 747 First Class—were the cockpit, relief crew, and the ten mechanics who always accompanied the plane on every flight. Mechanics with the proper clearance to service the plane existed at very few airports.

The rear of the plane included the communications and tech control area that could talk to the world. Aft of them, the crew rest area offered Business Class quality seats and enough bunks for them to sleep in six-hour hot-bunk rotation.

Below were the tech spaces for whatever didn't fit in the middle third of the plane.

The battle-staff cabin had large consoles to either side of the central aisle. Operations staff like herself sat in pairs at each console, each pair specializing in some aspect of world conditions: Air Force, Navy, Army, Space Force had been added recently, as well as intelligence sections reporting world conditions.

Every time aloft aboard the Nightwatch astonished her with the sheer volume of information at their fingertips. No ground-based training sim could touch this reality.

Desk Eight, her and Doyle's station halfway along the cabin on the port side, was all about aircraft security. Her half of the desk focused on the visual threats. During training she'd easily spotted details that washed others out.

Little Hawk, you could see a sparrow in a coal mine, Gamps always said when she'd point out something. He said it must be because she was part Cherokee on Gammie's side. There were family stories about that, but no one could pin them down. The slave heritage was plenty clear though. They were among the lucky ones who could trace themselves through the market all the way back to the ship and village. Most had lost their past beyond the plantation.

Whatever the source, her visual acuity had placed her aboard the Nightwatch—a true slice of heaven.

Tonight's long-haul flight from Joint Base Elmendorf-Richardson in Anchorage, Alaska, to JBLM and Bellingham, then Thule, Greenland, was a unique opportunity to practice her skills while aloft. A quiet passage, requiring only the most basic monitoring. The leg before that, from Okinawa (a mere hop and a skip from Taiwan and China) up past Russia to Alaska, had kept everyone on their toes. Over the Canadian tundra and Arctic islands was much mellower.

One of the four E-4Bs was always on alert, but at their age they rarely left their Nebraskan base. They had three possible missions under the single umbrella of National Airborne Operations Center, none of which occurred with any great frequency.

Like Air Force One, a war could be run from an E-4B Nightwatch. Unlike Air Force One, it carried twice the comm gear and there was nothing pretty about the inside of the aircraft, only the bare essentials.

Instead, every inch was dedicated to communications and security. Which was good because their three missions were ferrying the Secretary of Defense, the Chairman of the Joint Chiefs of Staff, or the President. Every time the President left the country, there was an E-4B lurking at an airfield within a hundred miles. He'd only come aboard once that she'd ever heard of, which had been her very first flight—immediately after last year's shocking death of the Vice President.

That had been a flight made on full alert as they'd scrambled from Joint Base Lewis-McChord near Seattle to DC. As far as she could recall, she'd forgotten to even breathe anywhere between the two.

This flight was the complete opposite. The Chairman of the Joint Chiefs had flown to Japan putatively to discuss North Korea. Based on the other aircraft she'd identified flying in for the meeting, she'd wager Taiwan had been the unannounced hot topic.

Now, after a layover at JBER in Alaska, they weren't headed back to DC, but rather to Greenland for some security conference so far above her pay grade that she had no clue what it might be. The only thing she knew existed in Thule was the Space Force base, mostly dedicated to watching for a ballistic launch out of Russia.

Not bad for a girl from Gibson, Arkansas. If only Gamps and Gammie could see her now—not that she could tell them anything about her job.

I fly highly classified missions aboard an aircraft that requires

Top Secret clearance to even step aboard. Nope, couldn't be squawking so much as a newborn-chicken's peep beyond that.

Her and Tech Sergeant Doyle Cowell's side-by-side stations were the oddballs of the battle-staff cabin. Everyone else covered the events *out there*. In case of war, they managed the flow of all data and communications about the status of any battlespace on the globe. She and Doyle managed flight security—she tracked the Nightwatch's progress from satellites and guarded against any direct threats to the aircraft.

Doyle handled electronic threats. She tracked physical ones.

At the moment, they were the only two required in the cabin. A few others monitored their consoles but most were back in crew rest as it was 1800 hours in some time zone or other—suppertime.

Something caught her attention at the edge of the screen. There...then gone.

"What was that?"

"What was what?" Doyle's standard operating procedure of repeating any question had been seriously annoying until she realized it was only to buy time. His fingers attacked his keyboard with a sharp burr of sound.

She began doing the same. Shifting center point and zoom even as she scrolled back through the recorded data feed. At Flight Level 45, the Earth's horizon lay four hundred and sixteen kilometers away. What she'd spotted was closer to half that. A flash, no more.

Doyle's fingers slowed for a moment. "I had a fox-three, duration four seconds. Time mark 1805:23 to 27." That was a very short burst for an active homing radar, unless it had been fired dangerously close. *Or...*

"Terminal homing?" She knew she was right as soon as she said it. The radar had turned on for the terminal part of the flight only. Fired, but not using an active signal that might attract attention until it was too close to do anything about.

She set her time marker to 1805:27—twelve seconds in the past. She froze, zoomed, enhanced, zoomed again—and was staring at a massive container ship. Once it filled her screen, she let the image roll in real time.

There was a bright flash at 1805:28. That must be what had snagged her attention. She was halfway to raising a shoulder to nudge Doyle aside. He was leaning waaay too far into her personal space.

But at 1805:41, a massive pink-red explosion blotted out the screen.

Their fists collided as they both punched for the Attack Alert Button at the center of their shared console. She ignored the alarm and the sounds of the entire crew rushing in from both the forward galley and the aft crew area.

Their station phone rang. Doyle took it and began explaining the events to the one-star sitting as watch officer. General Mitchell's post lay ten meters forward at the head of the battle staff cabin.

When the fireball had cleared, the stern of the ship was largely missing. What remained, continued to burn violently in great gouts of odd-colored flame.

Tamisha grabbed a second phone and punched for a station two rows behind her. She had time for nine *C'mon C'mon C'mons* before someone picked up.

"Chem analysis."

"Check my feed and tell me what's burning that color." She slammed the receiver back into the cradle.

She split the screen, letting one section continue to roll forward in real time. On the other section of her screen, she reset the data recording to 1805:28 and began scrolling the image backward.

At 1805:27 a fuzzy object, only a few pixels wide at this distance but at least twenty long emerged from the stern and tracked backward. She followed it away from the stricken container ship to 1805:06.

"There," Doyle leaned in and stabbed at the screen leaving a clear fingerprint exactly where she was trying to look.

"Duh!" She batted his hand aside. The man ate way too many Snickers but she didn't have time to wipe her screen.

The missile, for that's what it had to be, had emerged from nowhere as if it had magically appeared—or been fired from a submarine! Though the distance and angle were against her, she continued tracking backward in time and location as if she could pace the missile underwater.

If there was a sub, at this distance she couldn't spot any trace of it.

33

Four-star General Drake Nason, Chairman of the Joint Chiefs of Staff, slammed the phone into its flight-secure cradle in midsentence.

Shit! He should have said something more to Lizzy before hanging up. They'd both heard the alarm, and now she'd be left to wonder if her husband was about to be shot out of the sky.

Maybe he was.

Or just had been.

As he didn't disintegrate into a fireball and could still breathe the cabin air, he cautiously decided that the latter hadn't happened. And he sure wasn't going to find the answer to the former sitting here in his cabin.

Yanking on his jacket out of habit, he buttoned it as he hurried aft—a habit from years of having to present command authority in every situation. Past the small conference room where Miranda's team had spread out to attack the plane crash investigation. He didn't know anything, so he didn't slow down, only saying, "Stay here!" as he continued through the empty briefing room.

"What have we got, Bill?" He pulled up short beside the watch officer's desk.

"Desk Eight. Area security. Picked up a sub-launched missile."

Drake moved to the closest open seat. If they were in for hard maneuvering, he'd be battered to a pulp for standing here like some jarhead—he was a former 75th Ranger and he knew what action meant. He sat and snapped in the full five-point harness.

Everyone else was doing the same as they hit their seats. Several were still rushing to their desks. At least he was ahead of them.

"Not at us," Brigadier General Bill Mitchell informed him. "At least not yet. Hit a Chinese container ship down below us."

"Can we see it?"

Bill tapped a knuckle on the screen at his desk as he continued holding the intercom phone to his ear.

Drake took a slow breath and looked down at the screen.

Bill leaned over. "Sharp operator. On her way to being our best. That's a sub-fired missile, which she picked up visually at two hundred klicks. Harpoon, IDAS, a Russian SS-N-19 Shipwreck, who can tell. Wait, what?" He was listening on the phone again.

Drake spotted the man on the other end of the line, about halfway down the cabin. But he appeared to be interpreting for whoever sat beside him, all Drake could see was the top of the woman's head as she bent down, studying her screen.

"She says the launch, acceleration curve, and that the

homing radar only lit up during the last four seconds of the terminal flight phase strongly indicates a UGM-84 Harpoon."

"One of ours?"

"We sell those to a lot of people, Drake."

"The question stands."

Bill picked up a second line and punched the button for Sub Ops before holding it to his other ear. "Who do we have in the area?" He asked it without preamble, then grunted at the reply. "No one, Drake. Nearest is fast-attack Virginia-class boat half a thousand kilometers south, unless we have a rogue boomer up here."

The ultimate nightmare. Missile sub captains were under orders to go out there into the deep dark—and get lost. The best way to hide a boomer was to make sure that no one, foreign or friendly, knew where they were. However, the likelihood of one going rogue and choosing to shoot a cargo ship crossing the Arctic Ocean was comfortably low.

"There she goes."

Drake looked at the screen again.

The ship was massive, one of those supersized container carriers. The resolution was fuzzy at first, a low angle with the equally low evening sun beyond it dazzling the ocean surface.

Then the view shifted, high-angle, off-center at first, but it resolved and recentered until it seemed that he could see the rust on the container boxes. The console operator had found a satellite feed and centered it on the ship.

The stern, burning disco-pink—by which Drake knew he was dating himself—slid beneath the waves. But it didn't extinguish the fire, which lit up the water for a long way around. Massive bubbles rose to the surface and burst, feeding the tornado of fire consuming the portion of the ship still above water.

"Lithium, according to our chemical warfare analyst," Bill explained. "Maybe a load of lithium batteries catching fire."

"Ignited by a Harpoon missile."

Bill grunted his possible agreement.

In such hi-def that Drake was convinced he could hear the roar of the flames and the shearing metal as the back of the ship broke. The stench of fire amid the salt of ocean seemed to fill the cabin as they watched it die.

There was a stone silence aboard the plane as the ship sank, still burning, below the ocean's surface.

Drake was the first to find his voice. "Call the Canadian Coast Guard and whoever the Danish have on this side of Greenland. Get them out here to search for survivors. Scramble the Canadian's CF-18 Hornets out of Thule Air Base and see if they have any SAR component to send."

He tried not to consider the futility. The Hornets could spot ships, but were less likely than the Nightwatch to see a submarine, and had no chance of finding survivors. And if they did have a search-and-rescue C-130 there, it was forty minutes away. A helo would be twice that. Nobody now in the water stood a chance.

Bill punched for comms and passed on the order.

"How far away is the nearest airborne sub-hunter?"

Bill kept working the comms, then swore.

"Nearest P-8 Poseidon has no crew due to food poisoning. We have a couple of Orions but they're seven hours out." He listened again. "The nearest P-8 with a crew is six hours."

"This guy is gonna be a pumpkin in two hours, never

mind six." Drake pictured the strategic battlefield. The sub only had three possible routes of escape. Due north under the ice pack. That required a nuclear boat. West, deeper into the Canadian archipelago. Or south toward the Atlantic.

"Get our sub on the move. I don't want them escaping to the south. In fact, have him punch north and bring the pressure."

"And if they pick them up?" Bill hesitated with a finger on the comm button.

Drake wanted to say to blow them to Hell as they deserved, but suppressed the thought. "Tail them all the way home. And yes, I know that could take weeks."

Bill passed along the order.

Onscreen, Drake could see that the onboard operator who'd spotted the attack was already scanning the waves with her satellite view. It had sub-ten-centimeter resolution, could see anything bigger than a hand despite being in orbit —she'd used the Nightwatch's command authority to directly take over a KH-11 Kennen bird. The problem was that it would only see a narrow area to search in any one pass. But it meant she was trying.

"When she's done, I want to see her in my cabin." He pushed to his feet and went to his cabin to call Lizzy and let her know he was safe. As he closed the door to his small suite, he saw that his jacket was misbuttoned. Next time he'd leave the damn thing behind.

34

"Staff Sergeant Tamisha Ward?"

"Yes sir." Wow! She'd managed to speak. That was more than she'd expected to do when General Mitchell had told her to report to the forward cabin.

Three civilian women had watched her closely as she passed by the conference room on her way forward. She hadn't seen them come aboard.

She'd stuck her nose into the senior leader compartment once when it was unoccupied for a training flight. It had been impressively big on a plane where every square inch was packed with gear.

Now, with the Chairman of the Joint Chiefs of Staff sitting in his chair it was positively claustrophobic. She'd never been this close to him before, and certainly never alone with him.

General Drake Nason was a tall man when he actually unbuckled his seatbelt and rose from his chair to return her salute. Spare, with no extra weight on him, unlike General Mitchell. Like Mitchell, Nason sported a short brush of salt-

and-pepper hair a few inches long on top and close-shaved up the sides. She wondered if that haircut was in the *Senior Leader's Handbook for General Officers* as issued by the DOD. Every general officer who wasn't bald or black seemed to sport the same cut. He looked like an older Tom Skerrit from the first *Top Gun* movie.

"Tell me what you saw."

Right! Focus, girl!

He waved her to the seat across his desk, which she eyed carefully to make sure it had no more than the standard seatbelt buckles. No visible straps for lie detectors or immobilization. They were like eighty-three ranks apart and nothing in her training had included how to sit across the table from the military's senior-most officer.

Somehow she managed to fumble her way into the chair and buckle in. "How much detail, sir?"

"From the beginning, absolutely everything you can remember."

She spotted no recorder as she began.

He listened attentively. Pausing her narrative only when she tried to gloss over something as being too trivial. Man didn't miss a trick.

"You hijacked one of my wife's surveillance birds." For some reason he seemed very pleased that she used the Nightwatch's absolute command authority to commandeer the KH-11 Kennen imaging satellite. Essentially a Hubble telescope aimed at the Earth instead of the stars.

Rumor said the Hubble *was* an unused Kennen chassis provided by the Air Force and reengineered. One rumor said that the real problem with the unfocused first mirror wasn't a manufacturing issue, but rather that the one they'd launched was designed with a primary focal length of the Earth's surface, not the universe's depths.

"Your wife?"

"Director of the NRO."

Tamisha tried to imagine she could feel smaller, but didn't know how. She'd grown up in the same house that Gammie and Papa had, practically under the flightpath for the Little Rock Air Force Base in Arkansas. Gamps had been a bulldozer driver during its construction. Papa worked there at the USAF Weapons School as a C-130 mechanic and Maw as public relations.

General Drake Nason, a highly decorated Army 75th Ranger and a card-carrying member of the stratospheric Washington, DC, elite had married another of the same. The contrast was unreal.

Tamisha glanced at the alarm in the port forward corner of the room but it wasn't blaring out a decompression warning.

She did her best to continue the briefing despite her lack of oxygen.

When she was done, he stared at the large monitor mounted flush on the hull above his desk. Reaching some decision, he tapped a handy phone and punched a number. Then he ignored it. They sat for two full minutes in silence, during which her heartbeat was convinced she was pushing the top of the aerobic training zone at a hundred and sixty per minute.

The big screen flashed on. "Talk to me, Drake. I'm late for a dinner."

Tamisha's jaw dropped. Physically dropped. She snapped it shut with such force that when she caught her tongue it brought tears to her eyes and the iron taste of hot blood to her mouth.

She'd never seen President Roy Cole's face except on TV. Of course, that's all this was, wasn't it? He was dressed in a tuxedo. In the background stood an elegant redhead in a black sheath dress that screamed sophistication: his new fiancée, Rose Ramson. It must be one hell of a dinner. A glance at the four clocks on the cabin wall took her a moment to parse.

The Nightwatch and DC agreed that it was 1700, in the same time zone for the moment though DC lay four thousand kilometers to the south. POTUS—President of the United States—read 2200. A late dinner at a G-20 conference in London. Right.

"Just a heads up at this point, sir. Unknown aggressor sub just sank a Chinese Neopanamax container ship off Lancaster Sound."

"Where the hell is that?"

"What?" General Nason slapped a hand to his chest in mock surprise. "Did the Green Beret fail sixth grade geography?"

"Go to hell, Ranger," the President snapped back.

"Between Baffin Island and Devon Island. West of central Greenland," Tamisha blurted out to stop whatever the hell was going on.

"North...east Passage?" The President frowned.

"Northwest is the one over Canada, sir. As in Northwest from England seeking the old trade routes to the Orient without having to sail around Africa." She really had to learn when to shut up. "The Northeast Passage is the one that goes over Russia from Europe to the Bering Sea."

He glanced her way, then returned his focus to General Nason.

She bit down on her tongue to keep her mouth shut, which sent electro-shock pain along her nerves after she'd already bitten it so hard.

General Nason hesitated but didn't glance her way. Remonstrance or teasing? Damned if she knew but she wouldn't be speaking again until the next millennia.

"She's right, Mr. President. With the increasing Arctic ice melt, the Canadian Coast Guard are very worried about oil spills and conflicts. The Russians, of course, are celebrating by building some of the largest and most expensive shipping ports along their northern coast—including the hundred-billion-dollar mega-port fiasco on the Taymar Peninsula. They've also reopened dozens of Soviet-era Arctic bases, there's a hardship posting for you, and are building new ones along the Arctic Silk Road."

"Thanks for the status update, Drake. Get to the point or I'll ship you back to your damn unit."

"Ah, the old Green Beret is feeling threatened by a 75th Ranger. Good instincts, sir."

The first time Tamisha hadn't known what to make of such an exchange. This time she did a crap job of suppressing her laughter. The mutual respect and friendship shone between these two men.

Both glanced at her, neither smiled...except with their eyes. They were enjoying some aspect of this. Weird to realize they were human.

"The point, Mr. President, is who would attack the Chinese, our largest trade partner, in the territorial waters of Canada, our second largest trade partner?"

"Well...shit."

By not looking at them, she could start thinking again. While they discussed geopolitical ramifications she couldn't follow half of, and how to tell the Chinese *what* they knew without telling them *how* the US knew, Tamisha wondered at the incident.

An unknown submarine shooting a Chinese cargo ship in Arctic waters. That was deeply bizarre. Piracy in the Malacca Strait or the Red Sea, sure. By submarine? In the Arctic?

There was a roll-out drawer under her side of the desk that revealed a keyboard and flip up screen. Her desk would be more familiar but she hadn't been dismissed.

A quick scan showed no reports of other recent sinkings in the Arctic. Of course, there wouldn't have been news on this one if the Nightwatch hadn't seen it directly. She jumped on MarineTraffic.com and quickly located the *Fortunate Progress*—and the abrupt cessation of her tracking line. How long until someone noticed that?

There were few enough ships in the Northwest Passage for her to visually determine there were no other unusual anomalies. She reviewed the tracks of the ships that were in these remote seas. In the last forty-eight hours, each had sailed two days farther along their routes.

Staring at the screen harder didn't make any ships appear or disappear.

So it was an isolated incident in the Arctic Ocean.

No! It was an isolated incident in the Northwest Passage.

Tamisha started scanning the North*east* Passage over Russia. The Alaskan end of Siberia had nothing much going on. East of the central Siberian Taymyr Peninsula, a line of coast-huggers cruised along, Russian freighters shuffling between the oil fields there and the western ports on the

White Sea. And a whole mess of fishing boats. There were probably more out there with their trackers turned off.

But...

She set a filter to hide the Russian signals. The clusters of fishing craft and coastal freighters disappeared from her screen. Three American *fishing* boats were plowing the waters along the edge of the ice well north of Russia—in international waters. And if anyone thought they were actually fishing, they needed a serious lesson in spying and early launch warning systems.

There were two Chinese container ships. One just clearing the Lena River Delta in the east. And one a few hundred kilometers past Russia's Severny Island. She hovered over each. The first was trucking along at twenty-two knots. The other was making...six?

She found a satellite image. No ice to slow them down.

"What other reason could a ship have to move at six knots?"

Doyle didn't answer. Right, he wasn't beside her. They'd both formed the habit of asking hypotheticals out loud to garner the other's assistance. Being female, she wasn't his type, though it wasn't clear whether or not he realized that. But he was plenty sharp in the two-heads-better-than-one department.

No reason to travel so slowly that she could think of.

Tamisha pulled up its track. The speed-change location was abrupt and obvious. Twenty-two knots to zero and drifting sideways for a few hours. Then slowly rebuilding to six knots, briefly to seven, then back down to six.

"Had a mechanical failure, did you? But what if it wasn't?"

Playing the same game that she'd used on the missile

that struck the *Fortunate Progress* here near Greenland, Tamisha tracked back along the *Lucky Progress*' route over Russia from the moment they'd slowed to a stop.

"What the fuck?" She wasn't ready for it when she found it.

She grabbed a phone and punched for Doyle's station.

"Tell me what happened twenty-three hours and three minutes ago at 77.954 North 60.440 East."

On cue, Doyle repeated her request verbatim, but his keyboard sounded loud in the background. "Sorry. I have no monitors active in that area. Nearest surveillance boat is over five hundred klicks out. Maybe Sub O—"

She cut him off by punching for the Sub Ops desk.

"I need ears," she read off the time and coordinates again.

"Any ears I have up there will be deep. I'll need to deploy the antenna and get back to you."

"Fast." Tamisha hung up again. She could picture the giant spool down in the rear of the Nightwatch's cargo hold. It would trail out an eight-kilometer-long copper antenna wire, held up by a small drogue chute at the far end. With that, they could transmit on the ultra-low frequency necessary to reach a submarine no matter where it cruised the world or how deep.

"Sergeant?"

"Busy. Go away."

"Sergeant!"

Tamisha froze and turned very slowly to face the Chairman of the Joint Chiefs of Staff.

35

Drake knew that he really shouldn't be enjoying this moment quite so much. He kept a straight face but the one Tamisha Ward wore definitely made him wish for a camera. Hard to believe that eyes could go that wide. And he'd wager she was blushing brightly under that dark skin.

Christ, the last time he'd been that young had been as a fresh-minted second lieutenant leading a squad of Rangers into a Bosnian hamlet. Part of a UN peacekeeping effort back in '92. It hadn't lasted, either his youth or the peace. Knowing his team was getting close, the Serbs had killed most of the males and systematically raped every Bosnjak female over the age of five or so before evacuating. That memory replaced his brief amusement with the sergeant with a flash of hot rage that he'd never quite shed in thirty more years of service. Only a tight-clenched fist kept his hand from shaking.

"Would you care to share what you've discovered?"

She nodded. Shook her head. Then nodded again.

He waved toward the room's main display where he'd

pulled up a duplicate image of her laptop's screen, relegating the President's feed to a corner.

"A, ah, an, er, uh…"

"When you're quite done working your way through the alphabet could you explain what you found?" Some of the amusement returned, enough to unclench his fist.

She blinked twice, then her spine attempted to give her whiplash as she bolted to sitting at full attention. "General. Mr. President. A second Chinese cargo ship suffered damage north of the Russian island of Severny twenty-three hours ago. Perhaps to its propellor. Severny is the long one that projects north from the Urals separating the European and Asian continents. It's covered with the largest glacier in all of Europe. And was also the main test site for Russia's nuclear bomb program, including history's largest-ever device, Tsar Bomba."

"Less geography lesson, more what you found, Sergeant."

"Yes sir. Sorry sir. The *Lucky Progress* was targeted by a spread of six air-to-surface missiles—with two possible impacts. By size and speed, it has characteristics of an AGM-114 Hellfire or similar."

"Shit, Drake, are we now firing on Chinese ships in two hemispheres?" The President's look wasn't the easily pleasant side he showed the American people. This was a highly peeved ex-Green Beret.

"Unknown, sir."

"No sir," Sergeant Ward spoke at the same moment he had.

Well, she might be nervous talking to power, but she also didn't hesitate to do so. Drake could get to like her. "Explain."

The sergeant turned back to keyboard and zoomed in,

centering something he hadn't noticed at the edge of the screen. "The shape is wrong."

"It looks like an MQ-9 Reaper to me." It was one of the US's primary UAV attack drones.

"The lines aren't quite right, sir. The antenna layout is also wrong."

Drake squinted at the image...and had no idea what the sergeant was talking about. The image sucked, caught by chance at the very edge of a satellite's view. "So, what is it?"

"CASC Rainbow. The CH-5, I think."

"CASC."

"Yes sir."

"As in the Chinese Aerospace Science and Technology Company?"

"Corporation. Yes sir."

"Well...shit." President Cole voice was dead calm.

"Leave it to a Green Beret to repeat himself," Drake replied automatically but neither of their hearts were in it and the President didn't return the joust.

"Can you follow it out of the area?"

"Doubtful, Mr. President," the sergeant spoke directly to the Commander in Chief for the first time. "I have a satellite coverage gap. Picking it up again later would be pure chance. I might be able to follow it *into* the area. I'll try, but it will take time."

"So we have a submarine of unknown origin, but possibly Chinese—"

"No sir. The AGM-114 Harpoon would never have been sold to the Chinese." And now she was correcting the President? Only proper decorum appeared to keep her from pounding her forehead on the keyboard.

"Good point. So a sub of unknown origin, but *not* from

the PRC," the general's brief smile said that he was absolutely teasing her, "blew up one Chinese container ship while half a world away a Chinese drone disabled another Chinese container ship."

"Yes sir."

General Nason turned fully to the President. "The really fun part is that the only thing south of the attack point is Russia for a thousand kilometers in any direction."

"So Russia could be attacking China with a Chinese drone?"

"We've seen stranger things, Mr. President."

"I'm not so sure about that, Drake. And I'm about to have a friendly dinner with the Chinese president at my table."

"Friendly?" Then Drake couldn't resist echoing the sergeant, "Doubtful, Mr. President."

36

The ringing of Clarissa's phone sliced through the restaurant's cloud of chatter.

She and Kurt had talked long into the morning atop Mont Royal. Much like the other tourists, done with the view of Montreal in the first fifteen seconds but reluctant to move on after all the effort to arrive, they had stood at the rail and quietly discussed business.

It had been a long time since she'd spent an entire afternoon talking with a single department head. And Kurt was an enjoyable man to spend it with, especially as the head of the Special Operations Group would never be eligible for her job. Thoughtful, smart as hell, and utterly lethal. He also wasn't at all bad to look at.

As hunger of a missed lunch set in, Kurt had led her down the back of the mountain and into a crowded district bustling with student and artist energy. Sculptures and murals adorned every open space and blank wall.

It was also a cuisine mecca. Mexican and Greek rubbed shoulders with noodle shops and patisseries. He'd led them into a Jewish deli that someone had airlifted out of the 1920s and dropped between a pizzeria and a fast-food Portuguese chicken shop.

Schwartz's had a sitting bar down one side and tiny tables crammed down the other. They spent a long time eating a pair of impressive smoked pastrami sandwiches and she was now helping Kurt with his side of French fries as she sipped her black cherry soda. He was a root beer man.

He'd slowly unwound enough throughout the day to reveal his own thoughts. They'd discussed the world, breaking down global trouble spots and planning who to insert in each one, at what level: surveillance, propaganda, action, or a little judicious thinning of the herd. Kurt, as head of the SOG, was one of the few people she worked with able to discuss the *ultimate solution* without qualms. He wasn't bloodthirsty, he simply considered assassination as another tool worth consideration.

All of which was safely lost in the heavy buzz of conversation arising from every table to hum off the glass of the thousand framed newspaper clippings and photos that papered one entire wall.

She pulled out her phone and read the caller ID.

Clarissa answered with, "Go to hell, Drake." Only after she spoke did she hope this wasn't a conference call with the President.

"Same to you twice, Clarissa." Apparently she was safe.

Simply because they'd formed a tentative working truce over the last months didn't mean she had to admit to it. He apparently felt the same way.

"We're sending you a set of images. Two Chinese container ships were attacked on opposite sides of the Arctic Ocean. We want your best image analysts to extract all relevant data. I'll be in and out, but you can coordinate through the provided contact information for Staff Sergeant Tamisha Ward."

Clarissa thought she heard a brief "*What?*" in the background, but it was hard to tell over the noise in the deli.

"Sergeant Ward will know how to find me."

"Duh! I have your phone number, Drake." She considered if he merited a need-to-know about Ernie Maxwell being sabotaged in the midst of sabotaging his own flight. No. A purely internal CIA affair; she'd keep it that way.

"Call her first anyway. She'll know if anything you find is important enough to bother me." His sharp tone had her ready to fire back with both barrels. The CIA and the Department of Defense were never close bedfellows. Yet he had involved her rather than his own image analysts. Or perhaps both.

"Done!" She hung up on him.

Clarissa let it ring three times before she answered.

"Go to hell yourself, Clarissa," he said before she could speak, then hung up. She'd swear that she could hear the laughter in his voice.

Kurt smiled as if he could guess exactly what happened. She liked that he understood all aspects of the joke without any need to explain, Clark certainly never had.

It was an easy smile to return.

37

Heidi's phone rang. The caller ID announced a world of incoming pain.

"Here we go," she warned Harry before answering.

"No worries. We're only half a day into a literally impossible task. At least she doesn't expect much."

"Better than the fifteen minutes she usually gives us." Heidi kicked the call to speakerphone half a ring before it decayed into voice mail. She jumped straight in. "No, we still haven't made any progress on Ernie Maxwell's mess. Nor will we this side of Armageddon. Thanks so much for asking."

"Oh, I forgot about that. Keep up the good work." She was some place noisy that the phone's built-in noise suppression did only a fair job of compensating. But the mellow tone and words had been clear enough.

Heidi blinked hard and looked across at Harry. He slapped his hand against his chest, collapsed in his chair, and let his tongue hang out—a heart attack's worth of shock.

"Say what?"

"Ernie is now second priority. By the way, we know he

had help, but we're fairly sure he was bucking for the D/CIA seat."

"Which you have no intent of vacating any time soon."

"No, I don't."

"Too bad," Heidi teased her as the supposedly dead Harry rolled his eyes at her. Okay, not her smartest play.

"Yeah, I'm sure you two would much rather be doing ten thousand hours of community service for that last hacker job you pulled before I headhunted you into the CIA."

"She has a point," Harry spoke softly.

"I thought you were dead." She whispered back, then returned her attention to Clarissa. "Okay, now that you've made your point, what do you have for us?"

"General Nason sent me files. Grab them—because I know you to have your fingers in all my accounts anyway—"

She left a distinct pause. Heidi didn't see any point in arguing. With a stone-cold bitch like Clarissa Reese for a boss, she and Harry had decided doing so was simply self-preservation.

"Get them to image analysis ASAP. Then look them over and let me know if you see anything obvious. Higher priority than Ernie—for the moment." And she was gone.

"Well," Harry sprang back to life and turned to his computer, "at least she isn't a micromanager."

"Big screen," was all Heidi said. The big display hung beside the door, visible only inside the office. Their own sets of triple monitors also faced away from the outside world.

Their office windows let them look out over the Triple-F, the Fun Factory Floor. At least on the good days. On the bad days, the first F changed for the worse, FUFF for short. It was populated by forty of the best hackers and geeks that they'd been able to hire, all fighting to keep the CIA and America safe—in that order.

Her cyber-security team filled the righthand side of the room, Harry's cyber-attack team filled the lefthand side—a layout based on the Ursula K. Le Guin title *The Left Hand of Darkness*. Their attack team, if fully unleashed, could dump an unstoppable Zero-day virus on any country's infrastructure. The CIA could return most countries to the Stone Age on an hour's notice. That was Harry's job. Hers was to make sure no one, foreign or domestic, could do the same to them.

"Whoever assembled the package knew their shit," Harry muttered. "Dead clean info. Not a coder, but damn good."

He began playing the footage simultaneously: satellites and an unlisted aircraft.

Heidi figured it out about the same time Harry swore.

"That's live feed from an E-4B Nightwatch and KH-11 Kennen class surveillance birds. Which means either the Chairman of the Joint Chiefs or the Secretary of Defense had direct eyes on this."

Heidi fooled around with her data feeds for a full minute before she found it.

"General Drake Nason, DC to Okinawa to JBER in Alaska. Busy boy. For a dude who rarely leaves DC, he's on the hustle this week. Planespotters.net picked him up bouncing through JBLM this morning and a place called Bellingham a hundred and seventy klicks to the north." Then she checked the photos and time stamp on their website and had to laugh. "On the ground under three minutes at the last stop to pick up some luggage but no personnel. Why the hell is an E-4B Nightwatch moving around with a set of Tumi luggage worth several grand, a Montblanc briefcase, and a pair of REI backpacks? Weird!"

All that truly mattered was that he'd been over the Canadian Arctic at the right moment to catch these images, which—she did a little projecting—meant he was headed to Thule Air Base.

They got the folder isolated and passed it on to image analysis with a crash-priority code. Two Chinese freighters, one crippled over Russia and the other sunk over Canada, didn't bode well for how this day was going to turn out. Except it was already six p.m.

"I'll order the pizza," Harry punched speed dial on his phone.

Then Heidi began poking around in Clarissa's files since she was already in there—with actual permission for once.

When she stumbled on Clarissa's travel partner, Kurt Grice, the head of the SOG, she called out, "Order an extra large."

With the Special Operations Group involved, it could get messy fast. The night was going to be even worse than she'd already guessed.

38

"You weren't supposed to *sink* the damned ship!"

"I didn't."

"Well one of your stupid-as-shit people did." And if he caught them, he'd chop off their damn head personally.

He tried to imagine how China would react. They were Number Three of the nine nuclear nations. Ten actually, because Japan could probably weaponize within weeks, perhaps hours if pushed. Truth be told, he'd rather China was mad at them than the Japanese. Stealthy and lethal when aroused, they made the Chinese appear as clumsy oafs —very heavily armed clumsy oafs, he reminded himself.

Of course the Russians had become trigger-happy nostalgia-heads who thought they were still a superpower. Only the US remained reliably benign due to its military bumbling, as if someone had tied their bootlaces together when they weren't looking and they *still* hadn't noticed. When they did, though, there was always hell to pay as they lashed out unpredictably in every direction.

"It wasn't me. It was our submarine captain."

"Oh, like that makes it so much better."

"If your man hadn't splattered his brains all over a bulkhead, our man wouldn't be in charge. He's trained as a liaison, not a sub captain."

Which was a valid point. He sighed. "What does that asshole say?"

"Nothing. He's gone silent. A single message, *Returning to port*. Nothing since."

"So, no clue for what could be weeks. We've got days, perhaps hours to leverage our advantage."

"No," his counterpart fired back. "We agreed we had months to make this happen."

"That's before you deep-sixed a hundred-and-sixty-million-dollar Chinese ship carrying ten thousand containers."

"And what have you done?"

He hated to agree with his counterpart, but there was no point in arguing with the facts. "Targeting that ship off Severny Island didn't work at all." The stupid ship had motored out of sight unharmed and unaware of being attacked despite his best efforts.

"Look again. There's a crippled Chinese container ship crawling along the northern coast of Russia. At the rate they're moving, they'll be lucky to clear the Arctic before the ice refreezes this winter."

"I was told—" that the attack was a failure. He snapped his fingers several times to get the attention of his assistant. He covered the phone's mouthpiece, "Double-check the status of that container ship near Severny Island. Now!"

The assistant, properly cowed, raced away to do his bidding.

"I heard that," the man on the other end of the line sounded deeply smug.

"Go to Hell!"

"Hey, that's your department."

"I shall go to heaven for my great works. It's your religion that damns you to hell for murder, even of infidels. Besides, we've kept to the plan. *We* didn't kill anyone—yet." He let the threat hang.

The assistant came hurrying back with a slip of paper. Scrawled quickly, it said, *Lucky Progress. 20k TEU. 6 knots.* His assistant in turn raced in with another slip. *Failure 77 minutes post-attack.*

It *had* worked. Perhaps he shouldn't have shot the chief project scientist, though he'd been angry enough to feed him to a pack of feral dogs at the time. The man's plan had worked. Now operations, with no help necessary from the dead scientist, could launch a follow-up with some confidence.

Still, he couldn't let his partner in business off the hook so easily.

"When can they reengage?"

The man on the other end of the call sputtered helplessly.

"It's not even my submarine. It's yours, we only provided the first officer."

"Precisely. And it's *your* officer, now the captain, who has gone silent. Well, his boat runs on diesel power and must come up for air sometime. Find him and turn him around." Then he thought better of it. "This is too important for you to handle. I'll see that it's done."

He slammed down the phone before the weakfish could respond. It was against all of the protocols his commander had ordered, but the situation had become too fluid. Besides, the commander had insisted on being completely hands-off on this operation. So be it.

He surveyed his small operations center. Everyone was in their seats, focused on the job.

Stopping by the flight operations desk, he told them he wanted the CASC Rainbow re-armed, fueled, and turned around in time for the next Chinese container ship's passage. It was well clear of the Lena Delta and would be crossing the same area as the strike on the *Lucky Progress* in thirty hours. It was going to be tight, but they should be able to do it.

Then he went to the far corner and stopped beside the lone agent seated there looking bored out of his skull.

"I need to talk to our man on the sub."

The operator didn't argue. No excuses about the sub going quiet or being submerged so that it couldn't hear the radio like that idiot.

Instead he simply asked, "How badly?"

He debated for a long moment. The sinking of the Chinese freighter had changed everything. The plan of having every Chinese cargo ship to enter those waters suffer critical damage to the propellor or drive system would have done what was necessary over time. They would have come to believe the passages were too hazardous to traverse. Or perhaps—because who understood the Chinese—they'd decide it was too unlucky.

But now, with news of the fatal attack that his insider had sent, even providing damning footage, a different scenario would be required. Now the Chinese must believe that there was a war against their big freighters using the high Arctic.

Perhaps it could be as a collusion between the Russians and the Americans?

No, too far-fetched with the disaster now raging between them in Eastern Europe. Yet another final battleground for the US and Russia: Korea, Southeast Asia, now Eastern Europe… Fine, as long as they stayed out of his way.

Could he pass it off as an internal Chinese war?

There must be enough battling factions, though their President had focused on keeping the military firmly in his pocket by making them his greatest priority. It couldn't last. The world's second largest economy was pinned up by so many fingers in the dike that someday soon it would collapse and the world would change yet again.

No, the problem was the present, not who to make appear culpable in the near future.

He needed action. Concrete, effective, *immediate* action.

He looked at the operator responsible for reaching their man on the inside, who was wise enough to be patient as he himself ruminated.

"Top priority. So critical that I'll be in my office until you reach him."

"Yes sir."

He thumped the man on the shoulder and returned to dispatch his normal duties while he waited.

39

"You want me to *what?*" Doyle couldn't have read the message right. He sat at his station at Desk 8 in the middle of the battle staff section that filled the middle third of the 747 and stared at his phone.

"What was that?" Tamisha popped her head up out of whatever world she was immersed in, not that she was telling him shit. Some deep hush-hush for the CJCS. She'd been a long time up forward with the Chairman of Joint Chiefs of Staff, old man Nason himself.

However, he'd worked with her enough to know, if he kept his mouth shut, she'd forget he'd ever spoken as she slid back into work. Sure enough, twenty seconds later he was again alone with his own thoughts and the stupid damn message on his private phone.

A year sitting beside her and he'd never registered on her radar. Tamisha was pure business and had no interest in sharing those awesome dark curves or those powerful shoulders with his narrow white ass. He'd been seriously put out at first, but no one who came sniffing got the least green light. With time he'd come to wonder if she was asexual—though how someone built like that could be, he couldn't imagine.

She returned to her console without a word. Plowing through the Urals, looking for something so fast that he couldn't see what it was and she wasn't bothering to explain.

Didn't want to date him? Fine. Whatever. But ignoring his existence? That was fucking annoying, no matter how useful he found it at the moment.

He wished they'd get to where they were going instead of circling over this empty stretch of nowhere. Not that Thule, Greenland, was any kind of a prize, but at least he'd be off this damn airplane.

Near the top of the planet, Thule was the ultimate hardship post, the farthest north US military base.

And what did they do there?

Climate stuff, sure. He cared about that as much as the next Millennial who'd been shafted by the Boomers and Gen Xers who'd sucked the planet's teat dry for their greedy little lives. But the rest of Thule's task, watching for over-the-pole missile attacks? What Stone Age did they come from? The next attacks were going to come in over the wire—cyber doomsday.

He'd started in cyber security, back when he'd been naive enough to believe doomsday could be stopped. Now he knew better. If it came down to it, an E-4B Nightwatch command post's sole purpose was to stay aloft at least long enough to ensure that if the US lost, no one else anywhere on the planet won.

It would take a Boomer or an Xer to go nuclear, no other generation was that stupid. A Millennial would crash the infrastructure and let nature take her course from there.

Three meals from anarchy. Full crash? Without power, water, and all that came with it, two weeks from cave culture, less in the cities.

The only answer was to have a serious bolt hole of one's own, the kind of bolt hole built for the one-percenters. He'd heard about the Arab oil prince who had a blood-type-compatible slave locked up on his personal 747, his family already paid off, just in case the sheik needed an emergency organ transplant in the onboard surgical suite.

And he sure wasn't going to get there on a tech sergeant's pay—fifty-k per year was slave wages, even with health and benefits.

So he'd agreed to keep an eye out for anything unusual in the Arctic. Not like national security was involved, just anything interesting. Tamisha might have found it, but that hadn't stopped him from reporting it.

His new bank account had jumped half-a-year's wages just for the report and imaging of the shooting of the cargo ship. He hadn't included the high-res Kennen images, because the extent of that capability fell under state secrets. He wasn't going to risk tangling with that, unlike that loser of a former President waving them around in front of the media. The direct capture from the Nightwatch's onboard cameras had proven plenty graphic for the guys bankrolling him.

But now they wanted him to boost out a message to a submarine? No way could he pull that off.

Or maybe he could?

Because General Nason had them still circling their asses out over Baffin Bay, rather than on the ground at Thule, the sub must still be somewhere below them. In fact, because there were no dedicated sub-hunters in the area yet, the

Nightwatch was on the hunt themselves. This bird had more capabilities for detection than anything else aloft, even if hunting subs with a 747 looked ridiculous.

Tamisha was still head down in the Urals. About half of the operations desks were empty. Once they'd assured themselves there was nothing going on anywhere in the world beyond the two ships and the usual wars, terrorist bombings, and single shooter events, everyone was released back onto relief rotation.

Fourteen would be sacked out in the back of the plane for the remainder of their eight-hour time slot in the bunk. Another fourteen finishing their interrupted dinners. And the rest of them either relaxing or back at their stations. The only ones critical at the moment were sub ops, the comm techs' station that was manned twenty-four-seven, and Tamisha.

He was, of course, fucking superfluous.

A point the phone message had made. He was in it now and there was no backing out unless he wanted to be reported for breaking his security clearance—which would lead to a whole world of hurt. He had to do what they asked, but...how?

Doyle realized that he didn't need to convince anyone to deploy the eight-kilometer-long ultra-low-frequency antenna to talk to the aggressor sub. He didn't know the details about that system and didn't care, but he knew that only four countries maintained the capability to converse with the deepest-sailing subs via ULF. They needed antennas that were miles long, China's latest was bigger than New York City, driven by obscene amounts of power.

And ULF was so damn slow, allowing only four eight-bit characters per minute. The most common message sent via

ULF was to order a particular sub to surface so that command could talk to it at a reasonable rate via satellite uplink.

Any country other than the big four: US, Russia, China, and India—and he hadn't asked for an ID from his new benefactor—wouldn't even have ULF equipment aboard. A standard VLF could punch through forty meters of ocean. If they were deeper than that, then, well, he'd have to tell his newest clients to go to hell.

Well, maybe not tell them *that,* but he could at least say he'd tried. Also, a very-low-frequency radio was standard gear on an E-4B Nightwatch, and he knew exactly who to ask.

Lately he'd been chatting up one of the comm techs. Suzy was a lowly airman first class, overwhelmed to be noticed by someone as grand as a tech sergeant with over ten years of service compared to her sixteen months. He'd found a way in by playing stupid and asking her about her job and her comm gear. They all had top secret or better clearance aboard the Nightwatch, so she was most forthcoming.

At least about the comm ops. She wasn't hot the way Tamisha was, but she was plenty cute with her tangle of curly red hair and tight little body despite being almost pancake flat. And he'd been careful to be nice and funny; she always smiled easily at his approach. But that's where it ended.

Anyway, he had bigger, more financially important concerns at the moment. He drifted back along the central aisle, passing the mostly unattended pairs of desks until he reached the comm shack that separated battle-staff operations from crew recreation...mostly meaning chairs that tilted back and the freedom to read or play a video game.

Jackpot!

Suzy was alone at her station.

And there was that smile that gave him an odd buzz.

"Hey Suzy. I was just sitting there, bored out of my skull, and reviewing all of the cool shit you taught me. I can't remember how the VLF transmitter works. Could you show me again?"

"Sure, Doyle." She patted the open seat next to her with no hint of anything else. Maybe she and Tamisha both preferred women. That was becoming far too common in his opinion, but there wasn't shit he could do about it. He'd remember it for a topic the next time there was an all-guys group at the bar: *If women keep wanting each other instead of us, I'm telling you that the whole species is gonna go extinct someday soon. Sooner than we'd like anyway.* Yeah, that should play well, get some laughs at least.

Meanwhile, he focused on Suzy's lesson in what he already knew.

He even *made up* a sample message to punch in. "It won't hurt anything if we broadcast it?"

She'd shrugged. "No. It's not one of our sub identifiers, so they'll ignore the message if they hear it."

Doyle tapped the send key before she could say the next line, *But I'm not authorized to initiate any communication myself outside of a state of emergency.*

"Hey!"

But he ran a friendly hand down her back, feeling the clear definition of shoulder blades and the lovely dip of the spinal column between, but not sliding his hand lower. He sure didn't want someone yelling about sexual harassment, way too likely in this day and age.

"I get it now. Thanks so much, Suzy, you're the best. Hey, Jack," he called out as the man headed to his desk, two in front of Doyle's normal position. "Got a question for you."

Or he would as soon as he made one up.

40

THE CAPTAIN OF THE TYPE 209 SUBMARINE GLARED AT THE VLF message his comm tech had just handed him. It was about the only paper aboard other than personal books. His boat's identifier and two four-letter code groups that translated to: *Report immediately.*

Sneaking away from the accidental sinking hadn't worked, not that he'd thought it would, but he could always hope. And it was his own damn fault for forgetting that the Harpoon missile had been in Tube Two. The tube-status display code directly below the launch button reinforcing that hadn't made him feel any better. He'd been so glad to be able to take action—after the long cruise to the Arctic and the long wait there. He just hadn't slowed down enough to double-check everything.

The last hour and forty-six minutes since he'd sunk the Chinese cargo ship—*damn but that thing went down fast*—had left his gut in knots worse than his ex-wife. It was hard to blame her...the sea had kept him from home far more than she'd expected.

He checked the clock, though he didn't need to, the grumbling in his stomach told him it was dinnertime.

By any normal standard, he should stay submerged until nightfall. Except he was still north of the Arctic Circle and the best he could hope for was a couple hours of lame twilight. The order didn't sound like they were willing to wait six hours to tell him what he already knew; he'd screwed up and destroyed his career. His wife wouldn't have liked that any better than his being at sea, so it was still a lose-lose scenario there.

"Sonar. Any contacts?" They were already a hundred kilometers south of the sinking, so if anyone was about, they shouldn't care about him.

"Some small craft," Sonar answered. "At least I think so. Very far away. Certainly nothing of any size."

He took them up to periscope depth and took a quick look around.

Nothing.

"Down periscope. Raise satellite antenna."

He pulled on a headset so that the crew wouldn't overhear while command chewed him out. Entering the phone number he'd been told to memorize, then never mention upon pain of death, he took a deep breath and started the call.

"Ah, good. You received the message."

"Yes sir."

"What happened?"

He wanted to blame others, but they sat close in the tight Command Center. The only open space that didn't require jostling to pass one another was around the periscope itself. It needed room so that he could spin it around for observations.

"I fired the wrong tube. I launched a Harpoon missile instead of a SeaHake torpedo." Perhaps his honesty would save his son's career, at least.

"Ah, I thought so." The voice on the other end didn't sound upset. "Pity."

And here comes the ax. The man's voice was so calm that it sent chills up his spine.

"This has forced us to change our plans. It will vastly accelerate the consequences. Return to Lancaster Sound. Let *no* Chinese freighter pass. Not in any condition."

The captain readjusted the headset, partly to buy a moment and partly to test that his ears were still working properly.

"Do I need to repeat myself?"

"No sir."

"Good. Report when you arrive and the area is clear for operations." And the connection went dead.

He slowly pulled off the headset and stared at it in his hands. He couldn't have heard correctly.

They were declaring war on China?

But that made no sense. China could erase their two little countries off the map and no one would even notice.

The Minister of Public Security himself had ordered him to take command of the boat and to absolutely follow the orders of the man at the other end of that phone number without question.

Other than appealing to the President himself, whose number he did *not* have, the captain could only do as he was told.

"Con, turn us about. Sonar, make sure we aren't detected."

He saw Sonar's confused look.

"Orders," he softened enough to explain. "We go back to where we just came from."

Sonar looked no happier than he himself probably did.

41

"Why are we circling?"

"Not related," Drake tried brushing Miranda's question aside.

"Are we in immediate danger?" Andi asked like she was requesting a cup of tea.

Her mother looked up in startled surprise, apparently not having considered the possibility.

Drake needed answers about the attack on the Embraer airplane in Quebec that should be the only thing in Miranda's head, but he knew there'd be no answers until he stopped their questions.

"No. It's an unrelated matter."

"How unrelated?" Miranda again.

Seeing he wasn't going to avoid the topic, he kept it as simple as he could. "An unidentified submarine fired a Harpoon missile at a Chinese container ship transiting the Northwest Passage. The alarm earlier was because one of our people spotted it and was unsure if it was a broader attack; it wasn't. We've called out search-and-rescue teams, but the closest aren't here yet. We're circling to offer surveillance and search for any survivors until their arrival." *And to hope we spot the goddamn submarine that fired the shot.*

Miranda used her free hand to raise her arm in its sling and rest it on the conference room table. She didn't look merely tired, she looked worse than a platoon of Rangers after a patrol gone wrong. Her skin was almost gray with the pain of the motion.

"You should rest, Miranda. You could use my—"

"Not while there's work to be done."

"You never said how you broke it, Miranda."

"Andi did it for me." It sounded like a compliment, as if Andi had bought her a new set of clothes.

Andi, on the other hand, hung her head until her jaw-length hair hid her face.

"But that is definitely irrelevant. I'm less certain about the attack on the Chinese container ship. Are there any other irrelevancies I should be aware of?"

Ching Hui twisted to look at her, then at him. "You must excuse her for—"

Andi looked up, ready once more to go on the attack against her mother.

Drake held up his hand to silence them both. "You'll learn, ma'am, that Miranda doesn't generally understand sarcasm. It takes a little getting used to."

"I'm sorry, Drake," Miranda looked down at her cast. "Was I being sarcastic or did I miss yours?"

Ching Hui's eyes went wider. Drake could remember similar confusion from his early experiences with Miranda.

"Neither Miranda. You said something that someone who didn't know you might misconstrue. We're fine."

"Okay. Would this be an appropriate time to repeat my question?"

Odd that Andi's mother knew so little of Miranda. To the best of his knowledge, the women had been an item for over a year.

"No, Miranda. Actually, yes. It is an appropriate time but no I don't need you to repeat it. There was a UAV attack on another Chinese container ship yesterday, en route from Beijing to Rotterdam via the Northeast Passage over Russia. Their propellor was damaged."

"Time and location?"

He had to call Bill for those details.

Miranda didn't move to write them down, though Andi did.

"If we normalize these events to Eastern Time," Miranda didn't look at any notes.

Instead she unbuckled her seatbelt, stood slowly, pampering her arm, and picked up a small pad of sticky notes before stepping over to the large world map on the port-side wall of the conference.

"The Embraer went down at 1139 hours EDT near Montreal." She tried to peel a note free, but the cast gave her trouble.

Andi hurried to her side, took the small pad, and pressed a sticky note over southern Quebec.

"The ship over Russia," Miranda continued as Andi placed a second note, "was attacked by UAV at precisely 1700 hours EDT, and the one witnessed by this aircraft was within minutes of twenty-four hours after that. Furthermore, there are typically less than a hundred plane crashes per year across all types. The number drops significantly if we only consider commercial aircraft and by a factor of thirty again if we consider only those with fatalities. Commercial shipping numbers are similar. For all three of these to occur within a twenty-four-hour period is not impossible but statistically highly suspicious. How convinced are we that these are unrelated events?"

Drake stared at the three notes. Geographically thousands of kilometers apart, but what was distance in this day and age? "You think they *are* related? I mean...I suspect the two ships are, but the passenger jet in Montreal that Taz and Jeremy are chasing?"

Miranda simply stared at his left shoulder. As he wasn't wearing his jacket, all she'd be seeing was his white shirt.

"Okay, how?"

"Now you're asking for conjecture."

"I am." How had the world come to be a place where such was even possible? The CIA sabotaging a plane? Chinese superships targeted in two hemispheres?

"I don't have enough facts to create a reasonable conjecture." The answer he should have expected. Everything was going to hell. It made him feel old and slow that he couldn't wrap his fingers around any of it.

Andi was still staring at the map. "What if—"

42

"Sir?" Tamisha Ward stood at the conference room threshold.

"Sergeant?" Drake struggled to shake off the morose thoughts that crowded around him. He'd been in West Point the year that the Berlin Wall came down. With the Cold War over, everyone hoped for a safer, more peaceful world. The Eastern Bloc broke away from Russia with the collapse of the USSR. Ukraine returned all of its Soviet-era nuclear weapons to Russia for decommissioning.

Second Lieutenant Drake Nason, that sadly naive kid, had graduated top of his class with the dream of being a guardian for a better future.

Six months later he'd been forward-deployed in Desert Storm, then Bosnia, then... And now someone was blowing up Chinese cargo ships in the Arctic.

Though some fingers pointed to Russia, it was easy enough to argue for a dozen other state actors. Forty-one countries had submarines. Private subs lay in the hands of narco runners, but how long until someone began building personal attack subs—if they weren't already. A career as long as his was supposed to leave behind a more peaceful world, not a more dangerous one.

"Sir?"

"Sorry," he rubbed his eyes and looked at Tamisha. She remained in the doorway, neither in nor out. "Come in. What have you found?"

She glanced at the other three occupants.

"It's okay. They're cleared to hear anything you have to say. Miranda, Andi, Ching Hui," he indicated them in turn. "This is Sergeant Tamisha Ward. She's the one who spotted the submarine attack and has been tracking the UAV that carried out the shooting in Russian territory."

Tamisha sat down at the table leaving a seat between herself and Andi and two from him up the other side. He shouldn't like that he was scarier than the three unknown-to-her women, but he did.

The tone of the engines changed.

"The SAR team has arrived," Tamisha explained. "We've stopped circling and are starting our descent into Thule, Greenland. The CF-18s swept the area thoroughly and have returned to base ahead of us."

"Right. The SAR flights not going to find anyone, are they?"

Tamisha shook her head. Not a chance in the Arctic waters with the ship sinking so rapidly.

"Okay. What else have you learned?" She looked as happy to leave that subject behind as he was.

"The CASC Rainbow UAV was on station over the Arctic for eleven hours before it fired on the container ship. I lost it several times due to coverage gaps, but as it kept patrolling the same area, I was able to recover its track each time."

Back in their seats, and after Andi had buckled Miranda's seatbelt for her, they both leaned forward to listen attentively.

"Make your head hurt following it backward in time?" Andi ventured.

"Took some getting used to," she risked a smile. Tapping the computer awake, she put a global map on the conference room's big monitor. Then added a line composed of uneven dashes. "These are the confirmed tracks of the UAV during its passage to the Arctic."

The line blotted out a section of the Arctic in overlapping circles, but then it trailed south, carving a line south through the Urals.

"Tracking it against that rugged background would be difficult," Andi observed.

"It was, ma'am."

"I'm not a ma'am. I'm an Andi."

"Yes ma'am."

"It's okay to chill a bit, Sergeant," Drake told her.

Her level gaze called him an idiot.

What was he trying to do? He'd never have relaxed around a four-star general before he'd reached three himself. *Give it up, Drake. You're just some old fart with a lot of stars. Let the girl be.*

She waited with that perfect patience a soldier learned to show to a superior officer no matter what they thought of that officer.

He looked at the trail again. "But it ends in northern Kazakhstan. Is that it's origin?"

43

TAMISHA TOOK ONE LAST LOOK AROUND THE TABLE. GENERAL Nason had given no hint as to the identity of the three women beyond their names. Civilians were so rare aboard an E-4B Nightwatch that no guess was going to be accurate. Well, it was the general's ass, not hers, if they weren't cleared for what she had learned.

"Northern Kazakhstan is when I lost daylight. Or rather, because I was tracking backward in time, when I reached dawn and the sun hadn't risen yet. The UAV had no lights that were visible from orbit, maybe none at all—flying dark."

The general glared at the line. "Conjectures?"

"Me?" Tamisha swallowed hard and wished she'd stopped long enough to eat something, like a piece of dry toast to still the churning in her stomach. "I'm just a staff sergeant, sir. I can track it but—"

"You've spent more time studying this than I have over the last two hours. I want your opinion." He folded his hands on the table and stared straight at her. "How else will you learn to think? The first levels of Army training were about how to *not* think. Following orders, predictable behavior under a wide range of conditions, ingrained responses to a variety of crisis situations. Such training was about survival, not thinking. You now need to relearn that skill—"

"Which, let me tell you, is a major pain in the ass," the younger Chinese woman offered a half laugh. Military? Too casual around the general. Ex-military.

The general nodded but continued as if she hadn't spoken. "—hopefully in a more structured, efficient way. So, yes, I want to hear your own personal conclusions."

She looked from him to the screen and back. Took several deep breaths as if preparing for a deep-sea dive. What the hell. She'd lay it out and see how it all went down.

"Not Russia. They have no reason to fly a UAV so far over their own landscape. They may—or may not—have granted permission for the overflight. The Rainbow is no stealthier than our own MQ-9 Reaper but it doesn't particularly stand out either. Bring it in low over the border and slalom along the Urals, a common military flight training corridor, maybe no one questioned it."

"I'll have to remember that for future reference." He smiled. Her mouth threatened to do the same but she suppressed it in time. "Where beyond Russia?"

Tamisha drew an arc across the southern edge of the map. "It probably has the fuel capacity to have originated from and be returning to any of these countries."

"There are days I hate technology."

"Sir?"

"We have a remote-controlled armed UAV with enough range that it could have come from any of a dozen hellholes: from Pakistan in the east to Libya in the west."

"Yes sir. However, I note the final curve, sorry, first curve of the flight path I was able to observe." She zoomed in on the last link of the line before it disappeared into the darkness over Kazakhstan. "There *was* a definite course correction in the first hundred kilometers."

The general was damn hard to read. He appeared to get the implications, but was waiting for her to say it. Fine.

"What if the UAV had stayed with the Urals as long as they lasted to avoid drawing Russian attention, then turned for its actual destination, or at least the next most likely safe route? If it flew straight before my final observation, it would have crossed over Armenia and Azerbaijan, then slipped along the Turkish-Iranian border rather than originating from either one."

"Why do you think it didn't originate in them?"

Or maybe she *was* ahead of him on this one.

"No," the woman in the arm cast stated it flatly. Melanie? Monica? Something like that.

"Why not?" The general turned to her with as much attention as he'd shown to her.

"As Sergeant Ward pointed out, it was headed for the border between two of the only nations in the area capable of shooting it down. Overflying the countries that it did, before Russia, were low-risk choices. The high-risk factor, based upon the time marks of Sergeant Ward's observations and the fuel capacity / range of a CASC CH-5 Rainbow, was fuel usage. They would have adhered to the most direct route whenever possible. Therefore, by choosing to pass along the Turkish-Iranian border, they were following the only viable route efficiency permitted."

Tamisha nodded. She agreed, though she'd never have said it so neatly.

"South of that," Andi nodded, speaking to arm-cast lady,

(Melody?) "Syria is basically a Russian puppet state and if Lebanon had something like this, they'd use it on Israel and vice versa."

Marianne? shrugged, "I never understand such things."

The older Chinese woman's startled glance toward the woman must match her own. To explain so much so clearly and then not understand Lebanese-Israeli politics made no sense.

"Don't the Saudis and the UAE have Chinese drones?" Drake asked Andi as if that wasn't an odd statement at all.

"Yes sir. Primarily the Chinese CH-4."

Tamisha should have looked for that, yet this Andi knew off the top of her head.

"That makes as much political sense as…" His eyes traveled west. "You sure it wasn't Turkey?"

Andi shook her head. "If Miranda is guessing right—" (Miranda!)

"It wasn't a guess; it was a straight-line logical conjecture."

Andi smiled, "If Miranda's straight-line logical conjecture—which is a fancy way to say you guess," Andi bumped her shoulder against Miranda's "—based on Sergeant Ward's information is valid, they weren't coming from a base like Incirlik, but were rather dodging the edge of Turkish airspace. They turned awfully late if they were slipping out of Greece or Eastern Europe."

"Egypt or Libya, Captain Wu?" The general asked.

Andi shrugged. Captain? Tamisha was definitely in officer country.

Miranda shook her head. "Libya is outside the known range for a CH-5 UAV."

"But..." Sergeant Ward pulled up a large spreadsheet of calculations that she'd made of every stage of the flight.

After a single glance, Miranda shook her head before Tamisha even had a chance to scroll to the final range estimation. "The ground speed you measured along the north-south passage over the Urals is seven percentage points below the CH-5's nominal speed."

"Yes, I know that. I—"

"It wasn't flying forward slowly."

Tamisha pointed at the number right there on her screen.

"It was flying crabwise," Miranda explained, "to counteract the jet stream blowing it strongly from west to east. The aircraft was not flying at ninety-three percent power. It would be at full cruise speed and therefore using full fuel."

She was right. How had the woman shot down all of her work so fast?

Worse, Tamisha had just presented, and even tried to defend, an inaccurate range calculation to the Chairman of the Joint Chiefs.

"I'm so sorry, sir. I should have seen that. I don't know—"

He patted his hands downward telling her to mellow.

She put her hands to her cheeks to stop the heat flooding there.

"Sergeant, no matter how good you are, when it comes to flight logistics and aircraft capabilities, no one is as good as Miranda."

It was hard to believe. She'd looked directly at no one since Tamisha had entered. She spent most of the time staring down at her cast. Yet at a single glance, she'd detected an error in a very cluttered spreadsheet that Tamisha had spent no time organizing or labeling.

"So, what is the real range of possible origins?"

Even as she turned to start adjusting her numbers, Miranda spoke up.

"Based on Sergeant Ward's observations, there are four possible countries. Kuwait, Saudi Arabia, Egypt, and Libya. In the last, only the airfield at Tobruk in the northeast corner of the country is viable, and that's marginal at best. An unlikely choice."

Tamisha didn't know whether to look at the woman or her own numbers. There was no way that—

The general was smiling. "I warned you, Sergeant."

He had. Sure, some things needed to be seen to be believed, but she wasn't just yet discarding magic, fairies, or that Miranda had neuro-embedded supercomputers.

"General Nason," the older Chinese woman spoke for the first time.

"Drake, please, Ching Hui."

"Drake," she offered a pleasant nod that Tamisha couldn't have duplicated with a week's practice in the mirror. "There is one other possibility."

"No," Andi spoke sharply. "Weren't you listening to Miranda, Mother? If she said those are the only places it could reach, then that's it."

Tamisha winced in sympathy. She could get around Maw most times, but she'd tried to take on Gammie only once, and she could still feel the metaphorical scorch marks on her hide.

"Either one of those four sent it, Drake, or..." she didn't condescend to acknowledge her daughter. Instead she arched one perfectly plucked eyebrow.

The general sighed.

Then Tamisha finally got it. "Or someone wants us to think they did."

"Sergeant," the general said it harshly enough to make her snap to sitting attention. "Don't stop thinking, Sergeant. You're good at it."

She bit her lower lip. "Yes sir."

44

The comm's buzz jolted through Tamisha. *Don't stop thinking. Thinking wasn't the problem, keeping her mouth shut was.*

"General Nason here."

"Call for you, sir."

Tamisha started to get up even though she could feel the vibration of the flaps extending and the triple thunk of the landing gear locking into place. She shouldn't move during landing—and none of the three curious women were moving.

General Nason waved her to stay put as the screen lit up —with the President again. He looked as immaculate as he had two hours earlier when headed to dinner, except he looked exhausted.

"Oh. Hello, Miranda."

"Hi, Roy."

Tamisha's gasp was ignored.

"Hello, Andi." His eyes shifted on the screen to not quite

the right place to be looking at the older Chinese woman.

"And you'd be Andi's mother, I presume."

Andi groaned—softly.

"Ching Hui Wu, Mr. President."

"Interesting team, Drake. I see Sergeant Ward is back as well," he glanced aside in what Tamisha assumed was her direction but like all video conferencing, the camera perched above the screen never quite lined up properly. "You find a new one?"

"Might have," General Asshole Nason agreed happily. "She's got real potential. Gotta fix the staff sergeant thing."

"So do it."

General Nason turned to her. "Congratulations on your field promotion, *Technical* Sergeant Ward."

Tamisha opened her mouth, then closed it. She supposed if anyone could issue her a rank bump without going through a whole lot of hoops and evals it was these two.

But...*why?*

Was there some hidden agenda? Did they do it to keep her mouth shut about something? Were they pulling something like that drill sergeant she'd had to report for where his hands always landed during hand-to-hand-combat training? Who the hell would she report the Chairman of the Joint Chiefs to for—

She was careful to let nothing show on her face, but couldn't think her way out of this one.

"Sergeant."

"Yes, Mr. President." Now the hammer to come with the carrot of a rank bump.

"I can almost *hear* your thoughts behind that shield you just put up. Drake and I may be old and you may be an attractive young woman, but that has *nothing* to do with the present situation. Drake has an eye for talent and likes to help those people out, it's one of the main reasons I asked him to be my Chairman of the Joint Chiefs. That's the beginning and the end of it."

"And the price I've paid for it has been pure hell, trust me," the general offered her a smile and wink. "The only good thing to come out of the whole working for a mere Green Beret scenario? I met my second wife at a meeting. Now that woman is a standard for you to shoot for."

He'd said she was head of the NRO? That *had* to be someone amazing.

He turned back to the President, "How was dinner?"

Tamisha looked around the table. Miranda and Ching Hui were paying attention to the conversation, but Andi—retired Captain Wu—gave her a cheeky grin. That was actually the most reassuring sign of all. She looked to be way closer to her own generation and definitely knew the general and the President. If she said it was all cool, maybe Tamisha would believe her.

The President offered a long, heart-felt sigh. "If the Chinese President had heard a word, he gave no hint. That's when I decided that we needed another channel to slip it in."

Innuendo? Or an old fart missing the double entendre no matter how aware he claimed to be? A glance at Captain Wu earned her the slightest head shake. Not intentional.

"Sergeant Ward, if you could run the President through the short version of what you've found?"

She put the map back on the screen and spent several minutes briefing the President on what she'd learned over the last two hours, giving credit to Miranda and the general's comments as she went.

"Nice work. Seriously next level for the time you had. Drake, keep an eye on this one." Then, with no hint of anything inappropriate, the Commander in Chief turned to her. "Sergeant Ward, think seriously about OCS."

Officer Candidate School? The CINC was saying she was officer material? Couldn't get there without a serious command recommendation—which she supposed didn't get any better than the President and the Chairman of the Joint Chiefs. She'd never considered such a thing but, picturing the look on Gamps face at such news, she could only nod.

"Moving on, Drake. We need to get news of these attacks to the Chinese through a non-official channel."

"Direct?"

Tamisha didn't know what the general meant but the President had to chew on that one for a bit.

"No. I don't want you in the loop either."

"Yes sir, Mr. President. Hold on a moment." He turned to her. "Can you conference someone in, audio only, directly from here?"

"No..." Andi spoke up. "Can you link Miranda's phone and echo it to the speakers? We want the caller ID to be correct or he won't answer."

At the general's nod, Tamisha set up the link, wondering who the hell they were calling.

At her nod, the general turned to Miranda. "Are you up for this?"

Her nod was far less enthusiastic.

"As soon as you're done, you and Andi can take over my cabin and sleep as long as you need to."

Tamisha still had no idea who the odd woman was, but if

the Chairman was giving up his suite to them and the President trusted her, Tamisha figured she'd better be paying attention too.

Andi took Miranda's phone and selected an entry. Tamisha could see the country code—and her breath caught hard in her throat.

"Sergeant Ward," General Nason leaned in with no hint of amusement. "This is absolute highest security. Any mention of this phone call or the person called will be treated as treason. You may leave the room if you wish with no mark against you."

Tamisha shook her head. No way. Not with the President and the Chairman of the Joint Chiefs watching her. Then she flipped it in her head. She was being *allowed* to stay. She could get to seriously like being one of the general's chosen ones.

He then looked at the others. "No one is to speak except Miranda."

Then he began giving Miranda a precise set of instructions.

45

GENERAL LIÚ ZUOCHENG HAD LEARNED YOUNG TO BE A LIGHT sleeper. It had proved useful when he'd become provider at age ten for his mother and sister, working as a trapper after an Asian black bear killed his father.

It had served him well in the Sino-Viet War and in his long climb since, including three assassination attempts. Now, as the Senior Vice Chairman of the Central Military Commission, his every waking minute, as well as his sleeping ones, were well guarded—being the second most powerful man in China had its advantages.

Yet his habit as a light sleeper still paid dividends. When his personal cell phone rang softly, he was able to pick it up and head to his private office without disturbing his wife. The Mid-Autumn Festival had been a good day yesterday. Most of the family had come to visit.

He'd done his best not to show favorites, at least not until most had headed off to bed, some staggering. After that, there was no one to begrudge him time with his granddaughter Mui and her lovely wife Mei-Li. The three of them had stayed up late under the full harvest moon, talking of the girls' lives in the US and their interesting insights into global politics. When he had tried to correct one of their odd views, they'd pushed back.

You are not young, revered Grandfather, Mui had insisted with perfect decorum and perfect politeness. Mei-Li, as elegant as his daughter when she chose to be, instead had to struggle to suppress a laugh—before, much to his chagrin, nodding her agreement.

He was not young, but to have two such lovely young women remind him of the fact was not comfortable. The comment did cause him to listen more carefully. How soon their generation would control the economy with their buying power, then the businesses with their skills, and finally the nations. And unlike women in his generation, or the one that separated him from Mui and Mei-Li, they didn't hesitate to assume their own roles at heights no other generation had offered Chinese women since the time of Wu Zetian, China's sole empress, thirteen hundred years ago.

He checked the time, 0700. Only their long night, and more cassia wine than he'd drunk in years, had him sleeping so late. The two girls had made him feel old while listening to them, but young to watch. He'd forgotten what enthusiasm for the future felt like. A good lesson to recall.

Clear of the bedroom, he read *MC* on the caller ID. It was unusual enough that it took him a moment to recall the small quiet woman who knew more about airplanes and satellites than most of his top specialists—put together.

"Hello, Ms. Chase. To what do I owe the pleasure of this call?"

"I've been asked to communicate the following to you, *It wasn't us.*"

Any youthful zest that had rubbed off on him last night became a cold chill that had nothing to do with his bare feet on the marble floor. "I'm unsure of what you are referring to." There was a loud roar in the background that wasn't quite a flamethrower but a sound he should recognize. Then he did, a jet landing—

Miranda cried out.

"Are you okay?"

There was a clunk that hurt his ear as she dropped the phone on a hard surface.

He was left to listen to the heavy roar of engine reversers for several long moments, then someone picked up the phone.

"I'm sorry, General. Please hold." He recognized that voice as well.

He'd met Miranda Chase's companion, Wu Andi in Brunei last year. Despite her size, she had proven to be viciously capable against a much larger foe; a skill he'd been in the correct seat to admire rather than suffer.

After that meeting, he had requested a file on what was known about the whole team, but especially the two women. Ms. Chase's past was an open book and very impressive. One merely had to peruse the public NTSB database to determine that. Her deep knowledge of military aircraft was less visible, but still unassailable.

Captain Wu's past included a seven-year service gap during which she'd climbed from US Army First Lieutenant to a highly decorated Captain—destined for a great career, abruptly terminated. And no sign of where she'd been in those years prior to joining Miranda Chase's team.

The most interesting factor he was able to assemble only by conjecture and innuendo. Somehow, Miranda's team had been involved in his granddaughter Mui and Mei-Li's landing safely in the United States and receiving a most unlikely prize: immediate dual citizenship. He suspected that it would serve his future well to see what light they could shed about Miranda's team before they left.

During all of the movement, only one sentence could be heard clearly, in Mandarin, "Mother, stop fussing. I'll take care of her."

Wu Andi's voice finally said, "There."

Miranda's voice cracked as she spoke. "It hurts to hold the phone."

"If you'd take a painkiller, it would…" Andi's voice petered away and there was a brief noise as the phone was handed off once again.

Zuocheng circled to his desk. He'd been born a trapper's son in a high-country cabin. His desk was as simple and functional as a schoolteacher's. The marble entryway was because it was the most revealing surface for approaching footsteps. Even in his own home, he didn't want anyone sneaking up on him unawares.

He took out a pen and paper. Such things could be destroyed much more effectively than history on a computer.

"Hello, General. Andi Wu here. I'm sorry for the interruption."

"Is Ms. Chase okay?"

"She broke…her arm was broken this morning," her tone became grim. "The landing smacked it against the table hard enough to hurt despite the cast."

"Please tell her to be careful and heal soon."

"I do, General. Trust me, I do." Andi's tone almost made

him laugh. It was much like Mui correcting yet another *old-point-of-view* assumption he'd made last night.

"Here, Miranda."

"Hold the phone for me."

The two women were as suited to each other as the youngsters he had spent last night with. He could so easily picture them leaning together, seated on some plane, perhaps surrounded by Andi's mother and other passengers. Except there was no background noise of other passengers. Did Miranda have a private jet?

"You will become aware of two events," Miranda turned to business without preamble, exactly as he'd learned to expect of her. "You have lost a container ship to a sub-launched Harpoon AGM-114 missile at the east exit of Lancaster Sound."

"I *what*? No, I heard you. Where is Lancaster Sound?"

"North of Canada at," and she read off a series of coordinates.

He wrote them down as quickly as he could as she didn't pause.

"Approximately one day prior to that, you've had another ship partially crippled by a domestically-manufactured, that's Chinese domestic, UAV, tentatively identified as a CASC CH-5 Rainbow."

A different woman's voice whispered in the background.

"My apologies, *positively* identified as a CASC CH-5 Rainbow. It launched a spread of missiles with the flight characteristics of your AR-1 air-to-surface anti-tank missiles. At this time, we're assuming that they damaged the propellor or the engines. The ship remains underway at one-quarter speed presently at," she read off another set of coordinates that he barely managed to scrawl down in time.

"The UAV is now en route to somewhere in the Middle East, Arabia, or Northern African."

She paused, but not long enough for him to catch his breath. This was a horrifying series of developments. Chinese military hardware being used to attack a key link in the Chinese economic supply-and-delivery chain was unthinkable.

"We've had no contact with either ship. I was told to say that, which strikes me as counterintuitive as the first ship I mentioned—though the second one struck, it was the first one we noticed—had no survivors past the first few seconds. Therefore, there was insufficient time for us to have contacted them. The second ship, which was the first one struck, we've also had no contact with."

And she stopped talking.

Liú Zuocheng wanted to blame being woken from a dead slumber on his inability to fully unravel that. He couldn't, as he'd once been clear enough to drop an attacking brown bear within mere seconds of waking. Perhaps he *was* getting old. Or perhaps Miranda Chase's mind worked in stranger ways than he'd already thought.

But the meaning was clear—they'd spoken to no one before him.

"You've…been asked to communicate this to me by someone else?"

"Yes." Suddenly she was brief when he'd rather she remained verbose.

"Someone who would know about this but doesn't want to be in the loop."

"Hmmm… I would say that sounds like a reasonable hypothesis though I'm never clear on another's motivations. Any more than I am on my own, as recent events illustrated."

She didn't explain that comment as she continued. "I hope this helps. I don't know how that particular phrase would assist, but I was taught that was a polite thing to say after relaying information. If you'd like, I can call back if we learn anything more about the flight of the UAV or either attack. It is being reviewed by our imaging specialists."

He'd bet it was. A double attack like that, even if the US military truly had no involvement, would be ringing alarm bells at the highest levels.

Think, Zuocheng. Think fast. She'd said—

"You have images. Can you forward them to me?" The American's Earth imaging was far superior to their own. It might be a breach of national security to ask for help, but he suspected he might need it.

"Can I? Yes, if you provide me with a secure e-mail or online storage account."

He did so.

"May I? I don't know. I'll have to ask."

Miranda Chase obviously ended conversations abruptly when she considered that they were done.

"Yes, please ask. Take care of your arm." And then he remembered exactly who else had been at their sole meeting in Brunei and smiled. "And say hello to Drake Nason for me." Was he there? It would tell him a great deal of the American's view of these matters if he was.

"He says hello, Drake." And in that moment she was gone, which was good as it saved him choking on a laugh.

Two ships attacked. That sobered him fast enough.

That the Americans knew of.

Again the cold chill had returned.

Oh-seven-hundred in Beijing.

General Liú Zuocheng had to figure out what was going

on, using only Chinese assets at first to protect his source. The source, if she came through, would put him ahead of his analysts as well as the other members of the Central Military Commission, always a wise tactic. Then he'd set about waking everyone up on this holiday morning.

46

While Drake, the President, and Tamisha debated the resolution of images and information that could be provided to the Chinese general, Andi took advantage of their brief inattention.

The plane had taxied to a halt and the engines were cycling down.

"C'mon, Miranda." She eased her out of her chair.

Mother took her other side. Between them, they gently guided her out of the room and forward to Drake's cabin.

There were two doors in the forward bulkhead. The one on the left had four narrow bunk beds tucked in between the central divider and the tapering of the 747's nose. The right-hand door led to a small suite with a twin-sized single bed, a dresser, and a sink.

Between them, they seated Miranda on the edge of the bed.

The moment she pulled out the bottle of painkillers, Miranda clamped her mouth shut and shook her head.

"Miranda, you need these. They're just prescription-strength Tylenols."

"Nuh-uh!" Miranda objected as she tried to raise her hand to cover her closed mouth. Because she'd raised her right arm—the one in the cast—she gasped at the pain.

"Miranda!" How was she supposed to—

Mother rested her hand on Andi's arm. Her interference was the last thing Andi needed at the moment.

"Miranda," Mother said in a perfectly calm voice. "You will be a good girl and take two of these pills. Excessive pain can delay healing. If you do not do so, Andrea will force two of the Vicodin she has in the other bottle in her pocket down your throat while I hold your nose like an unruly puppy dog."

Miranda eyed her carefully. Andi had never argued with Mother in this mood as a child and she wasn't going to start now. Miranda apparently reached the same conclusion.

Andi drew a glass of water at the sink and held the glass for her as Miranda washed down the Tylenols. It only took a moment to get her lying down. Mother slipped a pillow between her stomach and the cast.

Miranda was asleep faster than Andi could finish brushing the hair out of her face.

"Thank you, Mother."

She smiled. "Was that so hard to say, Andrea?"

Andi sighed. Her mother had never acknowledged Andi changing her name at twenty-two. And yes, it was.

"You make a beautiful couple, Andrea."

She could *not* have heard that right. It had been too long a day. Too emotional. "What, no gibe or dig about Miranda being five years older or autistic or..." female?

"You make a beautiful couple, Andrea," Mother repeated.

"Nothing about grandchildren?"

And, impossibly, Ching Hui Wu of Wu and Wu Law smiled. "I would not be averse to one of you having children."

It was too much and Andi sat clumsily on the bed, though careful not to sit on Miranda's other arm.

Her mother sat on the only seat, between the dresser and the sink. Did she realize that beneath its padded cover was the toilet? Then she realized it didn't matter, Mother could look regal squatting in a Third World outhouse.

"We actually talked about that."

Mother's expression went to curiosity rather than the expected anticipation.

"What did she think of it?"

Was Mother simply being coy about not asking for her own feelings first? Did she not care about how Andi felt? Or perhaps she'd asked the most important question first. "Miranda is reluctant to carry the child because of how she might pass on her autism. She thinks I should carry it. *If* we have one!" She said the last quickly.

"Which doesn't quite answer the question, does it?"

Andi could have attacked had her tone been one of judgment; instead it was of sympathy and Andi could only shake her head. "Miranda knows so little of her own feelings. And lately, it's as if she's become afraid of them. She keeps giving them to me to figure out."

"Oh, my dear Andrea," Mother rested a hand on her knee. "It's because she loves you so much that she can trust you like that. Even if she doesn't know how to say so."

Andi looked up at her. "I think she'd be an amazing mother."

"So would you, Andrea." As usual, her mother's voice

brooked no denial. And for once, she found no motivation to fight back against it.

47

Ernie Maxwell was so tired but the drugs, and the beeping equipment wired to him, and the destruction of all his plans kept him from the escape of sleep.

"It happens with some metabolisms," he heard the nurse say just outside his curtain.

There'd been a shift change since this morning and he rather liked this one's sweetly French-accented English. Cute. Married, but cute. Was it drugs that made so many nurses appear cute or were the cute ones drawn to the profession? He should have married a nurse.

But instead he'd married Marni, who'd dumped him after the third multi-year field assignment rather than being brought to DC. She'd agreed to pretend they were still friends so it would look good on his record—better if the agency didn't know about all the pain and rage they'd both unleashed in the final years. Now that he was stationed in the US, they met once a month for him to hand over the alimony check in some chichi bar. Then they'd have drinks —on opposite sides of the establishment.

Back before Marni, he'd thought he'd be with Clarissa Reece. That woman's body never stopped. In those early days at the CIA Black Site, they'd used each other hard, but it hadn't lasted.

VP. She'd finally married the VP. Woman was amazing.

Also the one who'd fucked his own career.

She'd slithered inside the Beltway, then conveniently forgotten about those she'd left in the field. She'd used him, bouncing him around from one hellhole assignment to another until Marni wasn't the only one sick of his existence. In retrospect, he couldn't blame her for leaving; the real surprise was how long she'd stuck by him.

Then last year out of the blue: *Oh, Ernie. Come have the booby prize of the fucking Middle East Desk that no one ever lasts at.* Last guy stroked-out on her office floor for crying out loud. *And don't mind that I've already screwed my way to the directorship and I'm going to screw my way into the White House.*

He might have been the only person in the country to raise a glass to VP Clark Winston's death. He'd liked the guy well enough but, even more, he liked how it had shafted Clarissa's plans almost as thoroughly as she'd shafted his. That was worth a toast. He'd made several that night.

"Also," the nurse was explaining to whoever stood outside his curtained cell, "he was still in enough pain that we've been slower to taper him off. He appears coherent now, but be aware that he is still under the influence and may answer strangely. He desperately needs to sleep, but can't seem to settle."

Then he heard her sneakers squeaking away.

Get away from the boring slow-recovery patient and hurry on to the far more interesting newest members of the ward. With the curtains shut he didn't even get to watch her cute married French ass as she walked away.

Two people were whispering outside his curtain, then Clarissa slithered through the gap.

Why can't you be dead, Clarissa?

"Who screwed you, Ernie?"

No *How's your shoulder?* No *Can I get you anything?*

"You did. Long time ago." He managed through the haze of drugs. Her blouse was just unbuttoned enough to see her collarbone. He remembered how she'd moaned when he'd bit her there, and afterward how pissed she'd been that he'd marked her.

"I meant the sabotage to your plane sabotage. Who helped you, Ernie, then betrayed you?"

Same answer.

His vision blurred and swam. He'd learned that when it did that, he had to focus hard on something to not puke bile all over the cute French nurse like he had the first time. He picked out the joint where the steel rod down to his chest entered the cast at his forearm and stared at it until the spins eased off.

"Do you even know?"

Christ, if only he did. Then he'd know who to kill once he got out of this rig.

"You really don't?"

He must have shaken his head without realizing. He could feel the swimming sensation inside his skull that meant he had.

"And nothing about the two other dead men on the plane?"

Hadn't someone else mentioned them? But that thought

slipped away, too. At least this time he was conscious of shaking his head.

Then she leaned close and hissed like the serpent she was. "And you thought you could frame me for your botched job and you could so easily land in the director's chair?"

Close enough that he could feel her heat. That he could see more of that warm skin revealed by her sagging blouse collar. He tried to raise his head to see some of that cleavage, but couldn't. Clarissa had always had magnificent breasts. He hated everything else about the woman but…damn.

He dropped his head back to the pillow. Not worth looking even if he could manage it. Marni was the one he missed; she was the one he should have done anything for.

But he and Clarissa once had a pet phrase between them about her God-given breasts. What was it?

So close he could smell her. Pure animal in heat. The greatest memory trigger of all.

Finally the memory of their nickname fought clear of the drugs swirling through him.

48

Ernie whispered, "The place men go to die."

It sounded like a good idea to Clarissa.

The useless toad.

He'd never been more than obedient muscle. Assign him a task and he did it, but no imagination, creativity, or—as he'd now proven—care. To not know who'd hired him? That precluded any possible risk assessment. Even if you were signing a deal with the Devil, you damn well should know that the Devil's was the name on the dotted line.

"Go for a walk," Kurt whispered from close behind her; his first words since they'd left the deli.

They'd been walking all day. She just wanted to get away from Ernie Maxwell and put her throbbing feet up.

He leaned in until she could feel his warm breath tickling her ear.

"No, Clarissa. Go. for. a. walk."

She turned her head enough to face him. His soft blue eyes, which hid the lethal warrior behind them, studied her from inches away.

Oh. "Good idea, Kurt. I'll go out and get some air."

"South parking lot, row 4, space 32." Then he faded away as if he'd never been close at all.

Without her noticing as she questioned Ernie, Kurt had been moving about the area. It was equipped for almost any emergency. A wide variety of machines and a tall cabinet of supplies.

The only electronics still attached to him was the drug dispenser, which had a fresh bag. It would be some time before it ran down and alerted the nurse. He must have moved past the need for a heart monitor. Any temptation to jack up the drug dose died beneath Taz's imagined glare, *Don't mess with the nurses, you bitch.*

Fine, she wouldn't. Which left…

That's when she focused on what else Kurt had done.

The door to the cabinet was ajar. Gauze and bandages had been knocked off shelves and lay scattered upon the floor. A plastic-covered steel tray rested askew on the lone chair, its hygienic lid pried open. Inside lay a jumbled array of surgical instruments.

Kurt lowered the guardrail on the side of the bed toward the cabinet.

His big rough hands were now sheathed in blue nitrile. With one gloved hand, he held Ernie's undamaged arm by the wrist. In his other, a gleaming scalpel.

"A walk, yes." Clarissa stepped through the curtain.

Near the exit from the ward, the nurse looked up from her latest arrival.

"He's resting comfortably now," Clarissa assured her. "Finally sleeping. No need to worry about him for a while."

"Oh thank you for letting me know. We have several emergency cases coming out of surgery in a few minutes."

Outside the door, she dismissed the RCMP guard, and told him to thank his commander. They'd finished with questions and Ernie was free to go whenever the hospital released him.

Relieved to be freed from the boring post, he closed his book and was radioing the change in orders as he walked away.

Clarissa rode down in the elevator, wondering that Kurt would slash Ernie's wrist. That wasn't very reliable. If discovered soon enough, he would be easy to save.

Ah, but Kurt's grip had been *over* the inside of the wrist, to control not expose.

When she considered the angle, she knew what would happen next.

A scalpel handle laid across Ernie's palm, then closed into a fist; Kurt's hand wrapped tight over Ernie's keeping it closed. The other over his mouth, and then the joined hands ramming the blade up under his chin and into his brain. Perhaps even cutting the spinal cord. Minimal blood loss from the small entry slice, maximum damage.

Drag the sheets aside as if Ernie had struggled with the bedding to lower the bed rail and raid the surgical kit, legs askew, the suicide scenario would be complete. And because Kurt was SOG, no one would see him leave, if anyone had seen him arrive. Close by her side throughout the day, she'd lost track of him any number of times.

Yes, a capable man.

With powerful hands.

How would those hands feel on her?

She exited the elevator, and the lobby, thankful for the evening air of a September evening in Quebec to cool the unexpected heat in her cheeks.

Clark's office-soft hands that she'd had to teach him how to use.

A man like Kurt would need no training.

An hour return flight to DC aboard the CIA's Gulfstream V bizjet. Given the opening…

Ha! The man was stealthy!

Leaning so close had been a question as well as a suggestion to depart, one she *had* answered by *not* pushing him aside at such presumption.

A man of few words, she could easily imagine what he'd say as he boarded the plane.

"Hard or soft?"

With Kurt Grice?

Hard!

49

Taz didn't bother waking Jeremy.

He was stretched out across four of the five chairs in the basement morgue waiting room of the Hospital Brome-Missisquoi-Perkins. Besides, taking a man who couldn't stand to enter a post-op recovery ward full of live people on the mend, into a room full of dead people being cut open, would be a disaster.

Five hours.

The sun had set. It would be full night now. Again Knowlton and the surrounding countryside would be shrouded in darkness. She knew her duty, not only to her rank but also to Miranda and Drake. But she'd now missing the second night in a row and her mind kept wandering.

Daydreams as she'd sat in the morgue's outer office had helped pass the time. But now past sunset? Most of the stops she'd planned: the house, the bookstore, the charcuterie and ice cream shop in Sutton—all out of reach until tomorrow. And the abbey! She'd wanted to sit in the monastery at

Saint-Benoit-du-Lac, taste their handmade specialty cheeses, and listen to Gregorian chants.

Five hours and not a word on the autopsy.

She pulled a mask out of the dispenser and brushed through the door.

Past the row of coolers, two men lay on operating tables, each with a plastic sheet tossed over them. No one else was about.

A peek under the sheets showed that they were definitely cut into. She dropped the edge quickly.

Along one side of the room stood a row of test equipment that she didn't begin to understand. If she had to, she'd wake Jeremy and drag him in here blindfolded—so he would see the corpses—to then face the gear and explain them to her. Anything he didn't know, he'd figure out fast enough.

A computer screen was active. It had a long list of tests. She knew some of them, was learning them all too quickly with her pregnancy. *Iron, sodium, calcium, total protein...* All of them had helpful *High/Low* ranges noted in the next column. Almost everything was normal, except for *oxygenation,* which was zero and helpfully highlighted in red. As neither corpse had taken a single breath in at least eighteen hours, that number was unsurprising.

She scrolled up and found the report of the physical autopsy. Gerald had a C4/C5 break, Lewis a C3/C4.

"Their necks were broken, as I say." The coroner stepped up to look over her shoulder. "Everything else, it is normal. Broken wrist in one, three fractured ribs in another. Their knees were badly bruised. Blunt force *traumatisme,* how you say?"

"Trauma," Taz didn't know what she'd been hoping for, but five hours of waiting for no useful information wasn't it.

"Ah, is so? They hit the back of the seats in front of them. It would have hurt them very much to walk, if they weren't already dead." He laughed at his own dead-guy joke. "Blood work you are seeing? *Très* normal."

"And you couldn't have told me that sooner?"

He shrugged. "I have early dinner with my children from eighteen to twenty hundred hours."

Taz could no longer see the room, it was sheathed in a dark red. "You left us cooling our heels for two hours while you ate *dinner?*"

"Cool your heels? I do not know this one. I told my assistant to tell you. We finished all of the fast tests, but some take time to run, so I to eat."

It meant she'd finally found the target she'd been looking for all day. Looking for since the moment she'd found out she was pregnant and her whole world, everything she believed about herself, was tossed wholesale out the window.

She yanked her Taser and sighted through a narrow tunnel in the red haze at a point inches below the ridiculous mustache and beard.

"No, wait! Wait! I do find something," his voice climbed in panic.

Safety off. Her finger inside the trigger guard. She'd pulled the slack out of the trigger. But she hadn't fired yet. "Talk, fast!"

He had his hands up, crossed in front of his face, palms out. He didn't even know enough to realize she was targeting his center of mass. Of course, at two meters out, she couldn't really miss.

She tracked him as he shuffled sideways.

"See? See red light? Slow test. Run while I eat with—" He chopped that off before she *did* shoot him. Waving vaguely at one of the pieces of equipment off to the side that she hadn't been able to interpret, he mumbled. "It found something not normal."

Taz's vision was reduced to the tunnel leading to his chest. "Explain."

"Blood *analyse.*"

"You said it was normal."

"*Non!* I say that the blood work you look at is *très* normal. Those are all easy, fast tests. While I...um...I run spectrographic *analyse*. It is," he studied the equipment for only an instant but his gaze dragged back to her Taser.

She aimed it at the floor, but kept it double-handed in case she changed her mind.

He turned, tapped one key. Looked at her. Tapped another. Looked at—

"Just do it or I *will* shoot you. And so that you know, it will hurt like a son of a bitch."

He finally turned to the machine for lengths as long as five seconds. On the third look, his attitude changed as he blinked at the screen and stopped checking on her. "Impossible."

"What is?"

"He could not be alive at all with this in his blood."

"He isn't."

The doctor ignored her and tapped for more information. "Not him either. They both are dead."

"I knew that. They're lying right there on your tables."

He shook his head. "d-tubocurarine. I have studied this, but I never see it before."

"Leaving me in the dark here, doc."

"Curare."

"Like blow darts and pygmies with poison arrows?"

"What?" his brows were furrowed in concentration on the ceiling and his beard-fondling nearly frantic. His reply was absentminded and he certainly wasn't looking at her. "No. No. Pygmies are Africa. Curare is weapon of Colombia, Peru, Caribbean islands. Derived from *Chondrodendron tomentosum.*"

He shouted loud enough to make her jump and nearly shoot a perfectly innocent floor tile with her Taser. She clicked on the safety and pocketed it carefully.

"Hands, neck, face! Exposed flesh. A wound. Curare must have a wound." He made a digging motion with his hand. "Under, inside of the skin. On skin, very not much danger."

He yanked the plastic tarps off the two men, dumping them on the floor, then began inspecting the two bodies closely.

"In all my study, I never have seen curare." He lifted one dead hand, then another.

Taz tried to ignore the flexion of the exposed muscles along the broken forearm. "What does it do?"

"Stops the breathing. Makes the diaphragm *paralysé*. No breath. They asphyxiate. So slow, they never know. They sleep. They die." He stopped for a moment and stared at the wall. "Yes, that explains the low oxygenation level in the blood test you looked at. Blunt force *traumatisme* should leave oxygen in the blood. But if they asphyxiate, it is explained. That is why I ran this other test."

He patted the machine.

"Also it explains how they break so much. Already dead

but no rigor mortis yet. And not alive to raise hands to defend themselves. No broken wrists. Dead less than three hours before crash."

"As it was only an hour flight—"

"They flail against the seat in front and neck—" he snapped his fingers loudly enough to echo like a gunshot in the tile room.

He tipped a corpse on its side and sighed happily before pointing at the man's neck.

"Ah. See? See? There. Poison enters here. Maybe he brushes it away, thinking mosquito bite against his neck. He begins dying before crash, maybe before boarding plane."

He dropped the corpse onto the table with a slap of flaccid flesh against steel. Even by Taz's standard, this was hard to watch as bits of him moved independently of others.

The doctor inspected the other corpse.

"Same place. Three centimeter right of C3 vertebrae."

"That can't be a blown dart."

He held up a hand as if holding a knife above his shoulder, but with his thumb cocked back. He swung it forward as if jabbing someone in the neck, then shoved down his thumb against his fist.

"Up close," Taz breathed it out. "Someone injected each of them with curare from a syringe. Maybe during boarding and shuffling luggage into overhead bins."

"*Oui.* It fits." But still he looked puzzled. Then he looked down at the Taser on her hip and laughed.

Her temptation to shoot him roared back.

He must have seen that as he held up a hand asking for a moment and moved to a shelf where he pulled down a case.

"We have been testing this." He held up a device not all that different from her Taser, except it was white, not black.

"A good-guy Taser?"

"In a way. I have it loaded with water." He pressed a power stud and a green light came on. He walked over to the nearest corpse, pressed it against the man's leg, and pressed a button.

There was a brief *psst!* sound, like it was hissing to get her attention in a crowd.

"A syringe with no needle. In the future, this is how you will receive shots, vaccines, antibiotics, anything. Air jet instead of needle." He leaned down to look at the leg. "No sign of entry. The red on the neck would be the body reacting to the injection, not the injection itself."

"But it makes a sound," then it was Taz's turn to almost laugh. "Less sound than a jet taking off, though. Someone sat behind them, reached around the edge of their seat, and injected the curare into their necks during takeoff."

The morgue director nodded. "Now all of the pieces, they fit."

50

CLARISSA COULDN'T TELL IF THE RINGING SOUND CAME FROM the plane or her body.

As she'd boarded the CIA's Gulfstream V at Montreal Airport, she informed the pilots that she'd be in a classified meeting. It would restrict them to the cabin, not a big burden for the hour-and-a-half hop to DC. They'd closed the cockpit's soundproof door.

She'd selected one of the side-by-side armchairs in the middle of the cabin, expecting Kurt to sit in the pair across from her. A little wordplay, perhaps some champagne from the galley as they flirted.

He slid into the seat beside her.

He didn't ask. No questions at all.

He simply reached across her lap and buckled her seatbelt. The leading edge of disappointment slid through her.

But Kurt didn't lean away.

Didn't remove his hand from her hip.

By the time they taxied into position, her first moan

slipped out of her throat.

He drove her far enough upward during the takeoff roll that by the time they were punching into the sky, so was she.

Too long. It had been far too long.

But unlike Clark, Kurt didn't let her down so easily. Definitely not there and done. He drove and worked her body like a masterful warrior in pitched battle until all she could do was hang onto the chair arms and hope that her cries didn't penetrate that heavy cockpit door. Even if they did, to hell with them.

Twenty minutes to altitude.

At forty thousand feet, the only things she wore were her Louboutin ankle boots propped hard on the edge of the facing seat—and a seatbelt. Where the rest of her clothes had gone was a mystery she had no interest in solving. Her heartrate descended from some stratospheric altitude and she finally managed to open one eye.

Kurt remained beside her. Fully clothed. Watching. His near hand firmly buried between her legs and the other crossed over to caress her breast with a touch so light that it hurt like electricity and enticed like velvet.

The ringing was no longer in her head.

It sat in the cupholder beside her chair.

Her phone.

Alight, buzzing, and ringing. So few had this number, every call was important.

Before she thought it out, she pressed Answer, impressed that her limbs were even functioning.

Kurt did not stop what he was doing to her.

"What?" she closed her eyes and lay her head back. What the man could do with his hands should be illegal.

She smiled to herself. Actually, as poor Ernie had discovered, it was.

"Christ, Clarissa," Taz snapped out. "Did you just answer your phone right after sex?"

Perhaps she should have waited until her breathing rate had dropped.

Kurt didn't drive her up again, but he didn't let her settle either.

"What do you want, Taz?" She knew what she herself wanted. Without opening her eyes, she reached out her own hand beneath Kurt's pants. Hmm, just as much promise as she'd hoped.

"Oh God, you're *having* sex. You're unreal. Well, we found out what killed Drake's guys and thought you'd want to know."

"Sure," she said half to Taz and half to Kurt as he pressed against her palm.

"Curare. The same poison I'd use on you if I had any handy and didn't need to go wash out my ears after this conversation."

"Pygmies?"

"Not Africa. Latin America. Caribbean, too." Kurt's first words since telling her to go for a walk while he dealt with Ernie Maxwell's *suicide*.

"Your hunk has it right," Taz spoke. "Hi, Kurt."

"Ms. Cortez." How could he sound so calm and coherent when he was— Clarissa had to cross her legs hard to contain the sensation he sent roaring into her.

"We'll look into it when we land. Tell Drake."

Taz didn't speak for long enough to make Clarissa glance at the phone. Not disconnected.

"If you accidentally snap her neck, Kurt, I'll throw you a

party. Not a soul alive would blame you." And the screen went dark.

Losing her seatbelt, but keeping her Louboutin boots, she shifted to drive her hand as deeply between Kurt's legs as his was between hers. She wouldn't be satisfied until he was as helpless as he'd made her moments before.

She had him writhing by the time the plane began the long descent into Dulles International.

Then she straddled him and rode his gloriously hard body all the way down to the tarmac, to hell with the seatbelts.

51

THE PHONE BUZZED LOUDLY AGAINST THE TABLE.

Tamisha eyed it carefully. They were on the ground at Thule, but General Nason had neither dismissed her nor left. Instead he still conferred with the President.

"Answer it," the general spoke up.

"Not my phone, sir."

He slanted a look at her that told her to stop being an idiot. Right, he'd known it was Miranda's when she staggered out of the room, looking like a rag doll with the life drained out.

"Sergeant Tamisha Ward here."

"Who the fuck are you?"

"I could ask the same."

"This is Colonel Vicki Cortez, Sergeant, now answer the damned question. What are you doing on Miranda's phone?"

"She's sleeping."

"Where's Andi?"

"She and her mother departed with Ms. Chase."

That earned her a long silence. "Andi's *mom*? Oh shit. I hope she's okay."

"They're," Tamisha searched for a polite phrase to describe the fraught relationship she'd witnessed, "cooperating."

"No bloodshed?"

Tamisha could smile at that. "Not yet anyway."

It earned her a brief laugh. "That's good. Is Drake handy?"

"He's talking with the President," then she focused past the conversation to the wider conference room. They weren't speaking, instead they were both looking at her. "Hold please."

She patched the call into the speakers. "A Colonel Vicki Cortez for you, sirs."

Drake smiled. "Another life-threatening experience for you, Sergeant. Hello, Taz. What do you have for us?"

"I'm not life-threatening. She sounded nice, so no getting out of line with her, General Nason. Has he been teasing you, Tamisha? If so, let me know and I'll call his wife. Lizzy can make me look mild."

"I'm fine," how was she supposed to address the woman? "Colonel."

"Good. General, Mr. President, we've determined the nature of the attack on your two operatives. They were air-injected with curare—a northern South American, southern Central American, or Caribbean poison—probably during the take-off roll, though possibly while they were boarding and loading luggage into overhead bins. The coroner estimates that the dosage was sufficient that they were already dead before the Embraer 175's crash."

"Any idea who poisoned them?"

"I thought—" Tamisha clamped her jaw shut.

"Go ahead, Sergeant."

She shook her head until the general gave her another of his looks.

"It sounds like a silly movie scenario, sir."

"Worse than a spy novel," Colonel Taz Cortez spoke up before the general could. "On an Embraer 175, the First Class seating is three across with an off-center aisle between A and B. CIA with his ass parked in seat 2A sabotaged the plane, but was in turn sabotaged by whoever hired him. And no, he really doesn't know by who. Across the aisle, two dead Air Force contractors in 1B and 1C, poisoned with curare by an injection in the neck by—Shit! Hang on."

"Colonel Cortez?" the general asked above the banging sound of heavy doors, then someone grunting as if being shaken awake.

"Jeremy. Seating chart. Who was in 2B and 2C?"

"Huh? Why?"

"Gerald and Lewis were injected in the neck during boarding or the take-off roll. Three centimeters to the right of the C3 vertebrae in their neck. As if someone was reaching around the seat from behind each one."

"That retired Montreal couple," Jeremy replied. "Hang on… Yeah, here are their names and IDs in the check-in records."

"Can you do a name-and-face match on them?" Taz asked.

"Not with what I have here."

"I can, Colonel," Tamisha told her.

Seconds later, they pinged into Miranda's phone.

Tamisha ran a quick search on the names, found them in

the Canadian newspapers. "Canadian philanthropists. Big donor types." She finally found their photos.

Then she focused on where she'd found the pictures.

"Uh, two years dead."

"You sure?" General Nason leaned in.

"I'm looking at their obituaries. Which," she glanced at the images on Miranda's phone again, "do not, I repeat, *not* match the IDs the colonel just sent me."

52

DRAKE KEPT AN EYE ON TAMISHA WARD.

No panic, no hesitancy, barely even shock. A soldier taking care of business first and her questions later. And Taz had taken a liking to her. She might be doing it partly to goad him, but it wasn't something Colonel Cortez did lightly either.

Good. Her career was about to launch upward; he'd have to make sure that someone kept an eye on her. Maybe Taz would like the job.

"Let's call Clarissa. Get her people on identifying who these two really are."

"I wouldn't do that if I was you, General."

He could hear that she was baiting him, but didn't see a way past it. "Why not?"

"You really don't want to do that, General, or you'll need heavy-duty decontamination immediately afterward."

"I know your feelings about—"

"Her taking my call a few minutes ago *while* she was

actually having mile-high sex? Fine. Go ahead. Call that waste of space."

Drake looked up at Roy on the screen. "You've got to do something about that woman."

"You know how good she is at the job, Drake." The President didn't look any happier than he felt. "Besides, she isn't going to quietly fade into the night. If I replace her, you ready for that kind of ugly?"

Drake felt physically ill. Clarissa Reese, with the full resources of the CIA, was lethal. Dismissed and cut off from those, but harboring whatever she'd secreted away, she'd fight dirtier than a Taliban Mullah.

"Jeremy can send the information directly to her people. He's buddies with them." Taz announced.

"Do it!" Drake told her.

"I'll let you know as soon as I have anything. We'll call Miranda's phone."

"You can call mine directly."

Taz paused a moment, "I don't have the number, sir. On our teams, only Miranda does. And frankly, I don't want the headaches that comes with that. But sir…"

"Yes?" When Taz was paying him respect, he knew he was in trouble now. Roy's smile onscreen agreed with his assessment.

"I do have your wife's number if I ever need to kick your ass, sir." And Miranda's phone went dark.

Roy's chuckle might hurt, but Tamisha Ward's flat-out laugh cut deep.

53

General Liú Zuocheng sat in the basement office of the Eight-One Building in central Beijing. He'd chosen it as the primary workplace of the Chinese Military Commission for security, not comfort. They were the six most powerful men in the country's leadership other than the President himself.

All were his men now, and most were content with their present power. The President dealt with the politics, the men now entering this room *ran* the military. It had taken much maneuvering to eradicate the worst of the political element, only a little easier once he convinced the President that he didn't want challenges to his power from so close at hand.

Admiral Chen of the Navy was the first to arrive as always. They had both served enough decades that they needed to exchange no more than a nod to acknowledge that an emergency morning meeting after the night of the Mid-Autumn Festival was more befitting younger men.

The General of the People's Liberation Rocket Force arrived next, and shuffled straight to the tea service without the nod. The delicate way he moved said how he had spent his festival. Zuocheng would have to keep a careful eye on him.

Air Force and Ground Force arrived together, clearly ending a conversation as they crossed the threshold. He had no worries about General Zhao, as Zuocheng had trained him personally as a pilot and he'd always been a most loyal aide since. If Ground Force did anything untoward, he would find out about it very soon from Zhao.

No one quite trusted the final man to enter the room. General Wang Fu was the youngest in the room, barely turned fifty, but that wasn't what led to the mistrust. He commanded the newest branch of the Chinese military, the Strategic Support Force, founded in 2015. The PLASSF needed a younger mind at the helm, though Zuocheng suspected that Wang was the only one in the room to actually believe that.

The man had an arrogance that grated on the others.

Zuocheng recognized it as part of the nature of that generation, convinced of their own self-worth. It would be easier to knock it out of him if it weren't for the insidious nature of the SSF. Their responsibility for all space, cyber, and intelligence efforts far outbalanced their relatively small size—barely seven percent of the People's Liberation Army's two-point-three million members.

Well, this morning he would test that self-assuredness.

He didn't wait for Wang Fu to finish serving himself before he began.

"This is the ship *Lucky Progress*." He placed the official maiden voyage photo on the large screen.

Wang Fu barely glanced over his shoulder from the tea service.

"Twenty-eight hours ago, as it transited the Arctic Ocean

north of Russia, a CASC CH-5 Rainbow drone fired six AR-1 missiles at the ship."

Wang Fu spun to stare at the screen, spilling hot tea over his hands. As he cursed and wiped, he didn't look away from the image, though there was nothing new to see. Was it alarm that such a thing could happen? Or perhaps that he might be caught for having been a part of it?

"The ship was partially disabled," he continued, "but still drives ahead at low speed toward its European destination under full control. I have spoken with Captain Yú Ling about the attack."

Actually the man had been completely shocked. Woken at 0600 local time, it had taken him several moments to absorb that he'd been fired upon rather than having a propellor malfunction. A woman from his crew was able to confirm seeing a glint of light astern at the time. Zuocheng didn't mention to the CMC that she'd been unable to corroborate anything further. Let them assume that the ship was the source of the information as he'd found no convenient satellite imagery of their own.

"I, of course, expect the PLAAF and the PLASSF to focus all due attention on these events."

"Of course, General," both men echoed. But Zuocheng could detect no clear indication of Wang Fu's innocence or guilt. He'd have to trust his friend Zhao spotting anything amiss.

"Four hours ago, this ship, the *Fortunate Progress*," he placed a near identical maiden-voyage photo on the screen, "which left dock six days earlier, was less fortunate."

"It was steaming through the Arctic waters between Canada and Greenland at the time. I have not spoken with the captain for..." he flicked to a trio of images, "...obvious reasons."

They were self-explanatory. The resolution was terrible, but it was sufficient. It was a three-image sequence captured by their own satellite. The ship steaming along, the initial explosion, and the final sinking.

"Note the time stamps. Less than four minutes."

The silence in the room was deep. Wang Fu didn't so much sit in his chair as collapse into it.

"Note this." On the first image, he marked a small circle around a dot of light. "This appears to be a sub-launched American-made Harpoon missile."

If he hadn't had the American's help, he never would have spotted anything beyond the explosion in their own imagery. He would let Wang Fu worry about how Liú Zuocheng knew that smudge of light was a Harpoon.

"The Americans?" Chen gasped out.

"They sell as many of those as we do the CASC UAVs. We need accurate answers before taking definite action."

"But the Americans!" Admiral Chen insisted waving a hand at the screen. "They manufacture the Harpoon. Their submarines patrol those waters so close to their own land. They could easily be the ones to shoot our ship."

"And the CASC UAV? Did they send that also?" Zuocheng asked.

The man scowled at the screen but had been silenced for the moment.

Zuocheng had considered this. He trusted that Miranda Chase believed what she said when she'd insisted, *It wasn't us.* But did he trust General Drake Nason?

Absolutely not.

However, he could also think of no plausible reason for

America to perpetrate these two attacks, and they were definitely linked. The only possible outcome of such an action by the Americans was the destruction of what tenuous relations the two countries managed to maintain. China might wither, might even collapse without the US's trade. But the US would not fare well either.

"No," he spoke to the room. "That is the easy assumption, but it makes no sense. We need to find the real answer. Perhaps some nation who *wants* to ruin our trade relations."

"And then what?" Admiral Chen demanded. He was always the first to support action—the man was positively bloodthirsty, which in this case didn't mean he was wrong.

"Then," Zuocheng sat back to show he was prepared for any contingency. "We unleash Falcon."

The Falcon Commando Unit answered solely to the CMC and had been modeled directly on the US Delta Force.

Yes, Drake, Zuocheng thought, *you had better be telling me the truth.*

54

Miranda lay in Drake's cabin, unable to sleep. Every time she closed her eyes, she saw her past burning away. Hangar, garden, house, a thousand memories.

Not that all of the memories were good. The reminders of those she wouldn't miss at all.

But she'd miss the ones that told of her and Andi curled up on the couch looking out the big south window. Beyond the island to where the San Juans spread out and then all the way to the distant peaks of Hurricane Ridge on the Olympic Peninsula. She'd miss the joy of the big team meals in the great room. She'd even miss Mike never putting anything quite where it belonged in the kitchen.

But those were new memories, not so lost in the past. The people who made them were still here.

Weren't they?

Miranda tried again to imagine what Andi must be feeling after Miranda had nearly killed her and her mother. But she couldn't even guess.

Yet Andi had remained at her side.

Hadn't she?

Miranda opened her eyes, and there she sat. Slouched on the one seat, her feet propped on the edge of the bunk, reading something on her phone.

"You love me." It was the only logical explanation.

"I do." Andi didn't even look startled by the question. Of course, as a Special Operations Forces warrior, Miranda had found her to be very difficult to surprise.

"Thank you." It was all Miranda could think to say.

Andi smiled at her softly. "Are you feeling any better?"

"Better than what?"

Andi shrugged. "Than earlier?"

"Like when I tried to kill you and your mother? Where is your mother?"

"Asleep in the next cabin," Andi nodded toward the wall behind her, then frowned. "I'm really sorry about your arm."

Miranda had forgotten that and reached out to pat the cast. "Thank you. I wouldn't have stopped myself in time."

Andi shook her head so that her glossy black hair swirled and caught the light of the phone, almost as if she sparkled. "You're the one who saved us when you kicked that pedal at the last second."

"You're stubborn."

Andi smiled, "You just got someone else's emotions right."

"No, it's an observed pattern of actions. You are tenacious like...some metaphor for tenacity that I can't think of. You wouldn't let us die, even though you had to break my arm to do it."

"Let's just call it a job we're both glad is over and done with." But Andi was frowning.

"What?"

Andi shook her head. "If—"

The Nightwatch's engines, which she hadn't been missing, started up. And with the pain relief, she hadn't heard them land or shut down, therefore she must have slept despite the impression that she hadn't. "How long?"

"You were out for less than half an hour." Andi always understood.

"Where are we going?"

"I have no idea. Hang on."

Andi came back as they started rolling. She tugged a seatbelt out of the sides of the bed and clipped it around Miranda's waist before sitting on the lone seat and clipping in herself.

"Well?"

The plane reached the end of the runway, turned sharply, and then headed aloft with a heavy roar.

As soon as they could speak easily again, Andi grinned. "Sub-hunting."

55

Tamisha hadn't taken the time to leave her desk in the conference room when General Nason departed—honestly, she'd barely noticed. He said he was going to meet with the base commander and get some sleep before tomorrow's meetings kicked into gear.

She had everything up and running the way she wanted it here. Returning to her desk in the battle staff operations area meant having to close it all down and restart everything. Even though the drone's track was archived historical information, she still felt as if she'd lose any chance of tracing the drone if she so much as looked away.

She was banking on the drone operator making a mistake and was now working hard to leverage it. She'd traced the flight backward until it had disappeared into the predawn darkness close by the Turkey-Iran border.

What if they followed the same route when headed home? Her projection placed them over that border in the darkness as they'd gone north into the Arctic. What if they'd flown exactly over that same border on their return?

Nightwatch

At the engine startup, she called Monica at the other end of the Nightwatch in the crew rest area. She agreed to work the next shift at Desk Eight beside Doyle, though she didn't sound happy about it. "He's been mucking about at Suzy's comm station again. Actually sent a broadcast without clearance. Made her plenty mad."

"Huh," was all Tamisha could be bothered to say. "Thanks for taking the shift. I'm working on something for the general."

"No surprises there, girl's on fire. Sure. Sure. No prob." And Monica was gone.

The Turkey-Iran border might be three hundred kilometers as the crow flew, but it wasn't some neat line on the map. It ran over five hundred kilometers as it zigzagged through the Armenian Highlands like a ticked-off timber rattler.

She rubbed at her eyes. *Not blinking. C'mon, girl. You know better. Gotta blink to reset those eyes.*

Staring at the little details all the way since Okinawa had taken its toll. Pausing the playback, Tamisha rocked back in her chair, closed her eyes, and began cursing.

"Does cursing help ease eyestrain?"

Tamisha twisted to look at the woman…women in the door. Miranda, looking a little better for her rest break. "Yes, absolutely. I highly recommend you do that."

The Chinese woman, Andi, sighed.

"I'll try that next time," Miranda stepped farther into the room. "Is audible cursing required or is subvocalization sufficient? There are situations where incipient eyestrain might occur in locales less amenable to multiple epithets."

"Are you serious?"

"Always!" Andi's accompanying nod said that she wasn't

joking either. "Miranda, cursing does not relieve eyestrain. It can relieve frustration though."

"Oh, okay." She didn't look the least upset that Tamisha had been messing with her.

"But—" This wasn't making any sense.

Andi turned to her. "Miranda is autistic. Humor, sarcasm, and recognizing emotions are a challenge for her."

"Missing the sarcasm," Tamisha remembered. She watched the woman walk up to the big wall display and study it. "Then how…" She didn't know how to state her question with Miranda standing only meters away.

"Do *not* underestimate her other skills because of that."

"What do you mean?"

Andi winked, "You'll see."

"You're looking in the wrong place," Miranda spoke without turning.

Tamisha opened her mouth, but Andi shook her head. If it hadn't been for the slight smile, just daring her to step in it, she would have. But she'd be damned if she'd do the expected.

"Where should I be looking?"

"Unlike most of the year, September and early October winds in Turkey blow predominantly from the east. A good UAV pilot would know this and fly along the eastern edge of the mountain line to avoid heavy downdrafts to the west of the peaks that might crash the aircraft. You need to search one to three kilometers east of your current view. And I believe you failed to compensate for the lower airframe drag due to the release of the six AR-1 missiles. The CH-5 will be fifty to sixty minutes farther along the route than where you are looking based on the time signature."

Tamisha looked at Andi, who only shrugged.

Nightwatch

She shifted the view to the east and scrolled the view backward seventy minutes—then let it roll forward.

At fifty-eight-minutes-thirty, Miranda nodded, "There it is." And turned away from the big screen and sat at the table. "Andi, does Taz have anything new on the Embraer 175?"

Miranda might be done with the topic, but Tamisha could only stare at the screen.

How many hours had she been chasing that fuzzy little cross of fuselage and wings through these mountains? And Miranda had just—

"Warned you, I did! Hmmm." Andi whispered in a Yoda voice, then circled to sit beside Miranda. "Taz hasn't sent anything, but I'll check in with her. Maybe Jeremy's CIA buddies Heidi and Harry found some facial matches."

To prove to herself that it wasn't blind luck, Tamisha zoomed in to full magnification. It was definitely a CH-5 Rainbow, with no armament mounted under the wings—and no country insignia along the fuselage or tail.

She locked an image tracker on the object and let time travel forward again. As she gained confidence, she was able to follow it at twice, then five, then ten times speed. By the time she hit the next gap in satellite coverage, she had the feel for how the pilot was flying it and jumped efficiently to the next feed. She was picking it up after the gaps much quicker now.

Miranda spoke without looking up. "It will pass a few kilometers north of Mosul if it's headed to Tal Afar Air Base in Iraq. Otherwise, it will pass over Kalak, then the Al-Hajarah desert. It will continue due south for Saudi Arabia or skirt Syria. If it does the latter, it will then make a direct line over Jordan to the southern tip of Israel to cross the Gulf of Aqaba and land in Egypt. Most likely the Army airfield in

Hurghada as I doubt they have the reach left to make Berenice Military Base. Either route will be very tight on fuel."

Tamisha opened another screen to type in Miranda's suggestions before she forgot them.

"Here's Taz for you," Andi handed the phone to Miranda.

How? Tamisha mouthed the question.

"Her memory isn't photographic," Andi explained in a normal voice. "But she never forgets an airport or an aircraft specification. Being a math whiz helps, and never challenge her on codebreaking, she's *really* terrifying at that."

Tamisha decided that unless she wanted her ass humbled even more than it already was, she'd keep her head down and continue tracing the UAV across the Iraqi desert. However, with Miranda's tips, she was able to significantly increase her tracking speed.

Sure enough, it neither turned west for the closest Iraqi base or south for Saudi Arabia. Instead she could have laid a ruler from Kalak straight to Aqaba, then down the gulf to Hurghada, Egypt, neatly skirting Israeli and Saudi Arabian airspace.

On a leapt of faith, Tamisha projected the airspeed over the final fourteen hundred kilometers and scanned Hurghada's small airstrip. It only took her a moment to nail its landing. She could even see the little flurry of trucks racing out to service it.

"Egypt."

"I hate it when I'm right," Andi sighed.

56

TAMISHA GRABBED THE PHONE AND PUNCHED FOR SUZY'S comm station.

"Sub/Sat Comm."

"Tamisha here in the conference room. I need to talk to General Drake Nason. He disembarked at Thule."

"Give me a minute. Do you know what that asshole partner of yours did?"

Tamisha sighed, "He's not my partner."

"You sit at the same desk. Makes you his desk partner, Tam." She'd never liked that nickname but there was no stopping Suzy. "He sent a VLF transmission without authorization."

"To who?"

"Not one of ours. I didn't recognize the header."

Miranda held out her phone, it was ringing.

"I'll have to get back to you on that, Suzy. Never mind on the call, I've got the general coming in on another line here."

Rather than taking the phone, Tamisha punched for the

283

link she'd previously made to the conference room system. Halfway through the next ring, it was answered.

"What did you find, Miranda?" His voice was heavily slurred. She checked the clock. No way he could have been asleep for more than twenty minutes, probably less.

"Sergeant Ward here, sir, with Miranda and Andi. We have a trace on the UAV. It landed at the closest possible base in Egypt."

"Egypt?"

"Yes sir."

"Wait a minute," his voice came a little clearer. "Do they also have a sub that can reach the Arctic?"

"Andi here. Yes they do, the German Type 209s. It's a long stretch, but they're German-built so they can do it. I did some training with their Air Force and Navy back when I was still a Night Stalker."

Tamisha knew what that meant. The US Army's 160th SOAR were the only people who could outfly the Air Force's 920th Rescue Wing, the guys who *delivered* the PJs. She'd never met one in the flesh; they were almost as mythic in their deeds as the Pararescue Jumpers and Delta Force.

"And, yes sir, we've sold them Harpoon missiles."

That's when what Andi was saying sank in.

Tamisha punched for Suzy again.

"What now, Tam?"

"Doyle sent an unauthorized transmission on the VLF? On a submarine frequency?"

"Didn't I just say that?"

"Suzy, get the SF. Have the Security Forces drag him off that desk and get him cuffed somewhere he can't access anything."

"What? Why? Never mind. You know you don't have the authorization to do that."

"I do. This is General Drake Nason. Do what she says on my authority and we'll straighten it out later."

"Yes sir." And Suzy was gone.

"Let's finish this first," General Nason said over the phone. "Egypt launching two attacks in the Arctic. I'm not saying I don't believe you, but I want the reasoning."

Tamisha could start to see it. No. She could *feel* its rightness but knew she didn't have it yet.

Miranda looked completely confused. Then she must have noticed Tamisha looking at her, without Miranda ever quite looking at her in turn.

"I never understand people's motivations. Especially not when it's large groups, like governments. I understand planes."

Tamisha nodded her understanding. The woman herself was finally starting to make sense. A technical genius and the rest some kind of mash-up.

Then Tamisha turned to look at Andi.

Despite her earlier protests about it not helping, she was cursing quietly as she rubbed her closed eyes.

"Sadly, sir, it makes perfect sense."

And that was the moment the conference room went sideways—literally.

57

Tech Sergeant Doyle Cowell had a bad feeling since the moment the Nightwatch had fired back up.

Parked at Thule, he'd checked the balance of his new bank account. Six figures. He'd never seen six figures in his life. And the first digit was almost a three. Only a few grand shy of three hundred thousand! It made a guy wonder exactly what was possible.

But when the general disembarked, they'd sealed up and started to re-spin the engines. Tamisha was either still up in the forward conference room or she was off kissing the general's ass. Why had she shut him out? They'd made a good team. Every performance review said so.

But now they were headed back aloft and Monica sat beside him. A sexy name but not a sexy woman. Short, a little heavy, all chest and hips. He might have gone for her before. But he was a six-figure guy now and didn't need to settle. How long until he reached seven?

As the Nightwatch rotated and began the climb out of Thule, General Mitchell made a rare intercom announcement from his desk at the head of the battle staff operations area.

"Folks, you all know that we recorded the destruction of a Chinese super-freighter out in Baffin Bay. It was clearly a sub shot, but we don't know whose. The nearest Poseidon or Orion sub hunter aircraft is still two hours out. While we aren't rigged with sonobuoys or active attack, we fly some of the best radar equipment in the world."

Doyle couldn't argue with that.

If the sub's captain was dumb enough to run on the surface, the Nightwatch's radar could pin him down. If he transmitted a single peep, Doyle would have him.

The sea state was so smooth that even if he ran submerged, their radar could pick up the resulting surface ripple of displaced ocean.

His job would be to run that, and also hard pulse the ocean from the air. Capturing an acoustic backlash—just like a sub's sonar ping—was much trickier with a layer of atmosphere in the way, but they might spot the boat if they were close enough.

There was also the blind luck of looking down and seeing a shadow. That was Monica's job. He'd always sort of pitied Tamisha's job for visual security of the E-4B Nightwatch rather than the reach of his electronic security, yet she'd spotted that freighter explosion fast enough—faster than he had.

"Also," General Mitchell continued, "luck was on our side. We had a Virginia-class fast-attack hanging at the bottom of Baffin Bay. He's now driving north fast, running hard pings all the way. If this sub tried to run south, our fast-attacker will turn him around. Our job is to box him in by closing Lancaster Sound and north toward the ice cap with the Nightwatch. We need to pin this sucker down."

That's when the pieces all clicked together and he almost barfed on his console.

That code he'd been told to send out on the VLF! It had been to the sub they were hunting. The sub that had killed the Chinese freighter and everyone aboard. And he'd been the connection back to whoever ashore was commanding the sub home base.

Suddenly the quarter million added to his account didn't mean shit.

He looked around, as soon as he could do it without being sick. No one looking at him. No one paying attention.

Next time they hit the ground, he was chucking his phone into the ocean or a hot furnace, whichever he found first. He'd get a new number and never link the two, not like anyone except the Air Force ever called him anyway. He'd have to change all his social media, maybe he'd change his damned name to Betsy.

"Hey, what's that?" Monica asked.

"What's what?" he echoed to force his mind to focus.

There was a high-frequency alert tone of a sighter locked onto the E-4B. Half his console was lit.

Periscope on the surface.

A hard return of a motionless submarine mere meters below.

Then the rest of his console lit up in full panic.

Two objects punched out of the water, incoming fast with no angular variance in trajectory.

He slammed the emergency intercom to the cockpit. "Evade! Evade! Evade!"

58

MINUTES EARLIER, CAPTAIN ROMALDO SANCHEZ DECIDED that he must be in hell. Submarine hell.

"Sonar, what's going on?"

The mysterious man on the phone had ordered him back north to Lancaster Sound. Back to that quiet bay where he'd actually sent a ship to a watery grave.

There's another Chinese ship coming through in fourteen hours. Ignore the propellor, Captain. Two below the waterline.

He'd cruised north as slowly as he dared but could still justify that he was following orders. Romaldo had been a surface patrol-boat captain when he'd received this *special* assignment. He was supposed to be First Officer, not Captain. *You'll represent our interests on their boat.*

Two weeks out from port, the Egyptian captain had put a bullet through his brain. Romaldo remembered how the shot had echoed down the length of the submerged boat. They were all lucky that after passing through the chicken-shit bastard's head, it hadn't hit anything critical.

With a crew of only thirty, the ranks did not abound with

senior officers. He'd become the captain of the boat and been ordered to proceed with the operation.

None of the crew spoke Spanish and half of them didn't speak English. He sure as hell couldn't converse in Arabic and their names all sounded the same to him: Abdullah, Ahmad, Ayad… To survive, he called everyone by their job title.

Except creeping north hadn't worked.

Sonar, who Romaldo was now relatively sure was Arsalan Baghdadi, reported a faint contact to the south. Over the next few hours he'd made it clear that the ping energy measured stronger and stronger, increasing at a rate that said they were being hunted.

For hours after he'd accidentally fired the missile, he'd heard planes circling overhead. They could only be looking for him. He'd slid away to the south until the message to turn around had reached him.

And now? Sonar insisted that the only reason someone would ping as often as that boat to the south would be if they were hunting someone.

Him!

He'd punched north at flank speed.

If an American fast-attack sub had picked up his tail, he was screwed. The Type 209 was a diesel-electric that topped out at forty kilometers per hour. The American would be nuclear, meaning it didn't have to surface to recharge its batteries, and it would travel some highly classified amount faster, probably much faster.

Baffin Bay wasn't going to save him. The bottom was over two thousand meters down and the Type 209 could only reach a quarter of that. There'd be no hiding on the bottom as he had in Lancaster Sound.

"Sonar?" the man had become Romaldo's most trusted touchstone. He also had the best English.

He was tipping his head back and forth. "The ping from behind is stronger. But there is much going on ahead of us as well. I do not understand the sounds as they jumble one over another."

"Captain?" Electrics called out to him.

He crossed the two steps to that station. "Go ahead."

"Battery charge. Very low. Need to surface soon."

"But they're supposed to last seven hundred kilometers submerged." Romaldo had barely slept since the Egyptian captain had killed himself, but he'd read through every manual he could find in the man's cabin, even the ones stained with the mud-brown spatters of the chicken bastard's dried blood.

"That's at four knots, Captain. We travel at twenty-two."

It wouldn't do any good to berate the man, he'd been following Romaldo's order. Underwater, the submarine ran on electric batteries. They could stay under for a full week, if he dared move conservatively. But he hadn't thought about surfacing to recharge. First he stayed under to await the Chinese freighter, then to run, and now to return at speed. It was a wonder the batteries had anything left at all.

He wanted to blame Electrics, but the man would assume he was aware of all of these factors until it became a problem, like now.

When the batteries ran down, the boat needed to run the four big diesel engines to charge them, which required air. But the moment they punched a snorkel through the surface, they'd become visible to anyone looking.

He crossed back to Sonar. "Any luck with the other noise?"

"Sorry, Captain, no."

"Dead stop," he ordered.

The boat took forever to slow. He could feel the unknown submarine to the south growing closer by the second. Sonar guessed he was still six hours behind based on the ping noise, but that had been while running at full speed making their own noise.

When Conn finally reported full stop, he glanced at Sonar.

"Closer. Maybe two hours. Maybe one."

Yes, he was in hell.

Easing up to close below the surface, he raised the snorkel first to get the diesels running while he dared. Then the periscope; he looked out at the night, such as it was. At this latitude, the twenty-two-hour sun had only recently faded to a bright twilight.

To make sure that he missed nothing, he flipped in the night-vision enhancement. There was no need; it only took seconds to locate what Sonar was hearing.

It was so unlikely that it was no surprise the man hadn't been able to make sense of it.

A massive, blue-and-white 747 skimmed along less than a hundred meters above the surface of the ocean, headed away from him—no more than twenty kilometers away. He couldn't believe that they'd use such a plane to hunt his little submarine, yet they were.

And he would bet that they were hitting the surface with every kind of radar they could bring to bear.

To hunt him.

Their track was blocking his hoped-for escape back into Lancaster Sound. He followed the plane as it traveled east to west. Easy to see when it reached the far shore, turned as it climbed enough to catch the daylight, then settled on a new track—that was coming straight toward him.

It was too late to dive the boat. Too late to do anything.

Or was it?

They were flying so low...

"Weapons status," he called out without looking away from the periscope to see the crew's reactions.

"Tubes One, Three, Five, Seven loaded with SeaHake torpedoes. Tube Two empty. Tubes Four, Six, and Eight loaded with Harpoon Missiles."

"Prepare to fire Tubes Four and Six on my indicated heading."

"Sir?"

"Do it!" It was their only chance.

"Ready, Four and Six. *Harpoon Missiles,*" Fire Control said the last very clearly.

Captain Romaldo Sanchez centered the periscope—both horizontally and vertically—on the nose of the great bird.

He had been sent by Panama to act as liaison to the Egyptian submarine. His commander had explained the need to stop any Chinese efforts to avoid the two canals that supported their two countries.

But it was hurting the American's trade that had made him agree to the assignment, and his contact with the government's minister had known that.

The United States, who had placed the dictator Noriega over his country, which had cost the life of his freedom-fighter grandfather. Only after he had raped their country had the US military swept him aside.

As he stared at the plane approaching him head on, his three decades of service to the new order faded. All the ten-year-old Romaldo saw was his dying father, bullet-punched holes leaking red, because Manual Sanchez had stood in defense of the criminal the United States had placed in power to begin with.

He tapped the marker button that would transmit the exact aim of his periscope into the firing solutions computer. It, in turn, automatically set the missile's coordinates.

"Fire Harpoons in Four and Six."

He heard the thud and whoosh of the outer doors opening and the missiles launching.

Romaldo the man knew he should dive. Should try to save something. But the boy wanted to watch the plane die.

It kept coming as if it was blind.

Harpoon missiles were meant to break the surface, then fly at low, sea-skimming, ship-killing altitude until they found their target.

But with no ship to find, and with a clear target flying a hundred meters aloft and under twenty kilometers downrange, they climbed hard. At Mach 0.71, over eight hundred kilometers an hour, they also closed fast.

Then, as if waking up, the plane jerked up and to the right.

A blinding spread of flares bloomed from the aircraft.

Unknowingly, in his unpracticed grip of the periscope's controls, he held down the auto-gating override on the night-vision. The full brightness of the flares, enhanced by the night vision, blasted into his eyes, unlimited by the electronics designed to spare his vision.

When the Harpoons exploded, the pulse of light through the periscope's night-vision optics had him crying out like a wounded child as he collapsed backward.

It was the last thing he would ever see.

59

"Evade!" One of the eggheads in the back was shouting.

"Yeah, tell me something I don't know!" There were about eighteen things that Air Force Captain Ricky Malone hadn't liked about the present maneuver.

The E-4B Nightwatch was designed to get high up, move fast, and stay the hell out of sight. Everything at a nice and safe distance, even if it was a nuclear war. Instead, he was flying the 747 dog low, belly-dragging-dog low, creeping along at a bare two hundred knots instead of five hundred. And trying to pull off a mission that his baby was never designed for: sub-hunting.

But General Nason himself had come up to the cockpit and asked if he thought the Nightwatch's capabilities could be applied to the situation. How was he supposed to say no to a four-star who actually asked for advice and listened?

So, he'd been flying his grid pattern over the freezing waters of Baffin Bay, letting the eggheads do their dance.

Radar had showed a tiny blip ahead. No one was talking to him, so maybe it was a seal or a breaching whale.

Certainly wasn't an iceberg. He'd never seen such a quiet ocean.

But the tiny radar return wasn't moving and it wasn't going away.

When he was about to call down and ask what it was, two more blips painted on his radar screen.

And damn but they were on the move. Fast.

In his direction!

He hadn't flown C-17 Globemaster cargo planes into Bagram for three tours and not learned when someone was trying to off his ass.

"Countermeasures ready!" He'd shouted out to his copilot, Jim Hamlin, at about the same time that idiot had begun shouting, "Evade!" over the intercom. Wasn't anybody back there doing their job with all that high-tech equipment?

Ricky made the worst possible choice. He was too low to make any other.

Slamming in full power, which had a several-second lag time as raw fuel dumped into engines that weren't moving fast enough to swallow it all, he nosed up.

That exposed his underbelly, the entire expanse of his 747's big fat underbelly, directly to the incoming missiles.

The engine gauges were climbing, and the plane climbed like the champion she was. Large jets weren't intended to climb at seven thousand feet per minute, but she was doing it. *That's my girl.*

"Closing fast, Rick," Hamlin warned. "Inbound four-six-oh knots. Pair of Harpoons maybe. Lock. They have lock on us."

"Nav, transmit Mayday. Hamlin, Count it."

"Mayday. Mayday. Mayday. This is Nightwatch under

missile attack by unidentified submarine at..." Ricky tuned out the navigator.

"Fifteen, fourteen, thirteen..."

A 747-200 was a fifty-year-old heavy jet—light on people, heavy on shielding—not a ballet dancer.

At ten seconds he decided to wait two more.

Then he shouted, "Countermeasures. Now! Now! Now!"

As Hamlin launched the flares that would burn far hotter and brighter than the 747's engines, he began nosing over.

"Four, three, two..."

This was going to be so ugly.

By zero, he was nose-on to the two missiles, presenting the smallest possible radar profile. He was also moving at four hundred knots instead of two hundred and had climbed to five thousand feet from three hundred.

Whatever happened next was out of his hands.

60

The moment Andi had realized they had a traitor on board, she'd undone her seatbelt and leapt to Miranda's side. Because of her cast-encased arm, it took seconds longer to snap in her full five-point harness than it should have.

As Andi had reached for her own seat, every alarm on the plane went nuts. Each told her a story with ingrained body memory that she didn't need to mentally process. Someone had started shouting to evade long after the plane was already alerted and begun reacting. The power of the climb alone told her training the degree of danger.

By pure luck, her seat stood to the rear of Miranda's. She slammed into it. It spun, almost ejecting her out the far side, but she'd managed to grab the lap belt in both hands and buckle it rather than tumbling to the aft wall of the conference room. Using the seatbelt for leverage, she had the rest of her own harness in place quickly. She grabbed the edge of the conference table to spin her chair to face forward and lock it in place.

She then drove a foot against the side of Miranda's chair

to face her forward as well. The position lock was on the right-hand side, the side of Miranda's broken arm, so all Andi could do was keep a foot on the corner of the seat and press hard.

Beneath the heavy roar of the engine, Tamisha was bitterly saying that she was going to kill someone named Doyle.

Miranda's phone slid down the length of the conference table, gathering speed.

Over the conference room's phone, Drake was demanding that someone tell him what was going on.

That stopped when Miranda's phone shot off the rear end of the table, hitting the aft bulkhead and breaking the connection.

With no readouts or controls to provide more information, Andi was relegated to counting seconds.

Hard climb for eighteen.

Nose-over for eight, still under full power.

Her butt came off the chair but she rose no higher, pinned in place by the five-point harness and her foot still jammed against Miranda's chair.

She saw Miranda's arm float up as well.

And that's when she remembered.

"Mother!"

61

CHING HUI WU HAD NEVER BEEN ABLE TO GO TO SLEEP quickly. She would often lay awake for hours as her husband snored quietly beside her. He was a good man and a brilliant trial attorney. But she had never emulated his uncanny ability to leave the case in the courtroom and sleep without a worry. *I leave the fire up to you, my love.* He would then roll over and be asleep faster than she could turn out the light.

Aboard an airplane, there was no chance her nerves would ever settle and let her sleep. But she had agreed to lie down simply to remove herself from Andrea's sphere of worry. *Sorry, daughter, it is yet another trait straight down the matrilineal line.* Her concerns for Miranda overwhelmed her and Ching Hui didn't want to add to her burdens.

Too exhausted to even consider that once they'd landed, they'd go aloft again so soon, she had missed her chance to disembark. She lay, half awake, as the plane took off and flew once more.

Though she couldn't review the physical battlefield to prepare for the upcoming meeting, she could certainly consider it mentally. She began considering what she knew of each country's personality who would be there.

Her role would be far more challenging than the typical courtroom drama or facing down some Silicon Valley whiz kid. There were so many who didn't understand the legal intricacies of their new creation—or more often one that they *thought* was new but rarely surpassed derivative and more often than not infringed on other's intellectual property.

Drake had given her a dossier on the confirmed attendees. If this is what the military thought was a useful profile, they definitely needed lessons. For a major trial, in addition to any depositions, she would commission deep profiles on every opponent, opposing counsel, and witness. She did the same for those she represented as well. What they drank, what they drove, the name of their mistress, any bank balances...all of it.

Then the Wu and Wu attorney would know how to expose or hide weaknesses on the witness stand, shifting the order of questions and evidence to create the desired effect. *Nothing but the truth* didn't mean it was any less of an art form.

The military profiles were barely better than a *curriculum vitae* and told her so little of the person. Of course the mandate wasn't guilt or innocence, but rather to build a consensus. Which, so few people understood, required far more finesse.

But as she lay there, Ching Hui's thoughts drifted to her children.

Her other two daughters had proven to be nearly painless, moving smoothly through schooling into the ranks of Wu and Wu Law.

Emilia was already well on the way to matching her father's mastery in the courtroom.

And in Liana, following in her own footsteps, she'd found the future of Wu and Wu. Her youngest was already lifting portions of the firm management load from Ching Hui's shoulders.

Between them, they had provided her with three grandchildren.

Leaving Liana to experience the full load of running Wu and Wu for a week had been a perfect excuse to visit her troublesome middle child.

Andrea had never been a comfortable child. Middle daughters were supposed to be quiet and in need of a mother's coaching.

Not Andrea.

With more energy and imagination than Liana and Emilia combined, she had never once been at rest. Liana had ridden her first bicycle at eight. Emilia had never taken to one. Andrea had abandoned her tricycle at two and her training wheels at three. By twelve, she was racing go-karts, which had been terrifying to watch. But Ching Hui had rapidly learned that the more she voiced her worries on a topic, the harder Andrea dug in.

Go-karts had gone away at fifteen, when she'd allowed her daughter to ride beside the helicopter pilot en route to a meeting in Reno. Her relief had been short-lived, building to that horrid meeting about dropping out of Stanford Law to join the US Army as a pilot.

It had been overwhelming. Andrea was a four-oh student and was walking away from it. She would fly...*machines* into combat. Her choice for relationships was women and only women—which had explained Ching Hui's utter failure to create an appropriate match for her.

Losing her wild daughter: from law, from the family firm, from family, and into the Army, all in less than forty-eight hours—

Unable to tolerate the suffocating mass of the burden, for the first and last time she had lashed out. Not with a slap, never with a slap, but with words intended to cut and wound.

Andi hadn't responded.

Hadn't joined battle.

Hadn't given her a chance to do anything but regret the words.

Instead, her daughter had pulled a slightly crumpled envelope out of her pocket, set it on the Sunday dinner table, offered a bow of respect that she hadn't performed since she was six or seven, then turned on her heel and walked out of the dining room.

Minutes, perhaps hours passed before she dared touch the envelope. She could never recall the rest of the meal. Alone but for her husband at the cleared table, her good man sat patiently in the seat to her right, waiting.

The four thin sheets burned her fingertips. A four-page contract entitled *DD Form 4, Enlistment/Reenlistment Document - Armed Forces of the United States*. A contract with no escape clause. Her daughter was headed to war. And to think she'd been afraid of the go-karts.

And finally, all of these years later, she knew what she had to do. Wondered that for all her vaunted insight into the lives and careers of others, she hadn't seen it.

She unbuckled the lap belt Andi had insisted she don even lying down on the bunk.

There was no one in Drake's onboard office.

As she stepped out the door into the corridor separating the office from the conference room, some alarm sounded.

Then the plane nosed upward sharply, far more sharply than any takeoff she'd ever experienced. The narrowness of the corridor was all that saved her as she stumbled into the outer wall of the conference room. She lay stunned against the hard surface for several seconds.

And people wondered why she didn't like to fly.

Using her hands and shoulder, she managed to scoot to the closed conference room door. She felt lighter as the plane leveled and once again stood solidly on her feet.

As she opened the door, she heard Andi cry out for her.

Shoving open the door, she stepped into the room.

Or tried to.

Her feet were no longer connected to the floor. Instead, she was floating toward the ceiling.

"No!" Andi cried out.

The black woman, Tamisha, punched a fist at the round disk at the center of all the straps holding her to her chair. The straps flipped aside as she lunged upward. One hand on a seat strap, her other hand closed around Ching Hui's thigh and yanked her, from floating, down toward a vacant chair.

Then time seemed to blur into slow motion.

The loudest sound she'd ever heard slammed her to the floor.

Or had the floor slammed into her?

As if a giant had grabbed the massive 747 and simply tossed it sideways.

The room twisted at a crazy angle, tumbling her head over heels into the side wall.

A sharp cracking sound, no louder than popcorn popping, seemed of little consequence.

The pain she felt was her face hitting the wall.

Tamisha tumbled onto the wall above her as the plane tipped fully on its side.

Fred Astaire dancing up the walls and across the ceiling came to mind as they slid far less gracefully onto the ceiling.

Ching Hui looked down / up at Andi, still strapped into her chair. How she wished she could erase the horror painted there.

Then she attempted to hold on to a light fixture and her arm replied with a blast of pure agony.

With no grip possible, she began sliding toward the next wall.

62

Too late. Doyle had been too late.

Unspotted.

Unwarned.

Not doing his job, not reading the alarms blaring across his console.

The submarine had attacked.

Monica braced hard against her seat and console.

Fully harnessed.

Doyle still only wore his lap belt, the maneuvering threatened to cut him in two across the lap. He flailed about for the other belt ends but couldn't find them as the plane tumbled.

When he twisted to find them, he spotted two of the security forces sprawled in the aisle. One was bleeding from the temple, being tossed at the whim of the plane's maneuvering. The other still fought for a handhold.

Both were mere steps behind his own position.

They knew.

Definitely too late.

He tried to smash his phone on the corner of his console. At least he could hide that bit of evidence. The first blow cracked it, the second broke it thoroughly. At the third, the plane shifted unexpectedly and he caught his finger between the phone and the corner of the console. He yelped as his finger snapped.

As he turned his hand over to inspect the damage against the wild gyrations of the airplane, he realized that his only record of his new account number had been on that phone.

63

Captain Ricky Malone had seen this many warning lights on a 747's console once before in his life—in a simulator.

He didn't even know yet if the roll was controlled or perhaps he'd lost a wing and they were spiraling down into the ocean.

Unsure of anything's integrity, he continued the wing-over-wing roll as the lowest stress maneuver. Countering the plane's momentum with a correction might induce a critical stress that would kill them all.

"Still with me, Ham?" The artificial horizon was wholly inverted, the blue-sky side of the indicator toward his feet and the black-of-earth appearing right-side up to his upside-down position. Reverse thinking, he eased in on the wheel to keep that horizon indicator centered as it spun.

"Depends. Are we inverted in a 747?" His voice was slurred as if he'd fallen asleep...or hit his head.

"Yep!"

"Then I'm still with you."

Ricky began easing the roll, hoping to come out straight and level. The blood rushing to his head made him wonder if that was the next thing that was going to explode.

"Pull Two and Four."

"Say what?"

With a sideways glance, he could see Hamlin shake his head, then groan. "That was stupid." He pressed his hands to either side of his head, then looked up. "Both?"

"Roger that."

Getting with the program, Hamlin pulled the bright red Engine Two Fire t-handle located overhead. Its blinking lights went out as it cut the fuel feed and fired the extinguisher bottle for the leftmost engine. He then pulled Engine Four.

Ricky slid into level flight and was astounded that he'd only lost fifteen hundred feet in the maneuver—he'd spent half of it sideways with his wings providing no lift at all.

"Nav?"

No response.

"Marty!"

Nothing.

Hamlin twisted slowly in his seat and peered aft. "Out cold." He didn't need to add, *I hope.*

"Let's work the problem."

Hamlin threw several switches. "Still leaking fuel. We need land and we need it fast."

"Options?"

"Marty—shit! Hang on."

Ricky began testing other systems. Hydraulics were dicey. Something had deep-sixed a whole section of the flight computer as effectively as an EMP. Is that what had hit them? If so, the engineers had done a damn fine job, as more was working than wasn't.

Managing to free a hand from the wheel, he silenced the blaring Master Alarm.

To climb or not? It wasn't a question of falling out of the sky. If a wing broke free at a hundred feet or ten thousand, they'd be equally dead. It was a question of fly low and hope, or spend the fuel to climb and trust to glide if you flamed out due to lack of fuel. Gliding wasn't exactly a 747's forte, but he settled on a slow climb.

"Three choices, all bad. Four if you count landing in Arctic cold ocean."

"Three. Run them." *Back to five thousand.*

"Due west, seventy-five miles, Devon Island. Population: zero. It's the world's largest uninhabited island. You'll be on a glacier."

Six thousand.

"Northwest, a hundred and ten, Ellesmere Island. Population: one-forty, but nowhere near where we'd be landing. Mountains and ice there."

Seven thousand.

"East-northeast, a hundred and forty miles, Thule. With nearest land at one-twenty-five. Tundra and ice." Hamlin was still rubbing his head like it hurt and blinking hard.

Which meant critical thinking was up to him. Should he crash hours from help? Or make a reach for Thule at nearly twice the distance and hope the fuel stretched to shore because there was no chance of survival if they hit the ocean?

The fuel wasn't looking good but it should hold. His decision for a slow climb was still his best bet.

Eight thousand.

And the final decider? By pure chance he was already heading east and didn't like the idea of stressing anything with a big turn. He eased a few points to east-northeast, then told Hamlin, "Call it in."

"Where we going?" He was more dazed than he'd been letting on. He never looked at the heading.

"We're shooting for Thule. But tell them to be ready in case we fall short."

Nine thousand. Got ten for me, baby?

"Oh, right, good idea."

A new alarm had them both looking at the overhead panel. The Engine Fire indicator for Number One was blinking.

Hamlin placed his hand on Number One's t-handle before asking, "We sure about this? You know 747s don't exactly excel on one engine?"

"Is it blinking?" He knew full well that the plane needed at least two of its four engines to climb—or even maintain altitude.

Not gonna make ten thousand, are we, old girl?

"Blinking plus alarm." Hamlin confirmed and pulled the handle. "You're on one engine now. No more of that fancy pilot shit."

Ricky laughed, appreciating the *Top Gun* movie reference in this horrible moment.

That done, his copilot sat staring out the window. "Phone home, Hamlin."

No laugh of movie recognition. "Oh, right. Thule Air Base. This is the...ah...Nightwatch plane. We're a hundred miles, uh..."

"West-southwest."

"Right, west-southwest." Hamlin looked up at the fire

handles instead of down at the engine instruments. "One engine." Ricky had to prompt him, "Nine thousand feet. Uh-huh, right, fifteen minutes out."

He should have done it himself, but he wanted to keep Hamlin even marginally busy because he was going to need him if they were to have any chance of surviving the landing.

Whatever had blown up beneath them had thrashed three engines and riddled them with holes; they were leaking like a sieve. The crew would have to take care of themselves for a while.

The red lights on the landing gear hydraulics weren't the most encouraging either.

Captain Ricky Malone eyed the lone Engine Three throttle and engine readouts.

Stick with me, baby. Stick with me.

64

Drake stood in Thule Air Base's control tower and had never felt so useless.

Reports streamed in, several of them conflicting.

The copilot's report had been incredibly frustrating. The man was clearly hurting. That they were aloft at all was fantastic news. The six minutes of silence from the initial Mayday had been long enough for him to race up to the control tower and still spend five minutes pacing in the tiny space.

The ten degrees below freezing and the twenty knots of wind chill said he should have grabbed a parka before sprinting across the airfield, but he didn't connect that's why he was shivering.

His presence was superfluous, but his four stars had to be good for something.

The Virginia-class sub finally reported the aggressor sub was in range of its Mark 48 torpedoes.

Shoot them! He knew it was wrong, so he kept his mouth shut.

"Mark 48," the base commander informed him, "has a sixty-mile range, and moves at about that speed. The torp wouldn't catch them for an hour and they can be alongside in an hour-ten at their current speed."

"So, we wait, and shoot them if they so much as flinch."

"Damn straight."

Drake could live with that.

"We have a pair of Canadian CF-18s presently supersonic. They'll be overhead in another two minutes. As long as the sub remains on the surface, the Hornets can take it. If they dive, the Virginia can. They aren't going anywhere."

Drake tried to think of two minutes of his life that had been longer, but he couldn't.

The only break was the radar operator picking up the inbound Nightwatch at seven thousand feet and sixty miles.

"Hornet Red Leaf One, over target," crackled in over the comm. "Confirm sub at periscope depth, we can see its shadow close submerged. No wake. Coming around for a low pass to get their attention."

65

Arsalan heard as much as felt the slap of the passing jet.

Everyone in the control center looked nervously about.

The captain, who he'd helped into a chair, groped around in the air until he grabbed Arsalan's shirt. "Sonar?"

"Aye, Captain. It's me."

"Some captain I made. Listen," the captain shook him as he continued to stare straight ahead.

His eyes were blood red, not as if merely irritated, but like he'd stared at the sun until even the irises were sunburned. Tears still streamed from them. The captain didn't brush them away.

"Listen, Arsalan. You must surface and surrender."

"But—"

Again the captain shook him. "If you don't, they'll sink you. All of you. Blame me, lay all of the blame on me."

"They'll kill you."

He shook his head. "Just surface. Go out that hatch and wave like you are best friends. Or like you've been pirated."

Arsalan did as he said and took command to surface the boat.

The captain held the back of Arsalan's shirt as he moved to the ladder and began climbing up to the hatch. Not as if to hold him back, but instead letting Arsalan guide him.

Together they climbed out into the twilight.

The chill air, the first he'd breathed in weeks, tasted bitter.

66

DRAKE WATCHED WHAT THEY COULD SEE OF THE SUBMARINE through the circling Hornet's imaging system. The deepening twilight was making it hard to see much, but the boat had surfaced. Sixty meters long, someone had identified it as a Type 209 German-built boat, one they only built for export.

They'd tried various radio frequencies but received no response.

"Hornet Red Leaf One. I have movement on the tower. Hatch opening. One, two... Two individuals have emerged. One is waving his arms overhead. The second is— Holy shit!"

Drake's look met the base commander's. They were both praying they hadn't just lost the Red Leaf One and his plane.

"Sorry. This is RL One. No, I repeat, no aggression. The second individual appears to have tumbled off the conning tower, hit his head on the hull, then slid into the water. I'm seeing no signs of motion. The other man remains atop the conning tower, but appears to be looking toward his companion."

"Run the image back," Drake ordered the local controller. "Run it back, enhance and focus on the top of the conning tower."

Seconds later they were watching a replay.

Two men emerging. One waving. The other tumbling into the sea.

"Again."

Drake watched it closely. "Is it my imagination or did Number Two pat Number One on the shoulder as if in thanks the moment before he went over?"

"You're not crazy," the base commander told him.

They all watched it in silence again.

With no assets in the water, they had no way to help until the Virginia-class sub arrived in sixty-five more minutes. The man on the conning tower stood very still, making no effort to rescue his fallen comrade, but also not looking away.

Drake turned away from the scene to stare out over Thule base.

Ten hangar and service buildings fronted the taxiway. The sole runway lay beyond that. Behind the hangars, the base itself clustered tightly. Despite the vast stretch of the tundra, the buildings hadn't sprawled. At the height of the Cold War, it had housed ten thousand—now fewer than six hundred worked here.

Every year it was becoming less and less useful. Early warning of over-the-pole bomber incursions had evolved to ICBM launch warnings. But as technology advanced, those abilities mattered less. Now they were watching the polar routes with a thick net of satellites. Soon hypersonic cruise missiles, designed to hug the Earth's curvature, would make the base of marginal utility.

It might continue for climate observation. Perhaps the ongoing opening of the Northwest Passage would breathe new life into the base as a security outpost.

But at the moment he could deeply empathize with the tiny two-story abandoned wooden control tower that he could see far below. This was an era he no longer wanted to be a part of.

An Egyptian submarine in Canadian Arctic waters.

Why did he keep coming back to that? It didn't make sense.

No. It didn't make sense to *him*. Someone had said they understood it.

Recently.

They'd been talking about...*Think, Drake. Think!*

The Chinese UAV landing in Egypt. Captain Andi Wu had said she understood it, the moment before the attack on the Nightwatch had cut her off.

67

Andi eyed Miranda's phone ringing on the conference room floor.

Let it ring.

She'd helped a dazed Tamisha back to her seat and belted her in. Though she was little the worse for wear, the same couldn't be said for Ching Hui Wu.

Andi wasn't sure if she'd ever seen Mother disheveled before. Of course being tossed around the inside of a 747 as it did a full barrel roll didn't happen, well, ever.

One look aft convinced her she was on her own. A medic moved among battered crew members who hadn't found their seats in time. She risked a quick run to the command cabin and came back with one of Drake's sheets to create a makeshift sling for Mother's broken arm.

When she offered her one of Miranda's Vicodin, there'd been no hesitation at all. Her complexion remained ashen as Andi sent a silent request to the pills to work faster.

Andi was momentarily at a loss. Mother sat to one side of the table beside Tamisha. She wanted to take the chair to

Mother's other side, but that would leave Miranda alone on her side.

She let the phone decide for her. Crawling around to pick it up, she punched Accept, then scooted in beside Miranda and strapped herself in.

"Hello?" Drake's voice came over the speakers on the conference room table.

"You missed a hell of a ride, General."

"Is everyone okay?"

"Mother broke her arm. Tamisha is bruised and—"

"I'm fine."

"—and fine, according to her. The main cabin has some problems, a full barrel roll is a new one on me."

"A what? Really? Never mind. You said you understood what the Egyptians were up to?"

"I think so. It was more of a mental exercise to disprove it. It was so crazy that I kept it to myself."

Her own phone rang. She saw it was Taz, so she hit the Accept and handed it off to Miranda.

"Would an Egyptian submarine in Baffin Bay fit that scenario?" Drake asked.

"The one that fired on us is Egyptian?" Andi tried to swallow, but couldn't. "And sank the Chinese freighter?"

"Yes on both counts."

"Okay, it's no longer a theory. The only weird part is that they're both from Egypt."

"Someone threw himself overboard after the sub surfaced."

"Duh! Ask him why." Please tell her she hadn't just said Duh! to a four-star.

"He's dead. We won't have a waterborne asset there for another hour. So, does it make sense?"

Miranda was still talking to Taz.

Tamisha shrugged uneasily, and winced as she found some new bruise. Andi would wager that she had it figured but couldn't accept her conclusions enough to tell them to a four-star.

Andi looked to her mother.

Somehow Andi knew that Ching Hui's nod had nothing to do with understanding the situation and everything to do with trusting her daughter. Which was weird. Nice…but weird.

"I expect that you'll find out that the dead man was Latinate, specifically Panamanian."

"The two men who died on the crashed Embraer 175 were poisoned with curare, which comes from that region," Miranda spoke up from her conversation with Taz. "Also, Jeremy's friends at the CIA found a positive match with two dismissed operatives for the Panamanian Public Forces. That's their national security people."

"But…" Drake started to protest, but didn't finish it.

Andi was tempted to string the general along, but Tamisha spoiled it by speaking up.

"The canals, sir."

Drake harrumphed rather than arguing.

"Ah," Mother's color was returning. Either the Vicodin or her mental acuity kicking in enough to override the shock and pain. "Without the income from the canals, Panama slides far deeper into poverty. And the Egyptian authoritarian regime wholly collapses if it were to lose even half of the Suez income; it's a third of their economy. On top of that loss, both have made massive expansions and have to pay off all of the bonds they issued to finance those."

"So, sabotage anyone who tries to transit the Arctic to

avoid the canals." Drake's sigh was audible in the conference room.

"No, Drake," Mother spoke up again. "Merely convince them that it has unaccounted for hazards. Loss of a propellor, loss of a ship. Maybe make them think it's bad luck too. At our core, we Chinese are a superstitious people, especially the elders who remain in power. If they'd only hit the propellors, it might have worked."

Somehow Andi kept forgetting that her mother was a master strategist. Was global politics so different from the courtroom? Perhaps not.

"I don't understand," Miranda complained.

Andi tried to figure out how to explain the whole thing from scratch in a simpler way.

"None of that explains the double sabotage of the Embraer 175."

Okay... Maybe she didn't have to explain the whole thing. And Miranda was absolutely right. That sabotage of Ernie and the two US experts made little sense.

"That is easy, Miranda," Mother continued. "Our upcoming meetings are to make the Arctic safer with new aircraft designs. By killing the American experts, they would sow distrust and hinder that process."

"I'll be damned," Drake spoke over the conference call. "Okay, everything else will have to wait for later."

"But—" Andi almost had the whole picture.

"Wait for it..." Drake sounded very sad.

An announcement blared over the intercom. "This is Captain Malone. Air traffic control confirms my numbers, we have negative range to reach Thule Air Base. We should make shore and I can only hope that is to our advantage. Brace for impact and may your God be with you." Even as he spoke, the sole remaining engine stuttered, caught, and then fell silent as it began to spin down.

With no engine noise, the 747 was eerily quiet. But not silent. It creaked. Each flexion of the wings, every control correction echoed through the airframe in a thousand metallic adjustments.

68

"Tamisha, could you please bring up a satellite view of the area?" Miranda had only ever been in one true crash. It had been as the sole occupant of her father's Mooney on a snowy mountain meadow twenty years ago.

She'd known so much less then.

Now she wanted to see what the terrain would look like to better understand the dynamic forces she'd be experiencing. If they survived, that could prove useful during future investigations.

Tamisha found a satellite view and placed it on the big screen.

A moment later, she superimposed the flight path.

Miranda leaned closer to inspect the area.

The tundra's uneven surface was emphasized by snow that still lay in wandering runnels where meltwater had carved the land. She couldn't spot any landing area more than a few hundred meters in length. The landing would be very violent and damaging.

"Could you zoom back, please?"

Tamisha looked at her with some expression that Miranda didn't have time to ask Andi about.

Thule Air Base lay northeast beyond that battered terrain. Thirty miles away, definitely out of reach. To the south lay the long tongue of a glacier. She'd had quite enough experience with glacial crevasses in Antarctica and had no wish to revisit that particular hazard at the opposite pole.

Just south of that, past another patch of riddled terrain lay—

She picked up a nearby phone and punched the button labeled Cockpit.

"Hey!" Tamisha reached out to stop her.

"Don't," Andi snapped out. "Easy, Sergeant. Just keep your hands to yourself."

Miranda closed her eyes to avoid being further distracted. Which didn't help as she once again saw the image of her home being consumed by fire.

She opened them again and stared at the image on the screen while she waited for someone to answer.

69

"This had better be damned important!" Captain Malone sat alone. There'd been no response from Marty since the attack. And now Hamlin had slipped into unconsciousness. Even a shout didn't rouse him.

He himself was the relief crew. The primary crew for the leg to Thule had disembarked with the general at the air base. He didn't need a backup crew for what was supposed to be a couple hour out-and-back sub hunt, or so he'd thought.

"Please turn to a heading of one-one-seven." A woman.

"Why the hell would I do that?"

"If you choose to attempt a landing on the tundra directly ahead, you will destroy the aircraft and suffer a sixty-to-seventy-three-percent fatality rate. If you turn to, now heading one-two-one, you have an eighty-four percent chance of making a safe landing and a fatality probability below four-point-five percent. Each ten seconds you delay the decision will decrease the likely success rate by three-point-seven percent."

She delivered it all in a dead flat tone as if she was speaking God's own truth.

He looked out the windscreen in the direction of one-twenty degrees. Alone in the cockpit, he'd simply been glad to reach land at all. He certainly hadn't had time to investigate possible landing zones.

He glanced at the comm panel again. *Conf Rm.*

That was the seat of top brass. He might have brushed off someone in ops. In her favor, she certainly spoke with that perfect certainty like top brass.

Ricky considered asking who the hell she was, but he remembered Robert Duvall's line from one of the more realistic disaster apocalypse movies, and a big favorite of the unconscious Hamlin: *Deep Impact*. The solution to the crisis lay in Duvall's hands but he was missing a piece. When he calls for it, they start pounding him with questions and he states one of those great truisms that absolutely separated politicians and the military.

Mitch, we can do or we can teach. What's your pleasure?

He turned the plane in a slow bank, trying to conserve every foot of altitude as he did.

When he got closer, he finally saw where she'd led him. It was a deep embayment with hills rolling up to either side. But the center of the embayment was a smooth sheet of frozen sea ice.

"How good is the ice?"

"That's the sixteen percent chance of a failed landing. But fatalities should remain low as the ice should help float the plane to compensate for flooding through any hull penetrations caused by the missile strike."

"You've thought of everything, haven't you?"

"It's my job."

He didn't know whether to shift back to mistrust because of the pure arrogance of the statement or to...he didn't know what. But taking the turn toward the bay had removed all of his other options.

Step-by-step she guided his approach, insisting that he extend the landing gear.

When he'd tried to argue for a belly landing, she simply said, "That seems an unnecessary waste of the aircraft. If you land and don't punch through the ice, it will be a simple matter of replacing engines and patching the fuel tanks to shift the plane to a maintenance field."

"Lady, if this works, you're getting one seriously sloppy kiss."

"Oh. I'll have to ask my girlfriend if that's okay."

He laughed. "If she argues, tell her tough, you're getting one anyway. Hang on!"

The gear hydraulics were gone. So he punched the Alternate Release control. Without the engines, the heavy slam of the wheel well doors falling open vibrated the whole plane.

Three seconds later, the wind caught the front wheel enough to jam it into the locked position. The four main gear should have locked, but the Gear Down indicator light remained dark. Another dead system or—

Ricky took a deep breath, still unsure of the wings' integrity, and gave the jet a hard side-to-side shake. He slammed it first to the right, then the left. Each wheel carriage forced momentarily outward by the swing. Both locks caught and gave him the lovely green lit on the console.

Finally something had gone right.

He released the flaps, again needing the alternate release system, to the woman's requirements.

Now it was a balance of bleeding airspeed versus elevation. It was September, the height of the warm season, and he didn't exactly have a long stretch of ice for an extended roll-out.

He floated it in as gently as he'd ever kissed down a two-hundred-ton plane.

EPILOGUE

THE GUIDE HAD BEEN A FONT OF INFORMATION FROM THE moment the group had met in the lobby of Thule Air Base Top of the World Club. It was the social center for the six hundred people who worked at this northernmost US military base.

See this poster on the wall. It's actually a photo micrograph of Neodenticula seminae. *It's a species of plankton that hasn't been seen in the Atlantic for eight hundred thousand years.* Homo sapiens *and Neanderthals both emerged less than three hundred years thousand ago. Because of the melting of the Northwest Passage, it has migrated over from the Pacific for the first time in all those years. This image is of a sample collected right here in the bay.*

They had looked like curved stacks of golden glass blocks to make up a tube of warm color. Andi was glad that *someone* had made it safely through the Northwest Passage.

She now stood atop the peak, such as it was, of Mount Dundas overlooking that bay and Thule Air Base.

It is actually a tombolo. A distinction Andi still didn't

understand. It looked like a cool mesa at the end of a sandy spit to her. Apparently to geologists, it was the sandy spit, the tombolo, that they considered cool and the mesa was more of an afterthought. Just two and a half miles from Thule Air Base, it rose over seven hundred feet—*seven-twenty-four* the guide had insisted—to a half-mile-wide flat top.

The guide had been essential too. A polar bear family scavenged near the narrow section of the tombolo. *Now you know why we didn't hike over from the base. Remember, no one goes outside without a buddy and at least one person trained and armed with a shotgun or high caliber rifle.* Andi had kept her shooting skills to herself so that she didn't have to be the one to kill anything.

The flight had done enough of that. The explosion of the two missiles close aboard had riddled the plane with shrapnel. Three of the staff stationed on the lower deck in the belly of plane had bled out before help reached them. Four others in the crew rest area didn't survive, and the navigator had snapped his neck.

No one had died due to that barrel roll or the ice-field landing, though there'd been plenty of injuries—some of career-ending severity. Beside all of that, Mother's broken arm was trivial.

The craziness of the flight and the two days of meetings had finally drained out of her as she and Miranda had stood under the stars last night and watched the green aurora winding its sinuous curves over their heads. They hadn't said a word, hadn't needed to. They'd simply held hands and looked aloft in wonder that they were alive to see something so incredible.

She wished Miranda could have seen the polar bear cubs

this morning but she wasn't up to anything as physical as a climb. They'd been so damn cute, *first years,* that she wanted to go play with them. That the mom was about eighteen times her size had made her glad for the heavy steel rover they'd driven over to Dundas. Andi had taken several pictures.

Some sunning walruses had ignored them on the narrow isthmus, but were keeping a careful eye on the bears. She'd never understood quite how devastatingly ugly the walruses were. She'd cheered, quietly to not attract attention, for the mom polar bear. Also, the walruses stank even worse than the penguin colony had in Antarctica—which was saying a lot. They were so loud that everyone had to cover their ears as they drove past.

It had been a tough climb up Mount Dundas this morning, partly because today was a balmy seven degrees below freezing. They ascended by a straight shot up the eastern face, and then single file along a much-needed fixed rope through the mesa's hard cap. The climb had also been hindered by the heavy rock in her pack.

It's tradition. You pick up a rock at the bottom and you carry it to the top. You'll see why when we get there.

She'd been annoyed enough at one of the group, a Dane who wouldn't stop hitting on her throughout the meetings, that she'd chosen a big rock to goad his ego. He'd chosen a bigger one, and suffered horribly on the way up. Her continuing as much of her Spec Ops physical training as she could had definitely paid off.

Now she sat on her rock-filled pack at the mesa's edge, looking back down at Thule Air Base.

It would have been nice if Tamisha could have joined her, but she was pulling security duty on the Nightwatch.

There were far too many government secrets to leave it unattended even in northern Greenland.

Down on the runway seventy stories below, she could see the newest arrivals unloading the three new engines out of a C-130. The first repair crews to arrive were already out on the ice, patching the fuel tanks and hydraulic lines. Word was they'd be aloft within a week.

The relief at leaving all of that behind had been immense.

She'd hated being right.

The dead man had indeed been a Panamanian officer, trapped in his role by the real captain's suicide aboard the Egyptian submarine. The sonar operator had produced the poor man's phone, stuck into his back pocket the moment before the replacement captain had leapt overboard to his death. He'd left the phone with no password, the latest call had still been on the screen.

Harry and Heidi had traced the last several numbers with the targets none the wiser. One to a Panamanian minister and the other to a highly placed member of the Egyptian General Intelligence Directorate.

That traitor aboard the Nightwatch wouldn't shut up once he knew he was caught—sharp enough to remember the contact phone number, the same as one of the captain's, even while bemoaning his inability to remember his new bank account number, not that it would do him any good during the life sentence to Leavenworth that he'd earned for himself.

She and Drake had agreed that stringing him up on the yardarm would be far more satisfying, even if it was an ancient British Navy thing, not a US Army thing.

Miranda had refused to be a part of turning them in,

understanding full well what was going to happen to the men at the other end of those numbers. But Andi was glad to be the one to pass on the information about both contacts to General Liú Zuocheng, especially as they had almost killed her mother and Miranda, in addition herself and so many others.

It was an easy bet that one or both had bribed and betrayed Ernie Maxwell. Who had been pulling *those* men's strings she didn't know or care, that was General Liú's problem.

On a private call, Taz had told her about her final question for Ernie Maxwell. He'd built up quite a stash in an offshore account. Just a few hours ago—Taz had said she had no idea how it possibly could have happened, in her most innocent voice—a million dollars had mysteriously been deposited in the bank accounts of the families for the two dead men, Gerald and Lewis, labeled as Insurance Policy Payment. The rest had been given to the K9s For Warriors charity.

Andi had accused her of turning into a complete mush. *Don't mess with me, Wu, or I'll take your ass down!* Then they'd both laughed and talked about Taz's adventures around Lac Brome for a while.

Gods but Andi loved working with these people at least as much as she ever had working with the 160th SOAR.

And now she stood in this beautiful, amazing place and breathed in air that tasted so fresh and new—and cold—that it could never have been anywhere else but here. It had been hard to leave Miranda and Mother in their opposite-side arm casts, but they'd insisted.

Flummoxed by Mother's open acceptance of both her and Miranda, and unable to argue with Miranda's typical logic—*Between us we have a right hand and a left one. We can take care of anything we need to.*—Andi had gone on the post-meeting outing.

Had they been conscious of how much easier the two days of meetings had gone because of the sympathy factor? Well, Mother certainly would have. She was simply so elegant about it that no one would ever feel the subtle manipulations that had achieved so much. That Miranda would have no clue at all only made Andi smile more.

Mother had also unraveled the incident over Spieden Island's fire in the simplest of ways. Miranda had suggested forfeiting her own license, but Andi wouldn't hear of that. They'd been on the verge of their first-ever real fight about something, when Mother had stepped in. *Tell them only what they need to know. There was turbulence. Miranda broke her arm. Andrea dear, you managed to take control and save the plane from a dangerous dive. Done. No one else needs the details, and you have told nothing but the truth.*

She and Miranda had talked long and privately about future risks, but Andi had finally convinced her it was the best course by pointing out, *It's not like your childhood home is going to burn down in front of your eyes again.* They'd also agreed that Andi would continue her fixed-wing flight lessons and that Miranda would never again fly alone in the cockpit with others on board. When she flew alone in her old F-86 Sabrejet, which she did only rarely anymore, Miranda had been comfortable with the risks. Andi not so much, but it wouldn't be fair to forbid it either.

Andi tickled the petals of a small cluster of purple flowers shaped like tiny bowls beside her. She almost fell off her rock when a big, very hairy bumblebee emerged from the depths of one of the blooms.

"What are you doing here?" she asked the bumblebee as steps approached from behind.

"Northernmost species of bumbler," the guide replied for the bee. "*Bombus polaris.* Rare to see them out when it's below freezing. They'll be nesting down for the next eight months soon."

"You crazy little dude." She watched it choose the next bloom and dive in.

"Ready to get rid of your rock?"

"Please tell me I didn't carry this sucker up here just to throw it down."

The guide held up a can of white spray paint. "Put your name on it and add it to the pile over there."

Andi looked toward the middle of the mesa's flat top. A great mound of rocks, piled up like one of those old domed bee skeps stood at least a story high. Thousands, perhaps tens of thousands of rocks had been added over the last eighty years to form the mound—her thirty-pounder wasn't the largest but it was up there. Names painted or carved into each stone were visible on the outer layer.

As the two of them walked over to the other delegates from the meeting who'd chosen the outing, Andi began thinking about what came next.

Fly back to Washington and…

Spieden Island was gone, burned to the ground.

Well, maybe they'd design a place that was theirs rather than a home tainted with the shades of Miranda's past.

What kind of home would they make together?

Kids?

No. That one still left her squeamish.

But together.

With plenty of room for the team and guests—and other

people's children. Miranda would be as awesome an auntie as she would be a mother.

Andi took the paint can from the guide and stuffed it in her back pocket. Everyone else had tucked their rocks into open spaces or piled them around the bottom. With some of them the name didn't even show.

Instead, she chose her route and began to climb, careful not to dislodge anyone else's rock.

Once she reached the top, she was higher than anything in the area: the base, the mesa, and all of those problems that had threatened her in the past. That had threatened her and Miranda. She was going to leave behind the dark night of her PTSD after Ken's death and the miserable gray of her *past* relationship with Mother. She'd help Miranda grow out of her own pain-shrouded history and aim for a brighter future.

Remaining vigilant, on watch, was what she'd been most trained in, both by the law and the piloting. The old ways crowded in so easily, but she'd never cease resisting them.

She dumped the rock out of her pack, shuffled it to sit securely atop the very highest point of the mound, and took out the paint can.

Andi Wu couldn't stop grinning as she wrote *Andi & Miranda*. Below that, using a broken-off shard to etch with, two little stick figures holding hands and looking up at the crystalline blue sky.

AFTERWORD

*If you enjoyed NIGHTWATCH
please consider leaving a review.
They really help.*

*Keep reading for an exciting excerpt from:
Miranda Chase #13 OSPREY*

*A list of characters and aircraft may be found at:
https://mlbuchman.com/people-places-planes*

*A free bonus story/scene and a recipe from the book may be be found at:
https://mlbuchman.com/fan-club-freebies*

OSPREY (EXCERPT)

IF YOU ENJOYED THAT, YOU'LL LOVE THIS TALE!

OSPREY (EXCERPT)
JULY 17, 1996

THE SUN HUNG LOW AMONG THE TOWERS OF NEW YORK CITY casting final shadows across JFK International Airport.

At 2017:18 Eastern Daylight Time, Trans World Airlines Flight 800 from New York to Paris was instructed to hold short of JFK's Runway 22R. A landing 757 had kicked up some heavy wake turbulence that would take half a minute to subside. The 747-100, with two hundred and ten passengers and eighteen crew members aboard, held their position for a minute and three seconds.

While idling at the edge of the runway, the cockpit flight crew remained focused on completing the pre-takeoff checklist. The flight hadn't gotten off to a good start and the four men were all glad to finally be on the move.

The 747 had landed from Athens on schedule at 1631 hours. For cabin comfort, the APU—Auxiliary Power Unit, a small engine used as a generator to power the plane's systems—was kept powered up to run two of its three air conditioners to mitigate the heavy heat of the July sun beating down from the partly cloudy skies over New York.

Three of the crew had over sixty thousand hours combined flight experience, much of it in the 747. The fourth was relatively new to the 747, a trainee flight engineer. At twenty-four years old, he had over two thousand hours of flight time as an engineer, but only thirty of those were in a 747. His trainer on this flight was two years from retirement and did his best not to think how much he'd miss the big plane that had dominated his forty-year career.

Over the previous two and a half hours, the plane had been emptied, serviced, and reloaded with passengers and their luggage.

Rather than departing for Charles de Gaulle at 1900 hours as scheduled, there had been multiple delays.

First, a service vehicle had broken down, blocking the plane at Gate 27 until it could be towed clear.

Once it was clear, there was a further delay as gate personnel insisted that a piece of luggage had to be pulled from the hold because the passenger hadn't boarded. Eventually the luggage and its owner were both located. The owner sat already aboard the plane, seriously considering several scotches once they were aloft. The overexcited high school French class looking forward to their first trip to France were boisterously annoying. It was going to be a long damn flight and scotch was definitely in order. Despite the delays, he'd still be in time for his lunch meeting. The French would just have to take him in whatever state he was in.

The bag was returned to the hold.

Of only slightly more concern, the captain's weather radar wasn't working properly. Maintenance marked it as inoperative and, per regulation, ordered service at the next

Osprey (excerpt)

opportunity within ten days. The copilot's radar was operative, so the flight was finally cleared for departure.

At 2018:21, the tower transmitted final wind conditions and cleared TWA 800 for departure. They rolled down Runway 22R and lifted into the air well before midfield as they carried only two-thirds capacity. The final fuel load had been adjusted downward to avoid carrying any extra weight across the Atlantic. As a result, the large central wing tank sat mostly empty.

Over the next eleven minutes, as air traffic control routed the flight east to higher flight levels through the typical clutter of jet traffic, there was only one unusual comment captured by the Cockpit Voice Recorder.

At 2029:15, the captain remarked, "Look at that crazy fuel flow indicator on Number Four...see that?"

There was no follow-up comment captured by the CVR.

A minute and fifty-seven seconds subsequent to that remark, at 2031:12 after the flight was cleared to climb to fifteen thousand feet, the CVR abruptly ceased operation. For just over a tenth of a second before it did, a *very loud sound* was recorded.

It stopped recording because a frayed fuel gauge wire, probably chafed by a sagging air duct, sparked. The spark occurred inside the nearly empty central wing tank, now primarily filled with a highly combustible fuel/air mixture. The mixture had been further heated and concentrated during the overlong wait on the tarmac by the heat exchangers for the air conditioning units—mounted directly below the tank.

When the fuel/air mixture ignited, an intense explosion sliced the airplane in two, immediately ahead of the wings. This severed the wiring to the flight recorders as well as killing many of the passengers instantly—mostly by snapping their necks. Those who survived in the main body of the aircraft died from inhaling the burning air rolling through the cabin like a roiling wall of death.

Approximately five seconds later, the nose of the plane—including the flight deck and first-class passenger section—broke free and began its long, eighty-three-second fall to the ocean. Based on ocean water found in their lungs, some of these passengers may have survived long enough to attempt a breath after the impact with the Atlantic off East Moriches, Long Island, New York.

The main fuselage and wings of the 747, abruptly lighter in the nose, tipped steeply upward. With the engines still driving ahead at climb thrust, it ascended an additional three thousand feet over the next thirty-eight seconds before the wings broke free from the shattered central wing box that had enclosed the fuel tank. No one aboard remained alive as it too began its long tumble toward the ocean.

During the next four years, the largest investigation in the history of the National Transportation Safety Board recovered over ninety-five percent of the debris and all the bodies from the Atlantic. The plane was reassembled in a hangar piece by piece to determine the causes. Over forty recommendations were sent to the FAA by the NTSB, including several changes to all 747 wiring harnesses.

The most important? All future jets—civilian, military, by every nation—would eventually be redesigned to pump inert nitrogen into their fuel tanks as they empty to prevent the accumulation of a highly explosive fuel/air mixture. With that single design change recommendation, it is estimated that the National Transportation Safety Board has saved tens of thousands of lives globally.

Osprey (excerpt)

CIA Headquarters
Langley, Virginia

"Turn on the news."

Ron Klemens looked up from the file that was causing him such misery to glare at his assistant as he hustled into Ron's office.

Bert ignored the glare and hurried over to the television.

Ron must be losing his touch.

The set came alive with a bright red *Breaking News* banner. Some passenger jet had crashed into the ocean less than thirty minutes ago.

What the hell was it with planes going down all of a sudden? His two top agents, he resisted the urge to look down at the file spread before him, had gone down yesterday under conditions that could never be revealed. How was he supposed to explain their deaths?

Even as the Director of the Russia Desk for the CIA, one didn't stroll into the Director's office and announce such a thing without having a solution already in place. Besides, the bastard was too busy declassifying the Cold War and damaging the CIA in all sorts of creative ways. Ron couldn't fight back, but he couldn't let *this* get out. No, he wasn't going to the Director until this one was locked down and fully in the bag.

Wait. Did he have to explain it?

He flipped to the front of the file. Damn it. They had a kid, insurance policies, property, any number of loose threads that could never be allowed to be questioned.

The real tragedy? Nothing could be done to plug the

massive intelligence hole that their deaths created. They were irreplaceable.

He stared at the screen as dribs and drabs of information were gathered about the air crash.

Explosion.

A dead 747 plunged into the water off Long Island.

A French class field trip on its way from JFK to Paris.

"Survivors?" the news anchor asked.

After an explosion high over the ocean? Ron thought the man should be shot for offering false hopes. No one would survive that crash.

If only he could hide his agents' deaths there, then—

"Bert!" he shouted so loudly that the man less than five feet away jumped.

"Sir?"

"Was the flight full?"

"What flight?"

Ron jabbed a finger toward the screen.

Bert twisted his head like that green Muppet frog-thing, first to the screen, then back. Then he glanced down at the file on Ron's desk that had been giving them both headaches all day.

He bolted for his desk.

He was back less than five minutes later, and he was smiling. "The flight wasn't full. Two hundred and ten people and about three hundred and sixty seats."

Ron felt like a bit of a ghoul as he returned the smile—just another day at the CIA. "Make it two hundred and *twelve*. Get them confirmed aboard. Alter paperwork, flight manifests, all of it. Fast, before they can absolutely confirm the number."

"Assign seats. First class, I think. Fabricate some luggage

Osprey (excerpt)

and sink it in the recovery area..." Bert kept talking to himself as he hurried away. It was the kind of deep cover that the CIA had a whole department dedicated to creating.

TWA Flight 800 would now have two hundred and *twelve* passenger deaths, not two-ten. The agent's bodies should be repatriated within twenty-four hours. Divers from a Special Activities Division team could quietly insert them into the wreckage, even snap their seatbelts.

He could always wait for the next director before reporting it so that it stayed hidden; the current idiot couldn't last much longer. If he was careful, that director might well be him. Then he could add their stars to the Memorial Wall with no one in the wider world any wiser.

Ron flipped to the first page of Sam and Olivia's file. The emergency contact was some live-in nanny. Close enough.

He dialed the number and listened while it rang in the hell-and-gone Pacific Northwest.

As the call was answered, Ron glanced down to find the surviving kid's name: Miranda.

———

Keep reading. Available at fine retailers everywhere:
OSPREY

And don't forget that review for **NIGHTWATCH**
They really help.

MIRANDA CHASE SO FAR
AVAILABLE IN EBOOK, PRINT, AND AUDIO

ABOUT THE AUTHOR

USA Today and Amazon #1 Bestseller M. L. "Matt" Buchman started writing on a flight south from Japan to ride his bicycle across the Australian Outback. Just part of a solo around-the-world trip that ultimately launched his writing career.

From the very beginning, his powerful female heroines insisted on putting character first, *then* a great adventure. He's since written over 70 action-adventure thrillers and military romantic suspense novels. And more than 125 short stories, and a fast-growing pile of read-by-author audiobooks.

PW declares of his Miranda Chase action-adventure thrillers: "Tom Clancy fans open to a strong female lead will clamor for more." About his military romantic thrillers: "Like Robert Ludlum and Nora Roberts had a book baby."

His fans say: "I want more now…of everything!" That his characters are even more insistent than his fans is a hoot. He is also the founder and editor of *Thrill Ride – the Magazine*.

As a 30-year project manager with a geophysics degree who has designed and built houses, flown and jumped out of planes, and solo-sailed a 50' ketch, he is awed by what is possible. He and his wife presently live on the North Shore of Massachusetts. More at: www.mlbuchman.com.

Other works by M. L. Buchman: (* - also in audio)

Action-Adventure Thrillers

Dead Chef
One Chef!
Two Chef!

Miranda Chase
Drone*
Thunderbolt*
Condor*
Ghostrider*
Raider*
Chinook*
Havoc*
White Top*
Start the Chase*
Lightning*
Skibird*
Nightwatch*
Osprey*
Gryphon*

Science Fiction / Fantasy

Deities Anonymous
Cookbook from Hell: Reheated
Saviors 101

Contemporary Romance

Eagle Cove
Return to Eagle Cove
Recipe for Eagle Cove
Longing for Eagle Cove
Keepsake for Eagle Cove

Love Abroad
Heart of the Cotswolds: England
Path of Love: Cinque Terre, Italy

Where Dreams
Where Dreams are Born
Where Dreams Reside
Where Dreams Are of Christmas*
Where Dreams Unfold
Where Dreams Are Written
Where Dreams Continue

Non-Fiction

Strategies for Success
Managing Your Inner Artist/Writer
Estate Planning for Authors*
Character Voice
Narrate and Record Your Own Audiobook*

Short Story Series by M. L. Buchman:

Action-Adventure Thrillers

Dead Chef

Miranda Chase Stories

Romantic Suspense

Antarctic Ice Fliers
US Coast Guard

Contemporary Romance

Eagle Cove

Other

Deities Anonymous (fantasy)
Single Titles

The Emily Beale Universe
(military romantic suspense)

The Night Stalkers
MAIN FLIGHT
The Night Is Mine
I Own the Dawn
Wait Until Dark
Take Over at Midnight
Light Up the Night
Bring On the Dusk
By Break of Day
Target of the Heart
Target Lock on Love
Target of Mine
Target of One's Own
NIGHT STALKERS HOLIDAYS
Daniel's Christmas*
Frank's Independence Day*
Peter's Christmas*
Christmas at Steel Beach
Zachary's Christmas*
Roy's Independence Day*
Damien's Christmas*
Christmas at Peleliu Cove

Henderson's Ranch
Nathan's Big Sky*
Big Sky, Loyal Heart*
Big Sky Dog Whisperer*
Tales of Henderson's Ranch*

Shadow Force: Psi
At the Slightest Sound*
At the Quietest Word*
At the Merest Glance*
At the Clearest Sensation*

White House Protection Force
Off the Leash*
On Your Mark*
In the Weeds*

Firehawks
Pure Heat
Full Blaze
Hot Point*
Flash of Fire*
Wild Fire
SMOKEJUMPERS
Wildfire at Dawn*
Wildfire at Larch Creek*
Wildfire on the Skagit*

Delta Force
Target Engaged*
Heart Strike*
Wild Justice*
Midnight Trust*

Emily Beale Universe Short Story Series

The Night Stalkers
The Night Stalkers Stories
The Night Stalkers CSAR
The Night Stalkers Wedding Stories
The Future Night Stalkers

Delta Force
Th Delta Force Shooters
The Delta Force Warriors

Firehawks
The Firehawks Lookouts
The Firehawks Hotshots
The Firebirds

White House Protection Force
Stories

Future Night Stalkers
Stories (Science Fiction)

SIGN UP FOR M. L. BUCHMAN'S NEWSLETTER TODAY

and receive:
Release News
Free Short Stories
a Free Book

Get your free book today. Do it now.
free-book.mlbuchman.com

Printed in Great Britain
by Amazon